Live @ Five

LARRY BRILL

Black Tie
BOOKS

Black Tie
BOOKS

Published by Black Tie Books

Austin, Texas

Copyright © 2013 by Larry Brill

Cover design © 2013 Brill Graphic Design, Inc.

The Library of Congress has catalogued the trade paperback edition as follows:

Brill, Larry

Live @ Five / by Larry Brill

ISBN: 978-0-9888643-1-3

Printed in the United States of America

First Edition

10 9 8 7 6 5 4 3 2 1

www.larrybrill.com

For Kim

Live @ Five

Date: March 4, 1996
Lead Story: Jobless Rate Down

Anchor intro:

The jobless rate dropped by one the day Minnie Pearl died. It wasn't her demise that brought about the statistical change. No, her story was just one more item in the news of the day.

Since Minnie Pearl rated no more than twenty seconds and a bit of video pulled from the archives on the evening news—and not even a tasteful fade to black before the commercial break—her life on the fringe of fame, and her passing, could, in retrospect, be viewed as symbolic of what you are about to see.

Call it a coincidence of timing. But in the universe of TV news, as with every other segment of the entertainment business, timing is everything.

Roll tape
Sound full :03 seconds – cheer goes up in noisy newsroom

This was the scene today in the newsroom at KDOA-TV in Bakersfield, California. The sound you hear is a cheer bouncing off its dingy walls.

Minnie Pearl, dead?

Just came down the AP wire.

Who had her?

Who didn't?

The questions are bullets fired from every direction.

The answer comes in the dance of a lanky, prematurely bald news producer. Van Thompson. He's the one you see over there at a cluster of desks in the center of the newsroom. He's the one smiling with his index fingers pointing to the heavens.

"Minnie Pearl," he crows. "Right after the Pope on my list. That gives me three so far this year. Yessss!" Then he drops into his chair and begins typing at the computer keyboard as if nothing significant has happened. He has a menu of stories in front of him for that evening's newscast. "I'll give her twenty seconds. That is, if those chuckleheads at the network feed us some video on the satellite this afternoon."

A young reporter walks by and shrugs. "Minnie Pearl. Who knew?"

Hunter Riley is standing near the doorway of the newsroom. His lips are pressed thin as he tries to suppress a laugh.

"Death list," he says. "What's the jackpot?"

John Tuttle, the station manager at KDOA, is squeezing against the doorframe behind Hunter. Tuttle is round and soft, built with rolls of fat so that he looks like the Michelin Man. His skin is pasty white, and he has two button eyes buried above his fat little cheeks like the Pillsbury Doughboy. His hair is the color and consistency of a rusty Brillo pad. If God created a montage of his favorite prime-time TV commercials, it would come to life as John Tuttle.

"It's up to two hundred bucks," Tuttle says. "You know, we've had a death list in every newsroom I've ever been in. But these kids really get into it."

"Two hundred, huh? A nice chunk of change," Hunter replies.

"Yeah. Ten bucks for a pick thirty. I've only got one celeb in the grave from my list so far this year. Looks like I need to bump off three before Christmas to win the pot."

Hunter nods. "Back in Chicago we used the *USA Today* standard. If the poor slob doesn't rate a mention in *USA Today*, it doesn't count."

Tuttle nudges Hunter, and they roll into the newsroom. "Listen up, everyone. I want you to meet your new boss."

Only the voices in the newsroom's cacophony of sound die. Static-marred traffic on the police scanner ignores Tuttle's cry for attention. A fax machine behind the central cluster of desks grinds out a continuous stream of paper with a growl. Somewhere in the back of the room a noisy street scene is playing out on a videotape machine.

Little wrinkles of amusement, etched momentarily deeper by resignation, frame Hunter's dark eyes. You may guess what he's thinking. He has gray in his hair and more than twenty years in the business. Reporters and photographers, even the producers, just keep getting younger. So with the exception of the guy who was dancing on Minnie Pearl's grave, it appears to Hunter that the

KDOA news staff is made up of babies, practically. Right out of college.

Hunter reads their faces. If this is like every other newsroom he's been in, the reporters and photographers, following the lead of the older and wiser assignment editor or producer, have already feasted on the rumors of his hiring and formed an opinion. There is no time for a honeymoon in this business. You are already yesterday's news by the time you get there.

Do they like him? Do they hate him?

He knows most of them have already made up their minds but he can't tell where he stands. Hunter smiles at the group while his ego inside shrugs. Hell, a few months from now it won't matter.

He follows Tuttle to the middle of the room where Tuttle points to the lean fellow with a hawk's nose and a tired face—the beneficiary of Minnie Pearl's journey to the Grand Ole Opry in the sky.

"Van Thompson," Tuttle says. "Six and eleven o'clock producer."

Hunter Riley shakes Thompson's hand. Weak grip. Indecisive. Bad sign. "Minnie Pearl," Hunter says. "That was a good call. Who had George Burns?"

Thompson flinches. "Everybody had George Burns, for five years running."

Next.

"Kathy Wright," Tuttle introduces her.

Kathy Wright has big hair, somewhere between dark chocolate and caramel with curls that sway and jiggle as she steps forward.

Hunter is struck by her wide, dark brown eyes. He thinks they are happy, fun-loving eyes that meet your gaze head on and dare you not to smile.

"Kathy produces the five o'clock show," Tuttle says.

She's wearing a plain white cotton blouse dotted with half a dozen bright yellow sticky-notes on her bosom. Each one has a scribble of ink. Kathy arranges her curls and brushes her clothes quickly, sending two of the notes fluttering to the floor. She hesitates, undecided whether to pick them up or extend her hand to him. She ignores the notes on the floor. Her handshake is stronger than Thompson's.

"Kathy also runs the assignment desk," Tuttle explains.

Hunter nods and peels away a stray yellow note that had transferred to his palm. He glances at it before handing it back to her. She blushes.

"I think it says take the network feed at four o'clock," he smiles. Hunter is conscious of his shoulders, holding them straight and projecting strength, and he adds timbre to his voice the way tea drinkers add honey to their cup. It's thick and sweetening. It's his TV Anchor Voice.

Tuttle makes the other introductions more quickly. The two reporters are easy to identify because Andy Blackman and Valerie Watson are dressed for the camera while Lanny, the photographer, wears a t-shirt and blue jean shorts.

"You're on your own to meet the rest of the staff when they get in here," Tuttle says. "Including Kent Abernathy, the anchor."

Hunter follows Tuttle around the wheel of desks in the middle of the room, to the news director's office in the far corner. Hunter Riley's new office.

A large wall of glass with vertical blinds like the bars of a prison cell separates the office from the newsroom. Tuttle pauses at the door and waves at Hunter to go first.

A smaller window on the left looks out over the KDOA parking lot. Beyond that, Highway 99 and the brown hills of southern California stretch along the horizon, fuzzy in the noon haze like a vague dream. The two solid walls of the office are decorated with cheap western art and inspirational posters.

"When the going gets tough, the tough get going."

"Do it right, do it once—Do it wrong, do it over."

The clichés on the wall remind Hunter of his high school locker room. They didn't pump up the Clear Lake High School Fighting Weasels back then; Hunter suspects they only inspire jokes in the newsroom today. Go team go! Win one for the Gipper. Yeah, right!

Tuttle catches Hunter staring at the slogans. "Matthews, the last guy in here, was big on motivation but not what you'd call an original thinker. Moved up to Fresno."

Hunter runs a hand across the simulated wood grain desktop. It has been dusted and sanitized, leaving no trace of the previous renter. Even the small calendar propped up next to a computer monitor has a fresh page. Hunter bends and tilts his head, and finds the computer keyboard on a sliding track under the desktop. He uses his thumb to press the manufacturer's label where it had begun to peel away from the monitor's frame. He doesn't recognize the brand. Scratched and abused, it has the feeling of school surplus equipment.

Tuttle motions to him and Hunter sits down at the desk. He can look past his boss, through the blinds into the newsroom where Kathy Wright and Van Thompson are leaning close and sharing a secret over the desks that form the producer's "wheel".

"Let's talk about the ratings," Hunter says.

"Let's not," Tuttle replies.

During the last ratings period the KDOA Channel 13 Five O'clock Report was fifth in a four-newsroom town. Fifth place. Four newscasts.

"The other stations doing news finished one, two and three. We finished behind Bozo the Clown's Afterschool Clubhouse," Tuttle sighs.

They stare down each other in a familiar way. Neither is sure where to start. Tuttle's eyes narrow, and he holds up two fingers.

"Two things," he says. "I know you're used to being in front of the camera, but this ain't no anchor gig. And I know you're not in this for the long haul."

Hunter starts to protest but Tuttle cuts him off. "Look, you're broke and I'm desperate. So this is good. And, fuck. I still owe you for helping me get that network job with you at the bureau in Washington."

"Back when we were young and stupid," Hunter said.

"Like them," Tuttle jerks his thumb at the newsroom.

"Yeah," Hunter says wistfully. "Just like them."

"So what if it was twenty-five years ago, I still owe you."

Hunter gives the dreary walls of his office a disapproving look. "This isn't quite what I had in mind for a payback. Twenty-five years and what? Seven markets later. I would think you could come up with something better than Bakersfield, John."

"You should have stayed at the network with me. You would have made correspondent soon enough." Tuttle turns up the left corner of his mouth, his cheek is puffed out like Popeye the Sailor. "You'd be at the network today if you could have just been patient."

"Sure. Just sit tight, do all the leg work and have some prissy correspondent fly in just long enough to do a stand up and voice the script you wrote? They get in front of the camera and take all the credit for your work. And then maybe, if someone upstairs likes you, you get one shot at a correspondent's job? No thanks."

"I did eight years. It wasn't so bad."

"So I burned out faster."

"You didn't burn out. You couldn't wait to get in front of the camera."

"Whatever," Hunter replies. "But even you finally dumped the network for that producer's job in Atlanta."

Tuttle nods. "You were in Oklahoma City by then. What was that—your fourth market in eight years? Was that before or after Chicago?"

"After. After New York."

"Right. New York," Tuttle says. "It's like you've been living that song. You know, Route 66."

Hunter holds up a hand but it's too late to stop Tuttle.

"Go through St. Louie. Joplin, Missouri. Oklahoma City. Looks mighty pretty."

"Please, John," Hunter pleads.

But Tuttle sings, "Amarillo. Gal-up-New-Mex-ee-co. Get your kicks on Route 66."

Hunter takes a pencil from a cup on the desk and flips it gently in Tuttle's direction. "Okay. Give me a break. I never sank any lower than Des Moines."

This stops Tuttle. He shakes his head sadly. "Des Moines. How could you land in Des Moines?"

"I guess you could say I was working my way down the ladder of success." Hunter laughs without conviction. He realizes he has been thumbing the cuff of his white shirt where it was getting worn just below the monogram. E.H.R. It is his last good shirt. He picks at a loose thread and then stops. He self-consciously tucks it below the cuff and pulls at the sleeve of his suit jacket to hide the flaw. "At least you're in management now. General manager? Not bad," he tells Tuttle.

"Yeah. But, shit. It's only Bakersfield."

"Could be worse."

Tuttle disagrees, until Hunter adds, "You could be in Bakersfield *and* have someone like you for a boss. Now that's my personal vision of Hell."

Sober. Tuttle asks Hunter how long he plans to stay.

"Only as long as it takes."

His answer doesn't require explanation to a news gypsy, and that pretty much sums up most young, hungry reporters in small markets like Bakersfield. Young reporters. Hunter is uneasy with that. He's too old to be reinventing himself in this town, a television market where most of his "peers" are rookies with inadequate training and unrealistic expectations. He's certain it's worse than when he started paying his dues—how long ago now?

Before he leaves, Tuttle offers some advice. "Bakersfield isn't so bad once you get used to it. And who knows? Maybe you'll like being a news director instead of an anchor. You've been around. You've got all that pent-up experience and a lot you could teach them," he says, referring again to the bodies outside the glass wall of Hunter's office.

When Tuttle is gone, Hunter quietly closes the door to the office and pounces on the telephone. He stands with his back to his window on the newsroom while he dials. A woman answers his call on the second ring.

Hunter reaches down for a deep voice and tries to give it that touch of gravel familiar to millions of Americans. "This is Tom Brokaw calling for Murray Dell," he says to the phone. His wait is only a moment. Murray is on the line with the kind of friendly greeting usually reserved for favored clients and rich uncles.

Hunter stops him cold. "Murray, it's Hunter Riley. No, don't blame Dolores. No, I told her I was Brokaw so you'd pick up the goddamned phone. How come you'll take his calls but you won't take mine?" He runs a finger through the coiled cord of the phone while he listens to Murray in denial.

"No, it *is* true, Murray. You're my agent. You're supposed to be helping, but you haven't returned a single call for more than a month.

"Listen, I'm in Bakersfield. Bakersfield, Murray. You know where that is, Murray? That's halfway between Fresno and Hell.

I've been here two hours already, and I can't take it any more.

"I'm not hysterical but I am deadly serious. I can't afford to stay off the air too long. I need to get back into the anchor chair or nobody will look at me ever again. This news director's job isn't for me. Damn it, Murray. I'm an anchor, not a baby sitter."

Hunter's face is flushing. It becomes more noticeable next to the white in his knuckles as he grips the telephone at his ear. His voice is rising, and it's lost all of its calculated soothing tone of control.

"Murray. Let me set the scene for you here. I am standing in my office looking out the window. It's bare dirt out there and the wind is pushing tumbleweeds around like some spaghetti western, and in the lot next door is a goddamned oil rig, Murray. It's rusted and abandoned, probably hasn't worked in a decade and it's sitting there in the middle of nowhere just outside my frigging window. Get the picture, Murray? That is all you need to know about Bakersfield. Bakersfield is broadcast hell."

Hunter pauses, listens and then says, "Okay, purgatory. Don't make fun of me. That is where my career is right now. I wouldn't have taken this job if I wasn't so broke and Tuttle asked me to help him out while I'm on the shelf."

Hunter shifts the phone to his other while Murray is talking. "You'd bet your ass this has to be only temporary."

He is direct. "Murray, I want you to call Vesterhaven up there at WBFD in Cincinnati. I know they have an opening for weekend anchor. No, don't lie to me, Murray. They do have an opening. Aren't you married to Vesterhaven's cousin or something? Doesn't he owe you any favors?"

Hunter frowns. He doesn't like Murray's tone. "Well, no. He doesn't owe *me* anything."

One more exchange, and then another. Each one more heated than before and panic starts to rise. It's followed quickly by fear, desperation and finally resignation.

"Fine," Hunter says. He is breathing deeply now, deliberately, in an effort to regain control. It's easier now that the outcome is clear. "Go ahead. Tear up the contract. You won't help me. I don't really need you. I can get another agent. No, I won't call any more."

Dumped.

Murray is the only agent he's had in twenty years. Murray helped him land the job in Chicago. Murray was full of praise and optimism back then. He consoled Hunter after the management shake-up in St. Louis cost Hunter the job there, and even stuck with him while they tried to revive Hunter's anchor career in Des Moines.

Dumped. After all these years.

The telephone receiver hangs in Hunter's hand for a moment as if resisting gravity. Then it drops into its cradle the same way you watch a gunfighter's weapon linger on his trigger finger just before they both slump to the ground at the bloody end of a shoot-out on the late, late show.

Slug: Senior Bandit

Anchor intro:

They say that journalism is history in a hurry.

As such, it is the reporter's job to record the deeds of today's saints and sinners, and let time and history rewrite the story to tell us which is which.

Tonight, Bakersfield Police are looking for a bank robber. The media have dubbed him the "Senior Bandit" because; well, because it's required. Every journalist knows every serial criminal needs a catchy title to help viewers understand this is not just another run of the mill story. That helps sell news. As for the Senior Bandit, investigators have few clues about his identity, except that he may be the oldest, most polite and saintly robber you're likely to meet.

Roll tape

On the wide-angle picture of the bank security video, he's the tall one standing fourth in line in the lobby, checking his watch for the tenth time in eight minutes. A digital read-out of the time on the security video says it's 11:14 am.

Only three tellers are working the long marble counter at South Valley Bank's branch on Ming Avenue. It's a typical, cozy suburban-style branch office in south Bakersfield. The bandit picked it because it's surrounded by strip centers and the big mall across the street. Plenty of places to get away without using a car.

It is still too early for the lunch-hour rush, and he wonders where all these customers have come from. The bandit knocks his right knee repeatedly, rhythmically, against a tan leather briefcase he holds with both hands in front of him. His nylon jogging suit shooshes as he shifts his weight and rolls his neck to relieve tension. The movement gives him a good look at each corner of the lobby. The tinted lenses in his glasses make it hard to pick out details. He doesn't like that, but the lenses make him harder to identify. It's a trade-off he's willing to accept.

As if reading his mind, the short, round woman in front of the bandit turns and looks over her shoulder, up at him. She is exasperated with the wait, too, and apparently is chasing away the boredom of the moment by reading his face. He pulls his blue Dodgers' cap a little lower on his brow.

"How long does it have to take?" she asks.

"Seems like forever."

The woman squints one eye and tilts her head back. "Don't I know you?"

The bandit leans closer and invades her personal space. Almost nose to nose. It was reflex, mostly, but she retreats half a step. "No, I don't believe you do," he answers firmly.

She may or may not make a good witness. So be it. He makes no attempt to avoid her stare. She will remember the cap, and the longish gray hair that spills out beneath it, brushing against his collar. She can't possibly tell that his eyes are brown. The tinted glasses take care of that. She might remember the Nike logo on his nylon jacket, but she won't be able to confirm anything the security cameras haven't already picked up. They both see the disguise but not much more.

Right now he's just another customer. That is, until police come around asking questions. He steps forward, into her space again.

"I believe you're next," he says. He smiles and points to where the second teller on the right is waving.

The bandit draws a breath and steps to the front of the line. A gold-plated sign tells him to wait there for the next available teller. He has two other customers behind him, corralled in the area roped off by velvet cords. There are no butterflies in his stomach this time. Now he knows what to expect, and how simple it really is. Sad that it has come to this, but God has his reasons.

Psalm 39. "Surely every man walketh in a vain show. Surely they are disquieted in vain; he heapeth up riches, and knoweth not who shall gather them." He sighs.

Melissa, according to the nameplate on the counter, signals him from her teller's position. Good fortune. She is separated from the other tellers at the far end; more convenient for the private kind of transaction he has in mind. The bandit takes four long and sure strides to her station and squares to face her. His voice is raspy, not much stronger than a whisper, but firm.

"Melissa," he says. "My name is Chester. Chester Fields."

He smiles.

She smiles.

He sets the briefcase on the counter, careful not to touch anything he won't take with him. "I used to work at South Valley Bank, the branch over on Rosedale," he says.

"Really?" She seems genuinely interested. "I worked there a few months before transferring here. I don't remember you."

"You wouldn't; it was a while back. Quite a while, when we were a nice local bank. Much more friendly. More personal, I'd say." He snaps the latch on his attaché. He continues. "The point really is this: I know where you keep the clean money in your drawer, and I know where you keep the dye packet. And I even know where your alarm is." He opens the briefcase. "I also know you are trained not to upset a robber in the course of a crime. Good training, that is. Don't you think so, Melissa?"

She nods, the smile now frozen on her lips.

"So please, just put a few bundles of your best fifties and hundreds in the briefcase here." The bandit pulls out a scrap of paper and rotates the briefcase to a more convenient angle for her to deposit the money. It also makes it easier for her to see the funny looking package of tubes and wires inside, wrapped in duct tape, about the size of a paperback book. Explosives? She might think so.

The bandit holds the paper at arm's length for better focus. "I need exactly three thousand-seven dollars and forty-six cents," he says. He turns to her. "Well, let's just make it a nice, round three thousand and seven dollars." He watches as she takes first one, and then a second bundle from the cash drawer. He leans against the counter to let her know he is watching each move.

"I'm so glad it turned out to be you today," he says without taking his eyes off her hands. "I can see you're a smart girl and won't do anything wrong."

He was as gentle as a dentist with the most soothing chair-side manner, drill in hand, about to extract a bothersome tooth. They will both feel better when this is over, although he forgets to say, "This won't hurt a bit."

It doesn't.

He walks out of the bank as the counter on the security video reads 11:26.

Slug: News Zoo

Anchor intro:

Television news is a crazy business. Crazy. Every day is unpredictable, and that is exactly what makes it so attractive to the wide variety of characters drawn into the career.

It takes a special breed to live with the pace of a newsroom that can leap from dull to electrifying in a heartbeat. The pay is frequently peanuts, but it feeds the ego well. To survive, you need the heart of a lion and the humor of a chimpanzee.

Few in this business have ever been to the jungle, but most will tell you they work in a zoo.

Roll tape

"And how may I piss you off today?"

Kathy Wright asks that question every morning of the reporters and photographers who approach her desk to get their assignments for the day. She figures it's only fair, because it seems most days pissing people off is what she does most. No sense being diplomatic.

Reporters want more help, more time and more information to complete their assignments.

"Sorry," she says. "I would if I could, but I can't give you the"—fill in the blank here—"to make your life easier. We'll just have to deal with it."

Photographers want more help, more time, more information and maybe a real lunch break.

"Sorry," she says.

She says it with a dollop of wry humor that tells them some way, somehow, she'll pull a rabbit out of her butt and find them the help, time or whatever else they need to do their jobs. That is, if it exists. Lately the rabbits have been in short supply.

They call her the Assignment Wench. Goddess of all that gets covered and subsequently put on the evening news. Her job is to make sure the reporters and photographers are armed with at least the basic details of each story and the equipment they need to get them on the road and to news events on time.

Kathy Wright's job is to feed the beast.

The beast is that thirty-minute window of news they produce three times a day at five, six and eleven o'clock. It's a daunting task with only twelve people on her staff. Half as many as other stations in town. That irks her.

And thank God for commercials. Commercials not only pay the bills for the TV station, they eat up time. So in a regular thirty-minute newscast, if you subtract the commercials, the sports and the weather, and all the padding—like time spent telling viewers over and over what is still to come on News-13—you actually have a mere twelve minutes left for news. But some days, when her file of story ideas is empty and the reporters are unable to dig up anything worth putting on TV, that twelve minutes looks like the Grand Canyon to Kathy Wright.

"Nothing that a little spot news wouldn't cure," she says to her reporter Andy Blackman.

Spot news is a fire, a bus wreck (a bus wreck involving kids is a bonus), or any other unscheduled calamity that sends the news crews running. Crime is good.

Kathy waves an empty assignment folder in front of Andy Blackman's nose. "I hope you have an idea for a story today."

Andy suggests a follow-up to last night's school board meeting. Boring.

Melissa Ling, the third reporter on the staff, joins the discussion. Another meeting tonight on funding for a community center to be built on the west side?

Done that. Move on. Nothing seems particularly newsworthy to Kathy today.

She wags the file at the reporter and tosses a half-hearted threat in his direction. "If you don't come up with something, I'll send you over to do a story with Reverend Sam."

"Reverend Sam? That publicity pig?" Andy shudders.

"He says the senior citizens' housing program is out of money. Broke! Kaput! He swears this time it's for real. They'll all be homeless soon, and he says we need to do a story."

"He always says that."

Kathy presses the middle finger of her right hand against the tip of her nose to create a piggish scowl while simultaneously flipping off her young reporter. "I didn't have the patience to deal with him today, so I sent the phone call to the Big Cheese. Let him handle it." She points to the news director's office where Hunter Riley has been at his desk behind a closed door all morning.

"Kind of cranky today, are we?" Andy asks.

Kathy replies, "Yep. And I'll probably stay that way all day unless you come up with a lead story we can put on the news tonight."

She likes Andy Blackman. If Kathy set up an official ranking, she would score him as the second best reporter on the staff. Andy will jump to a larger market soon. All the good reporters do. Andy has been here nearly two years, and Kathy has watched his enthusiasm erode over the past few months. It's a symptom of the Bakersfield Burnout. That's her term for a condition that affects most of them at News-13. Working at the station with the worst ratings, the worst equipment and the lowest pay in town wears down even the best of them.

Andy says, "So I don't know if this is a good idea, but maybe we could go out for a beer after work. Or something. It might help with that nasty crankiness."

He says it sweetly, almost shyly. A date? She wonders. It's been a long time since a man has looked at her that way—especially one as young and good looking as Andy Blackman.

"That's a great idea, but I just have too much to do. Not tonight, thanks." Although there is a tickle of temptation, Kathy sees two major problems with the proposal. First, there is the age factor. She's thirty, and Andy is only two years out of college.

And the last thing she needs is another fling with someone who is just passing through town. The first couple of times Kathy didn't think they were flings until she had been flung. It's taken two broken hearts and a year of therapy to accept the fact that the newsroom in Bakersfield is not fertile ground for lasting romance.

But when you're married to the TV news business, you don't have much opportunity to meet anyone on the outside. So what's a girl to do?

Kathy takes a sticky-note pad from her desk and writes, "Get a cat." She peels the top page and places it on her blouse next to one reminding her to call the mayor's assistant for an updated city council agenda.

The sound of a door latch draws her attention to the news director's office. Finally. The new boss is coming up for air. Hunter Riley is a mystery to her. Kathy doesn't mind a good mystery if it can be solved—preferably in the span of an average prime time TV show. She always wanted to be one of Charlie's Angels. Kathy would be the brown-haired smart Angel. The one who gets to rescue everybody else.

Hunter Riley isn't the villain, but he is definitely a mysterious character who will have to open up before the final credits roll. Hunter has had very little to say or do with the staff since he got here a week ago. He hasn't been unsociable. Just busy.

Kathy Wright is on the case.

Hunter is sitting with his head in his hands, rubbing his eyes with his palms when she taps on the door.

"You should get more sleep," she says.

"Just what I was thinking."

"You're working so hard I feel guilty," Kathy says. "I even came in extra, extra early today and here you were."

Hunter looks a little guilty himself. "It's nothing. He reaches out and pulls videotape from the machine on a cabinet to his right. He places the tape on a small stack near the computer monitor on his desk.

Kathy says, "You've been going through a lot of audition tapes. Any luck yet?"

"Luck?"

"Finding an anchor for the Five O'clock Report," she explains. "I'm glad you're working on that first. Kent hasn't had a co-anchor since Betty Updike left. That was almost six months ago."

"Kent?" Hunter pauses. Kent Abernathy. News-13 anchor at five, six and eleven. "Oh yeah. No, I haven't seen anyone yet I'm dying to hire."

Hunter smiles. It's the crooked smile of a rapscallion, suggesting there is some warmth beneath the surface. Kathy thought she saw a flash of it before; now she's certain. And it improves her mood.

After a reasonable lapse of silence, Hunter notices Kathy is holding one hand behind her. He tilts his head and leans to the left, trying to peek past her hips. She whips her hand from behind her back and sets a gift on the desk in front of Hunter. It's a coffee mug with the station's logo.

"In honor of your first week here, I scammed this from the sales department for you," she says. "Sort of… a welcome-to-KDOA present."

Hunter picks it up and turns it in his hands. Someone has neatly painted the word "Boss" in bold letters.

"It's nice." Hunter thanks her, tilts the cup upside down and winks. "Too bad it's empty."

"That," Kathy responds tartly, "is not my department. I only supply the mug. You're on your own for the coffee."

Kathy lingers, tempted to drop into the chair across from the boss. "It's a real change to have someone with your experience sitting in this office. The network and New York and Chicago and all that..." she says. "What do you think about us so far?"

Hunter studies her with his hazel eyes. He has long lashes that look a little feminine. Kathy thinks they're thoroughly cute.

"I think the newscast is pretty typical," Hunter replies. "Not bad. What do you think?"

"I think it's darn good considering we have half the staff of everyone else in town. And we pay less than everyone else too, so morale is bad. We can't keep the good reporters. They either go across town or to a bigger market. You already know about the ratings. But they've been in the dumper for so long, it's okay. We're used to it." Kathy pauses long enough to suck a quick breath. "So I hope you're going to fix all that. Do you have a plan yet?"

"Nope. If things are so bad, why do you stay here?"

It's a question Kathy has asked herself from time to time. It makes her stop to think now, because she's never had a news director who cared enough to ask. "I can't help it. I can't imagine doing anything else for a living. How come you don't have a plan? Usually the news directors come in and want to change everything around right away."

"I suppose it's because I'm not like them. But if you like doing news so much, why Bakersfield? How long have you been here, and why aren't you in a bigger market yourself?"

They are two people fencing with words. Their questions are pointed but not really lethal. Kathy hadn't planned on talking about herself.

"I was born in Bakersfield. I'll probably die here. It's a great town to grow up in. Great if you have family, or if you want to start one. It's a great place to raise kids and all that. I take it you're not married?"

"I was once," Hunter replies. He lets the matter drop.

"Just curious. You know what a small business this is. I checked with friends in other places. You've worked in six other cities. Now you're here in Bakersfield. Haven't you wanted to settle down?"

Hunter shakes his head and laughs. It's a forced laugh. "I got away from the network with the idea of settling down in one of those cities. Things didn't work out. That hurt the marriage. Satisfied? This isn't some story to cover. Are you always this bold?"

"I'm a reporter. Do you always do that? Breeze over the answer to a question and follow up with a question of your own?"

"I'm a reporter too." Then Hunter raises a finger to his lips to shush her. "I'm just masquerading as a news director right now. Don't tell anyone."

They both laugh as Kathy retreats to her desk at the head of the newsroom. The image of her face lingers with Hunter. It's wide open with high, round cheeks and dark eyes. With her dark hair and innocent air, Kathy reminds him of someone.

As he studies her through the blinds of his office window, the newsroom morphs into a New York City apartment. The characters moving about doing what? Nothing, really.

Yada, yada, yada. Kathy reminds him of the neurotic TV character Elaine on Seinfeld. Hey, everyone is neurotic on Seinfeld. That was the show they pitched as a show to be all about nothing. He thinks he wouldn't mind doing nothing with her.

He picks up a few pieces of paper from the in-box on his desk but doesn't give them any significant attention. He tosses them back. Hunter stretches and wanders into the main newsroom to check the clock on the wall behind Kathy's desk. 11:25. He looks at Kathy. She looks at the clock.

"Lunch?"

He nods.

She holds up a finger and dives into a folder on her desk. A moment later she's waving a fistful of take-out menus. "Okay, let's see what we have here."

Kathy stops abruptly. She lays a finger along side her temple and closes her eyes. She squeezes them tighter. Tighter.

"What?" Hunter asks. "What is it?"

"Shut up!" Then, "Bank robbery." Kathy wheels and races back to her desk. She raises the volume on the police scanner that has caught only her attention. She snatches the phone from its cradle. "Did anybody get the address on that?"

Hunter had been oblivious, tuned out to the white noise of the newsroom. He had missed the call completely. He leans casually against the doorframe to his office, despite the wave of adrenaline building somewhere deep inside him. He watches as Kathy, with a phone pinned to her ear and furiously jotting notes on a pad in front of her, she sends the troops into battle. She points at a photographer and shouts at a reporter. "Head south to Ming Avenue. It's across from the Mall on the east side of the highway."

Hunter glances at the newsroom clock. 11:26.

Nothing turns into everything. The newsroom crackles with excitement. Even with all his years of reporting on cops and crime, disaster and distress, Hunter isn't immune to the jolt that hits with every opportunity of breaking news. For anyone with a reporter's heart, it is a call to action.

But Hunter is cautious, like someone who has just asked the prettiest girl in school to the dance. She accepts, but he worries she may turn out to be less than the perfect date of his dreams. Hunter knows that unless the robbery turns into a drawn-out hostage situation, a remote possibility at best, they won't get more than a bit of video of police milling around outside the bank building, a shot of the yellow police tape flapping in the breeze and a close-up of a hand-written note on the door to customers:

"This bank is temporarily closed due to robbery. We apologize for the inconvenience."

In the end, it will only fill thirty seconds on the evening news. He listens more closely to the scanner, hoping officers will put out a call for backup, or an ambulance. He waits for signs of some actual mayhem, something worthy of the newscast lead story. Instead he gets a calm description of the suspect—approximately six feet, 170 pounds with long gray hair. Wearing a dark blue or black wind-breaker and nylon pants. Last seen leaving the bank on foot.

The dispatcher's description is by the book, detached, almost robotic. This one has a Texas twang. Why is it police dispatchers, if they have any accent at all, seem to migrate from Texas or Okla-homa? You never ever hear of one with, say, a British clip:

"A tall chap, rather thin with longish gray hair," Hunter imag-ines they would say. "Casually attired in a shade a bit beyond royal. Escaped the scene in a brisk walk. Be good fellows and detain him if it's not too taxing, and do take care. Cheerio!"

Hunter shakes his head and searches for the menus Kathy had discarded in her dash to the assignment desk. The South Valley Bank robbery is over. Just another two-bit heist.

Oh well. Better luck next time.

Slug: Job Search

Anchor intro:

If you are like most Americans, you have already changed jobs, or even careers, at least once. Experts tell us we have become a nation of vocational nomads—free agents, if you will—where the job security of our parents is dying off with their generation, and the average American spends only seven years employed at a given company. And nowhere does that revolving door move people more quickly, more efficiently, than in television news.

Roll Tape

The face on the TV screen has classic good looks, a strong jaw and perfect teeth. It's a long, lean face, the kind the camera falls in love with. His hair is a light shade of brown, and the studio lights overhead weave streaks of gold into it. If it were darker, the silver that is slowly taking over would be more noticeable. Still, there is enough gray showing to mark the kind of experience and wisdom that should win the trust of both men and women in the key demographics of TV news viewers. Hunter watches the videotape and thinks, all in all, it is everything you'd want in your news anchor.

It is, of course, his own face on the monitor.

It's afternoon. Kathy and the others are busy stuffing the bank robbery and the other stories of the day into the evening newscast. Hunter is locked up in his office again.

He hasn't watched himself on videotape this closely for years. When he first started anchoring, he would race to a tape machine immediately after each newscast and analyze his performance frame by frame. Back then he was eager to learn and to improve. As experience and self-confidence took hold, reviewing tapes of his work on a regular basis became pointless.

Hunter stops, rewinds and starts the tape again, this time with the volume turned up. When he critiques his work, he likes to watch the tape twice—the first time without sound. It's a trick he learned from Fred Pleasant, the ageless network icon who once took ten minutes to coach him when Hunter was a rookie in D.C.

"Those ballsy voices are overrated," Pleasant had sniffed. He explained that you can tell everything about an anchor's personality and ability to "sell" a story just by watching all the subtle signals from their posture, facial expressions and the light in their eyes that leaves no doubt they are communicating one-on-one with you, the viewer. Hunter believes it.

Hunter is watching a newscast he did during his last week in Des Moines. He isn't happy with the lighting and the outdated news set, but it's the most recent anchor work he has saved on tape. This newscast is more than six months old. News directors in the *real* TV markets—the top fifty markets, in Hunter's mind— might prefer to see something more recent, but he expects they'll understand. Six months of unemployment is not an insurmountable handicap in this business. Hunter will even survive having to dump Murray the agent-weasel who wouldn't take his calls after Des Moines.

Satisfied with the second run-through, Hunter rewinds the tape, takes it from the machine and adds it to a half dozen others stacked next to his computer monitor. One is headed this afternoon to KCRA in Sacramento. Hunter had talked with an assistant news director there yesterday, and yes, they still need a male anchor for the weekend shift. Weekends. Oh well.

Hunter has mailing labels typed up for the other tapes in the stack. Albuquerque and Columbus, Baltimore and Rochester.

This tape, the one on top, he plans to hand-deliver to Walter J. Redmond, vice president in charge of news for the Universal Broadcasting Network—UBN. He is building a news empire and running it out of UBN's flagship station in Los Angeles. Hunter, like so many who are on the move inside the industry, has been keeping an eye on the trade magazines with a keen interest in UBN's recent acquisitions and expansion plans.

Ever since a cartel of Internet moguls from Silicon Valley bought the majority stake in UBN, the network has been buying TV stations across the country and signing working agreements with others, hoping to create a powerhouse like NBC, CBS and the rest. The experts are predicting that cable television is changing everything, that the news networks will expand and migrate there.

ESPN is cool, Hunter thinks, but not much more on that side of broadcasting shows much promise. For now, news is still a four-horse race with UBN just getting out of the gate.

Redmond has been spending the network's influx of new money like an addicted shopper with a line of credit on an Internet auction site. The new owners up in Silicon Valley are led by Bill Goliath and his billion dollar-deep pockets at MegaScan Software. His vision is to marry a network of TV stations with the World Wide Web. Its showcase will be a 24-hour cable TV news operation called MS-UBN. And while Hunter isn't entirely sold on the concept, Redmond needs to hire several top-notch anchors for the studios in Los Angeles. To Hunter, that is Anchor Opportunity-dot-com.

So he sits in his office in Bakersfield, and his mind flies down the valley like a crop duster over the vineyards and the olive orchards that have been forced to grow in sporadic patches along the desert floor. He soars over the brown hills at the southern end of the San Joaquin Valley to the Promised Land.

Geographically, the Tehachapi Mountains are all that stand between him and a big-market job in Los Angeles. Professionally, they may as well be on different planets.

But working at KDOA, a United Broadcasting Network affiliate, has a strategic advantage. As a member of the UBN family, Hunter is only 112 miles away from a plum job, with a newly minted resume, a solid audition tape, talent, and the experience for a big-time anchor job. Most of all, he has an inside opportunity to network his way onto Redmond's short list of applicants. UBN is holding a premier party for all its west coast affiliates tomorrow night in L.A. Walter J. Redmond will be there. So will Hunter Riley.

Hunter takes one of the industry journals from the top drawer of his desk and begins searching for the classified section—job opportunities. Kathy interrupts him with a knock on the door before he can find it. She barges in before he can tell her to go away.

Kathy drops a small stack of papers on his desk and ceremoniously plucks a yellow note from her breast. She crumples it one-handed and pitches it into the wastebasket.

"Overtime sheets," she announces.

Hunter blinks at the stack she delivered. Oh goody. More paperwork. Every day of the week someone brings in an equipment requisition form, budget form, vacation request form, work schedules, engineering reports and forms to order more forms. All this work is seriously cutting into the time he needs to find a job. On top of it all, he keeps getting written suggestions from the sales staff to provide news coverage for preferred clients. At least he can file those away immediately in the trash can.

"What, exactly, do I do with these?" he asks.

"I've already initialed each one, but you'll have to make sure it matches the person's time sheet before you send them up to payroll. They'll want everything approved and signed and upstairs this afternoon."

Hunter has been doing his best to ignore the pile of paperwork growing in a shallow wooden box on his desk, saving his energy for only the most important stuff.

Payroll is important stuff. Money is good.

Hunter reluctantly tosses his magazine aside. As Kathy turns to leave she bumps into a short, rail-thin, young black man. It takes Hunter a moment to link the figure to his mental roster of staff members. Ray the WebGuy.

Ray drops one more form onto the pile in Hunter's in-box. "The Avitar-2000 crashed again. But I downloaded a MegaScan patch kit and debugged the proprietary code-a-phone with a little data wrap of my own device, and the icon-click, Windows vernacular piece-of-shit program jazzed space in a nano-tech second."

Hunter squints one eye shut and raises an eyebrow over the other. He needs a translation. "What?"

Ray points to the invoice he delivered. "Problem solved. Log off in ink on the hard copy. Kill another tree. We'll snail-mail it back to headquarters and let them pay for it."

Ray is gone before Hunter can get an explanation. "Does he always talk like that?"

Kathy nods. "It's not so hard, once you get used to it."

"Well, at least the problem is solved. Whatever it was."

"Yeah. But what now? The network paid for all Ray's fancy equipment and had it installed here so we could do more Internet stuff. Take a look at it some time. It's pretty impressive. Big bucks. We could never afford that, but so what? We still haven't figured out what to do with it. Right now Ray just takes the scripts we run on the newscast and rewrites them for the web site."

"But it is a good-looking web site. And this is all MS-UBN," Hunter says. "They have a plan."

"Even God has a plan. It's just not too clear."

It is an interesting point that Hunter doesn't have time to explore. A shouting match has erupted in the newsroom.

Kathy and Hunter join the others just as a videocassette flies across the room and lands with a clatter near shelves of identical tapes on the far wall. Valerie Watson, the station's number one reporter, is about to launch a second missile when she spots Hunter nearby.

Her adversary is Kent Abernathy, KDOA's main anchor. He's decked out in summer anchor attire: crisp white shirt and rep tie with a navy blazer over baggy gym shorts and flip-flops. Fortunately, you'll only see him on TV from the waist up.

"Just keep your foot off the teleprompter pedal until I finish my story! That's all I'm asking," Kent says loudly, but his voice wavers. His arms are folded and he attempts to hold his ground, but leans slightly toward the exit as if keeping his escape option ready.

"If you didn't drag out the end of every story, I wouldn't have to cue it up to my stories so quickly," Valerie shouts. "You do that deliberately. Everyone knows you hate me."

Valerie swings her finger in a wide arc at others in the room. They cringe as if expecting a lightning bolt from her accusing digit.

"Don't be ridiculous," Kent says. "I don't think enough about you to hate you."

Valerie growls.

Hunter, having seen enough, steps into the fray.

"What's going on?" he demands.

"Valerie's been the fill-in anchor on the five o'clock news with Kent," Kathy mumbles, as if that is all the explanation Hunter needs for the outburst.

"How am I supposed to finish reading a story when she runs up the prompter like that? A hundred miles an hour." Kent whips the back of his hand from his waist to the ceiling and snaps his head back as he follows its movement. "Zip!"

Hunter is still confused.

Kent, Valerie and Kathy take turns explaining that the newscast script for the studio teleprompter is controlled by two separate foot pedals at the anchor desk—one for each anchor. That way the anchors can roll through the stories they're responsible for, and read at their own pace. Apparently Kent and Valerie have been wrestling for control of the script like two children fighting over a favorite toy.

"You mean you don't have someone to run the 'prompter for you?" Hunter asks. This is a new one on him.

"Maybe they do it like that in the big city, so you wouldn't understand," Valerie says with a nasty snort. "We don't have the luxury. This station is too cheap, okay?"

Hunter decides he isn't going to like this woman.

"We wouldn't have this problem if you'd hire a new anchor for the five o'clock show," Kathy says in a low voice as she leans close to him.

Hunter looks at her, then the others. Clearly this is a minor crisis to be resolved immediately. He's only been on the job a bit more than a week. What do they want from him—leadership? So soon?

Somewhere in the back of his mind he hears a deep voice. "This is a test. This is only a test. If this had been a real emergency, you would have been instructed where to tune in your area…" No threat of nuclear fallout here.

"Kathy," he says. "Weren't you just telling me what a great reporter Valerie is, and that it was a shame we had to pull her of the streets for this fill-in gig? That means we're losing a top asset—her stories every day." Hunter wonders if Kathy had really said that. It sounds vaguely familiar.

"Uh, sure."

Hunter continues, "Do we really need *two* anchors at five o'clock right now? Kent. You're strong enough to anchor alone until we can find a replacement for Betsy."

"Betty," Kathy corrects him.

"Betty. Kent, can you do that? Can you shoulder the load for just a while longer? That way Valerie can get back to doing those killer reports that have everyone in town talking."

Hunter shovels the shit pretty thick. In return, he gets muttering but no serious grousing. Eventually he gets half-hearted agreement. Still, it's half a heart more than he would expect from a seasoned, more experienced staff.

"That's good," he says. "Griping just takes all the fun out of this business. Let's have a little fun and stop wasting all this energy on the small things."

No one has a response, so Hunter suggests they get back to work. He returns to his office, moving slowly and listening for the sounds of computer keyboards clacking and videotapes editing.

They come slowly and then pick up pace as everything gets back to normal. It's the sweet sound of a news machine.

"Children," Hunter mutters as he crosses the threshold to his office. He knows he has just sugarcoated a problem away. Like Ray the WebGuy's software program patch with its introverted layup digital fan belt doohickey—or whatever Ray called it—Hunter isn't sure he understands what kind of patch he has just applied to the newsroom problem. It just felt like the right thing to do.

It's a temporary fix at best. That's all right. If Hunter can use the UBN affiliates' conference this weekend to network his way into a job in L.A., this will be the last KDOA crisis Hunter will have to face.

He turns and looks back into the newsroom. Too bad, he thinks. That was kind of fun. A slam-dunk for the boss.

Hunter reaches across the desk for his *Broadcasting Magazine*. He remembers being interrupted in his search for the classifieds. Then Hunter spies the stack of overtime sheets Kathy had dropped on his desk.

Oh yeah. Payday is coming. Money is important. Can't put that off.

He takes a pen and picks up a page from the top of the stack. Hunter wonders, who has time to find a real job when work keeps getting in the way?

Slug: Road Trip

Anchor intro:

> More than five hundred broadcasters, from the smallest town to the network penthouse, have turned out in Los Angeles for Universal Broadcasting Network's West Coast Convention. UBN launched the event with a party for its affiliate stations. One part business, one part pep rally and at least two-fifths whiskey, it is a perfect cocktail for wheelers and dealers and brown-nosers alike. The network's top executives mingle with representatives from the affiliates and, in the process, open themselves up for praise, criticism, advice or hustle from anyone with an agenda. And that, of course, is everyone.

Roll tape

Zoom in on Hunter's face. His jaw is set; his eyes are narrowed as he stares out at the highway, pensive. Distracted. You can see he is miles away. His mind is racing ahead, already passing through the doors of the Ambassador Hotel in Los Angeles.

Tuttle is driving and, despite the blast of cold from the car's air conditioner, he keeps wiping sweat from his brow. Tuttle flings it from his finger across the car, splattering Hunter's knees and lap, raining minuscule drops of perspiration on the passenger window. Hunter barely notices.

He is thinking of the three or four solid contacts from his past who will be at the UBN convention, mostly about the three or four people who have a pipeline to the network's brass and at least a small amount of influence to help Hunter. By far, his best chance may be Ryan Billings. Billings is the golden-boy correspondent who once subbed for Brokaw on the Nightly News. UBN stole him away from the peacock network a few months ago to anchor its own evening newscast.

Hunter takes note of the road sign: thirty-one miles to L.A. One entire continent and a lifetime away from the days when Hunter and Billings shared a desk in the Washington bureau. Back then, they were underpaid and overworked cub reporters at the network. Hunter glances over at Tuttle. He was there, too.

At the bureau, they got very little exposure on camera while doing the bulk of the legwork for correspondents, but it was a start. Two years with too much travel and too little appreciation were enough for Hunter. He got married and found out Joyce didn't like being the wife of a network news hound who spent more time on the road chasing stories than he did at home. Joyce pushed hard to settle down in some local market. Hunter resisted the idea until New York offered him a job in front of the camera with regular hours.

New York is the country's largest local television market. In retrospect, Hunter should have realized his career had nowhere to go but down. By the time his career reached Oklahoma City, Joyce had had enough and Hunter found himself down-sized out of a marriage when she headed back to her old job with a law firm in Chicago.

"Schumer and Roy the Lobster Boy will be there. That'll be fun," Tuttle says, as if he could read Hunter's mind.

"And Ryan is headlining. The star. Who'd have thunk it?" Hunter replied.

Ryan Billings stayed behind at the network when Hunter left. He eventually earned a promotion to correspondent by working long days and developing a reputation as a competent but sometimes overly dramatic reporter. Good timing and a couple of lucky scoops for the network catapulted Billings into the limelight.

Now he is settling in at his new UBN home, anchor of the *Prime Time Report with Ryan Billings*. More importantly for Hunter, Billings has become a frequent tennis partner of the network's news chief, Walter J. Redmond. Hunter suspects Billings served and volleyed his way into the anchor job at UBN, and that he won Redmond over more with a slicing backhand on the court than with his delivery of the news.

Hunter doesn't particularly like tennis or playing that social suck-up-to-the-boss game either. But with the job in L.A. at stake, he isn't about to take chances. Twenty-six miles from L.A. now, and he is armed with a resume and audition tape for Redmond, and his battered but serviceable tennis racquet just in case. It's not what you know… Hunter nibbles on his upper lip. There are others he can lean on, if necessary.

"Maxine Currigan. Jake Brown. Dusty Simon," Tuttle recites. "It'll be good to see them again. The big names sure move around a lot more these days than in the past."

They had left Bakersfield late, but Tuttle is making good time, slowing only enough to keep all four wheels on the highway where I-5 cuts through the Angeles National Forest before dropping into the L.A. basin.

"Happy hour waits for no one." It is Tuttle's slogan for the day.

* * *

The noise in the ballroom at the Ambassador Hotel reminds Hunter of the flamingos at the National Zoo in Washington. He can't tell if anyone in the room is actually conversing or if they're honking just to hear themselves make noise. It sounds much the same to him. Robby the Robot, the Universal Broadcasting Network mascot, is greeting conventioneers at the door and handing out goodie bags.

"Just what I need," Hunter complains. "Another coffee mug."

"I've got a buddy with an impressive collection," Tuttle replies. "One from each of the stations he's worked at. Three networks and eleven different station logos. Not bad in sixteen years."

Hunter asks about the KDOA station owner. "Is Don going to be here? I've been at the station for a week now and still haven't met him."

"Old man Andrews? Shit, what's the rush?" Tuttle wants to know. "I was hired by the guy I replaced. So it was a good four months before I bumped into Andrews in the hallway. Until then we had a wonderful relationship—a few memos and voice mail. If

I went looking for him in his office, he was never around. He pretty much ignored me, and that was friggin' fine. Once I met him in person, it was a different ballgame. Now I can't keep him off my back." Tuttle sighs.

"So he'll be here?"

"Oh, he'll be here all right. Bet the house. He may not be much for socializing with riff-raff like us, but he wouldn't miss a party like this, except that…" Tuttle lifts his massive frame a scant inch to peer over the crowd. "The bar is that-away." He points to the right.

"And since Andrews doesn't drink, I suspect he'll be over there," Tuttle then points left, to the opposite end of the room where banks of giant TV monitors frame a stage and podium. "But I *do* drink so I'm going this way, partner. Besides, it's not polite to mingle with drunks without something of your own in hand. Bad form. Tell me if you spot The Don-ster."

Hunter yells after him. He doesn't even know what the station owner looks like, but it's lost in the noise.

After making his own brief trip to the bar, Hunter circulates through the room with a Lite beer wrapped in a UBN-embossed napkin. The drink is really just a prop. One sip. Then two. That's all. No telling who he will run into, and he wants to have a clear head. There will be time to relax later.

Hunter drops in on one clique and then another. Station owners, managers, news directors, anchors and reporters. The conversations fall into two categories. One is current events and the game of one-upmanship to see who has a better grasp of today's headlines.

The other, dominated by the anchors and reporters, consists of war stories from the trenches. Hunter listens, nods and sympathizes. Pessimists by nature, journalists love to share their failures. Better still, they love to feast on the failures of colleagues.

Hunter watches them, and he recognizes the class system shapes the interaction, even the very formation of each group. And he thinks about the Japanese.

In Japanese business circles, strangers exchange business cards with company names and corporate titles that, in some unspoken way, have come to define their society's pecking order. From that point on, they continue to acknowledge each other with a bow. The rules dictate that a junior executive, or one from a lesser corporation, must bow lower than his more esteemed colleague.

At a gathering like this, television news insiders use market size as their calling card. For easy reference and advertising purposes, each city in America with a television station is conveniently ranked by size. New York? Number one. Houston? Number eleven. Lansing, Michigan, is halfway down the list, coming in this week at 105. At the bottom is number 211: Glendive, Montana. Two hundred-eleven markets and each one is fully aware of its rung on the industry ladder.

Hunter thinks about the Japanese executives as he circles the room, because in all the overly sincere handshakes and nervous small talk, he can see a lot of implied bowing throughout the ballroom tonight.

A nice-looking blonde is holding court in one small circle. She grabs Hunter with a glance and draws him to the group. She's wearing a bright red dress with spaghetti straps. Her hair is shoulder length and permed in that wild Hollywood style that makes you wonder if she simply forgot to brush it, or if two horny squirrels had run circles in a mating ritual before settling down to nest in her locks. She returns Hunter's gaze as she moves to his side. She must be an Anchor, with a capital A.

She coos. "One of the nice things about a hoop-de-doo like this, is you can go up to someone and ask, 'Haven't we met someplace before?' and really mean it."

Hunter nods. "I can't say it occurred to me, but I'll have to give it a try. Whether I know them or not."

She has an intoxicating laugh. He runs a finger down the length of the bottle in his hand, catching the edge of the label.

"I'm Angela Powell," she says. "I do the six o'clock news at Channel 11 in Tucson." (unspoken: market size 78) "And you really do look familiar."

"I guess you could say I used to be somebody." He offers his hand. "Hunter Riley. I was with NBC a few years back." Too many years, but what the heck.

Angela nods and looks at him the way a good tailor measures a man for a suit. Then she gets it. "Of course. Hunter Riley. You were with Eyewitness News in Chicago" (market size: 3). "I grew up in Highland Park. I can't believe it! Hunter Riley."

She rolls her eyes and flirts. Angela touches Hunter's arm and the first hint—a vague suggestion, really—of late night possibilities creeps into his head.

She asks Hunter what he does now.

"I'm in management these days. A news director."

Her face brightens. "There are a lot of you here. Do you know John Shoulders, over there? He's the news director at channel three here in L.A." (market size: 2) "He wants to see my resume tape. I think this is the kind of market I could fall in love with."

"Ah, but would it love you back, Angela?"

That stops her for only a moment, and then she laughs again—a glorious, uninhibited laugh. "That is the question, isn't it?" The buzz of conversation and the rattle of ice in a thousand glasses force Angela to move closer. Her hair is perfumed. Hunter smells roses. She asks where Hunter is news directing.

"Bakersfield."

Her smile falls. "What market size is that?"

He swallows. "130."

Her grin hits bottom, and Hunter watches his stock plummet with the corners of her mouth. He is no longer good enough for the girl from Tucson.

To her credit, Angela makes a little more small talk before making her retreat. When she's gone, Hunter fortifies himself with a long, hard draw on his beer. He drifts without a rudder through the sea of bodies, picking up bits of industry gossip and exchanging thoughts on technology or ethics with people whose names he will never remember. And he keeps watch over the crowd for the arrival of UBN anchorman Ryan Billings.

The sign is anything but subtle when Billings arrives. You could set off rockets. Strike up the band. The buzz in the room takes on a different, frenetic pitch. Billings is the queen bee, attracting the largest cluster of drones at each stop around the room—the bar, then the stage, or at the table of an affiliate station owner who wants his picture taken with Billings. The crowd is thick wherever he goes, even in front of the men's room where relief has to be delayed several times by good-hearted folks who take pleasure in just shaking his hand.

On a smaller scale, a much smaller scale, Hunter had felt that kind of adoration during his short stints as a news anchor in Chicago, and even Des Moines. Face time at social events is part of the job. So is being kind to viewers who recognize you with a forkful of spaghetti halfway between your plate and your mouth at your favorite Italian restaurant. It is a pain, and a pleasure. The demands on your free time, the interrupted meals, movies, the occasionally rude intrusion on your solitude are the pain. Hunter watches the Billings circle drift closer, and he sighs. He misses the pleasure of Anchordom, the friendly smiles, the unconditional respect and the bonding with total strangers who want nothing more than a moment with the town's celebrity.

"Celebrity, my ass." Billings responds to Hunter's gentle ribbing with a firm handshake and thousand-watt smile when Hunter catches up to him between the clusters of humanity. "You know better, Hunter. It's good to see you again."

"It's nice to see you finally make it to the big chair. I'll have to check the numbers and see if I won that pool we started back in D.C. Everybody knew you'd make network anchor some day. I think I had spring of 2001."

"Did anyone bet against me?"

"If I remember right, Doris Carter thought you were too… too flashy."

Billings has a glass of something gold and expensive-looking in his hand. It is a far cry from the six-pack special of the week they shared whenever they could afford it so long ago in Washington. Billings clinks his glass against the bottle in Hunter's hand and laughs again. His eyes are full of enthusiasm and interest, and so attentive that something special passes between the two men. They connect, truly connect, as if some supernatural charge has obliterated everything around them and only their joint fate and fortunes mattered at that moment.

And then the moment is gone. Just like that.

The eyes that Hunter had captured are darting away again as Billings asks, "So what are you up to these days?"

Hunter gives him the ninety-second version of his road to Bakersfield.

"Bakersfield?" Billings snorts. "You can do better."

"Well, Bakersfield is only a temporary thing." Hunter counts to five slowly. He wants to avoid coming across like every other job seeker. "It presents some interesting challenges. And it's given me a taste for life here on the West Coast. After all those years living back east, I think I could really get to like it out here and settle down someplace like Los Angeles."

"Uh-huh. You know Redmond's looking for an anchor here in L.A. You ought to have your agent give him a call."

Hunter cringes at the thought of Murray the weasel-agent. "Sure. But I was wondering," he begins.

Hold that thought. A short, thin and slick suit slithers in and steals what is left of Billing's attention. He's dressed in black from his wing tips to the very stylish onyx button cover on his black, banded-collar shirt. Hunter recognizes the type, but not the face. Definitely network. Probably Promotions, Publicity or Programming—one of the flashy divisions.

"Ryan. I have someone you simply have to meet," Slick Suit says.

Hunter catches a whiff of roses and a streak of red satin. Tucson Angela is at the man's elbow. He introduces to Billings the woman who had jilted Hunter for a bigger market prey only an hour earlier.

Billings takes her hand. "I've been watching you all night," he says in the voice that is rapidly making Ryan Billings one of the most trusted men in America. "I was hoping I'd have the opportunity to meet you."

He hands his drink to Hunter without taking his eyes off the woman. Billings quizzes her about her background, her career and her life in Tucson. They share small talk while Hunter, for a lack of something better to do, ponders the melting ice in Billing's discarded drink. It does little to cool his palm and his fingers as they tighten their grip. Two executives from New York crowd into the group and Hunter surrenders as little space as possible in making room for them. The intimacy now destroyed, the circle begins to grow and take on a new life as others join in.

"I seem to have lost my drink," Billings announces. The group declares it a terrible shame. Without so much as a final nod to Hunter, they march off to the nearest watering hole.

Cheaper barware would have shattered from the pressure in Hunter's hand. He takes aim at the back of Ryan Billing's head. If he had any skill at all as a quarterback, he thinks, he could drill the pompous son-of-a-bitch.

If he had been any more of a man, he would at least try.

Slug: Pistol Pete's

Anchor intro:

>*If success breeds contempt and adversity builds character, the life of Hunter Riley should be a springboard of inspiration to everyone treading water in the shallow end of the talent pool. You might think one more humiliation is not the foundation for rebuilding a dream, but salvation sometimes comes from unlikely sources. The real talent may be in recognizing a life preserver when it's thrown at you, even if it comes wrapped in a wig and a g-string.*

Roll tape

Thump. Thump. Thump.

The sound you hear is the bass pulsing, straining the speakers of a multi-watt, state-of-the-art surround-sound system. It rattles your teeth, and only the whiskey softens it in your head. Somewhere, ten or twenty decibels below, synthesized fusion is trying to make music with the bass, but it gets lost in the thump, thump, thump. The sound is heavy and it is primal.

Pencil-thin spotlights dart out of the ceiling. Streaks of white heat, they catch you and make you flinch as they sweep across the nightclub. They bounce off your table, the bar in the back of the room and the skin of three mostly naked women dancing on separate stages at Pistol Pete's Gentlemen's Club.

"She wants you, Hunter," John Tuttle shouts. "She wants you bad." He sits back in his chair and slurps his drink. He wrinkles his face with an impish grin and pushes a dollar bill across the tabletop toward Hunter.

"Go on," John says. He waves at Hunter to tip the blond dancer on the stage two tables away. She is watching them, judging them and smiling. She dances to the edge of the stage and tugs provocatively at the waist of her g-string, in effect issuing Hunter a challenge. When he slides the dollar bill back at Tuttle, she stops and pouts like a little girl momentarily denied candy from a visiting uncle.

Hunter is cruising on an alcohol high somewhere just above the cloud of reason, but John had taken off like a rocket from the moment they walked in to Pistol Pete's. He will hate himself in the morning when he wakes up from the crash landing.

"Go on. She wants you," John says again.

Hunter waves him off with the glass in his hand, splashing whiskey on the table. "Not my type."

That satisfies John. In fact, it pleases him greatly to spend that buck on a moment's ecstasy for himself. He snatches the dollar bill and weaves his way past a table of businessmen with beer-stained ties who are shouting come-ons at the dancers. The blond perks up immediately and begins a slow, rhythmic undulation in front of Tuttle. She draws closer and guides his hand to a safe spot between her hipbone and heaven's gate. He wedges the dollar under the ribbon of flimsy fabric. They laugh and whisper and share a secret.

She nods and, looking past Tuttle, blows a kiss to Hunter before dancing away to grab the adoration and money of her other customers.

"C'mon, Hunter, loosen up!" John says when he returns. He does a shimmy and bounces his head up and down like one of those spring-loaded dashboard dolls. "Titties. Uh huh. Uh huh. Gotta' love those titties." He drops into his chair, exhausted, wraps his fist around the whiskey glass and leans heavily on the table in Hunter's direction.

"I swear. You put those babies on the set, and the ratings would go THROUGH THE ROOF! Yeah! Bring it on, baybee." A bodacious redhead has replaced the blond on the nearest stage. Big Red now owns Tuttle's attention.

Hunter puts a hand on Tuttle's arm to keep him from howling, if nothing else. He is pretty far gone himself, but he isn't ready for total abandon. "Wrong demographics, John. You won't get the eighteen-to-thirty-five-year-old women that way."

Tuttle shakes his head. "We've already got Kent Abernathy and all his teeth and his plastic hair and his... his... well, hell. We'll have him take off his shirt, too. Naked news. I love it! Through the roof, baby. Ratings. That's what we'd have."

Hunter tries to detour the waitress when Tuttle orders another round. He doesn't need to fly any higher and wants to throttle back.

"Make it a beer," he says. "Lite beer."

He runs his tongue across his front teeth and wonders when they started growing fuzz. His nose is getting numb, too. Hunter glances around the club, where firm bodies in alternating pools of light and shadow are working their clientele amid the audience. He sighs. Despite all the alcohol in his system, one part, lower on his body, is tense enough to remind Hunter he hasn't spent a night with a woman since, well, since somewhere in the middle of Bill Clinton's first term.

The music changes, and Bob Seeger's voice bounces some old time rock 'n roll off the walls. Call him a relic; call him what you will, but Hunter relaxes at the sound of the familiar music. That's more like it. The D.J. segues from Seeger into something more soulful. Hunter doesn't recognize the music, but it's soothing and sexy.

Then a long, lean leg comes out of nowhere and crosses his lap. He ponders the shin and then the knee, moving north to the thigh where it meets the hemline of a short, light blue dress with lots of sparkles on it. He scans past the waist and breasts and into the face of the blond he had left pouting on the stage a few minutes earlier. Her hair is straight and brushes gently on her shoulders. She is wearing a Cleopatra-style tiara. Her eyes are too heavily lined, but it works well with a beauty mark in the crease between her cheek and upper lip. She puts her hands on the back of Hunter's chair and leans forward until her mouth was next to his ear. Her breath is warm.

"Hhhhhhhhhhhhh," she exhales slowly, tantalizingly. "Hi."

"Hi, yourself," Hunter responds.

The dancer stands and pulls the dress over her head while rocking gently to the rhythm of the music. Hunter is flushed. He hasn't paid for a private dance and isn't quite sure how to avoid the embarrassment when the time comes to pony up twenty bucks, or thirty, or whatever naked bodies cost these days. On the other hand, she never asked. He looks to Tuttle for guidance, but Tuttle's face is buried in the cleavage of the big redhead. His arms are spread in total surrender, and the hand near Hunter is waving a pair of sawbucks in his direction. Hunter has been set up.

Cleopatra discards her dress on an empty chair, takes the bills from Tuttle and presses them into Hunter's hand. Her touch lingers, carbonating Hunter's hormones. It is one of those moments in time that the mind captures and replays in such detail that you can never tell if it lasts a few seconds or a few years. Her every movement is drawn out and seems to be in slow motion. Exotic. Erotic. Unlike the other dancers Hunter has watched, she moves with a grace that is sensual without being lewd. And he is absolutely convinced that she wants him as much as he wants her.

Until the music stops.

She laughs with an unexpected and awkward embarrassment, and kisses the tip of his nose the way you would kiss a puppy. She gives him a look of... what? Relief? Gratitude? The sensual confidence she exhibited a moment ago disappears as surely as if someone had cut it off with the flip of a switch. She takes the twenty dollars from his hand and sits in the chair next to Hunter, shyly draping the blue gown across her body. She holds it tight as she extends her hand.

"My name is Sugar."

Naturally, Hunter thinks.

"Sugar Kane," she adds. Of course. She points to the redhead who is dancing again and working Tuttle for another twenty. "That's Candy. Candy Kane. We're supposed to be sisters, but we're not really."

"No?" Hunter tilts his head to look at Sugar's partner. "But you look so much alike." He looks at the blond again. Even in the dim light of the bar, Hunter can tell she is a little older than he thought, probably closer to thirty than most of the dancers working the room. Her face is lean, and her nose sharp enough to cut paper.

"You could do me a big favor if you buy me a drink," she says.

Right. A seven-dollar, watered-down cocktail.

As if reading his mind, she adds, "See, if you buy me a drink I can stay here, and I won't have to work out there." Sugar waves absently at the room.

"Won't this cut into your tips?"

She nods and flags down the waitress. She orders rum and coke. Hunter holds on to the beer in his hand. Tuttle comes up for air from between the redhead's breasts and orders another round for everyone.

"What's your name?" Sugar asks.

Hunter leans closer to be heard over the music. He breathes in her perfume. It's gentle, like an orchid petal kissed by a spring rain. She stays close to Hunter while they sit there searching for a word to break the ice.

"I'm a student at See-Sub," Sugar says. "I'd guess you're a

lawyer, but you don't seem that smarmy."

Hunter shakes his head. "No, not a lawyer. What's See-Sub?"

"The university. C-S-U-Bakersfield."

Of course.

Hunter ponders how quickly they had gone from a couple sharing an excruciatingly intimate moment to an awkward pair with nothing in common.

"So how long..." Hunter begins.

"Have I been dancing?" she finishes. "Not very. How long have you *not* been a lawyer?"

Hunter smiles. "Forever."

Sugar leans closer and studies his face. She nods, her approval unspoken. Then she turns her head to give him a sideways glance. "Am I going to dance again, or can I get dressed now?"

"If you're going have a drink with me, you may as well do it with your clothes on. My name's Hunter."

She stands and slips the slim dress over her head. "Nice to meet you, Mr. Hunter."

He starts to correct her, and then lets it pass.

"You know, you really should loosen your tie a little more," she says.

Hunter hooks a finger over the knot and pulls it down half an inch. "I keep hearing that."

"You're a control freak," she decides.

"How can you tell?"

"You came in wearing a suit and, even though you took off your jacket, you hung it on the back of your chair. You loosened your tie enough to relax, but the knot is still tight. And when you pulled it down just now? You straightened it and adjusted your tie clip."

Sugar reaches over and taps the NBC peacock logo on his tie clip. She leans for a closer look and then raises her eyes to meet his. "You've had three beers and a couple of shots, and you have all of the bottles lined up in a neat row. You're not like your friend here," she points at Tuttle. "And you're building a fence with the bottles between the two of you. Symbolically speaking, of course. You're trying to put some distance between you because you're not really comfortable here."

"What are you, a psych major?"

Sugar nods. "We're studying compulsive behavior this semester. Did you know that everything you do, right down to the tiniest detail, says something about your personality?"

"I don't buy it."

"It's true."

"Learned that in class, I suppose," Hunter says.

She shakes her head this time. "No. Actually I saw that on *60 Minutes*. Or *Dateline*. One of those news shows. And why do you have that NBC thingy on your tie clip?"

Hunter explains he used to work for the network.

"So why are you in Bakersfield?" she asks. "Some big assignment?"

"I got out of the network rat race," he says. He thinks of Ryan Billings and adds, "The rats won." Hunter tells her he has taken over the news operation at KDOA. "It's something of a fresh start for me." Why did he offer that? She doesn't care. It must be the alcohol talking, he decides.

"You're not taking Kent Abernathy's place, are you?"

He is surprised Sugar made the connection between the station and anchor so quickly. If the last ratings book was any indication, only half a dozen people in all of Bakersfield could tell you KDOA had a news operation. "No. I get to boss him around. I don't do much in front of the camera these days."

Sugar's eyes widen just as one of the pencil-thin spotlights sweeps across their table. It catches the tiara on her head and makes it sparkle like a silver halo. "I'm a big news junkie," she says. "I even majored in journalism for a year."

"Before psychology."

"Yeah. Before psychology, and before pre-law. And English." Sugar stops to purse her lips on the small cocktail straw sticking out of her drink. She nurses the last of the alcohol from the glass. "I guess you could say I'm a professional student. I've had six majors in eight years. I have degrees in three of them. But News-13. Wow!"

Sugar rattles off the names of the anchor team and tosses out a couple from the KDOA archives of past talent that Hunter doesn't recognize. She brightens like a lighthouse beacon. Even through the thickening fog in his mind, Hunter can see it coming: the inevitable gush of a news groupie. She is overly impressed.

"News-13. I think they do okay," she says.

Only okay?

"But I don't know anyone who watches Channel 13 that much. If I'm home in time for the news, I watch Channel 17 with Jim

Scott and Robin Mangarin. They're married, you know. But really, I only tune in to get the weather forecast. Then it's CNN. I mean, where else are you going to find out what's really going on?"

Channel 17? CNN? Her opinion of local news stings more than he expects. The booze is urging him to take issue with the little lady.

"You don't think you can get decent news from our station?" Hunter challenges. "And as for the weather, who needs it? What are they going to tell you out here that you don't already know? It's summer. It's hot. It's dry. And it's going to stay like that until it's wet and cold for two weeks in the winter. That's all you have out here in California. Summer—hot. Winter—-wet. Get over it."

Sugar looks away. "Well, it just seems the local news is all the same. And it's not really news most of the time." She gathers a thought and then lifts her head to look straight at Hunter. She picks her words carefully. Words like "superficial" and "sensational-ism". When she starts lumping local news anchors like Bakersfield icon Jim Scott and News-13's own Kent Abernathy in with the likes of Jerry Springer and Sally Jesse Raphael, Hunter thumps the table.

In a more sober state, he might admit her criticism wasn't far from the same arguments Hunter has shared with other seasoned reporters over bourbon and brags, whiskey shots and news scoops. But they are in the business and they have earned the right to knock it. He doesn't have to take this from some floozy who dabbles in just enough college journalism to feel self-righteous about the sad state of the media today.

"Now wait a minute." Hunter sets his bottle down with a thump so hard the beer gushes like a geyser from its long, narrow neck. "Comparing us to daytime, white trash, talk TV is like... it's like comparing the *New York Times* to the *National Enquirer*. It's like comparing the Mona Lisa to a velvet Elvis. It's like comparing a filet mignon to Alpo." He pauses. "Well, okay, maybe we're more like Hamburger Helper—but we're certainly not dog food."

Sugar tosses her hair. "But it's not exactly news, either." She ticks off two examples from the past week. Neither of them had made the News-13 broadcast. Scooped again, he thinks.

Hunter ignores that and picks up the thread of his argument. "And we may not be Mona Lisa. More like Norman Rockwell, or maybe a nice piece of hotel-motel art. The kind they have in those big auctions." He is rambling now. He recognizes the liquor has stolen control.

Sugar is pretty and passionate, and much too articulate for a stripper in a rundown club like Pistol Pete's. Hunter wonders what a nice girl like this... He loves watching her talk. She is opinionated and animated and punctuates her points with a smile or a frown that Hunter reflects back at her to show he's paying attention.

He challenges her. Does she think...

No, she doesn't think she could do better. But how hard can it be?

Wrong. Wrong. Wrong. It only looks easy. The good ones make it look easy.

Well, anyway, coming back to her original point, it may be a little bit of news wrapped around a lot of entertainment.

Hunter picks at the label on his bottle of beer. "That's because it's a business. If we don't entertain, nobody will watch. And we won't make enough money to stay in business. That's what it's all about. Ratings and money. Mostly money."

"That's sad," she replies. "It shouldn't be like that."

"Why? It's like you and your dancing. You dance and smile and make nice with the customers because you make money. This club makes money and everybody's happy. It's the American way. Good for the economy. It doesn't matter whether we're selling cars or widgets, or sex or news. We're all whores for the greater good of the company, using whatever skills we have to turn a buck."

Sugar asks him to repeat that.

He sees a spark in her eyes. Hunter likes that. She has spunk.

"Widgets or news?" he wants to know.

"What you said about whores. Is that what I am?"

Hunter snickers. "Well, sure. You. Me. In the grand scheme of…"

Without warning, ice cubes pelt his face and what was left of Sugar's drink stings his eyes, runs down his nose and cheeks and into his lap. There is a commotion and an overturned table.

Tomorrow he won't remember much about the hulk of a man who yanks him from the chair and drags him out of the club. He will definitely remember the hard parking lot asphalt, still hot to the touch from a Bakersfield summer day, that skins his elbow and knee and takes a patch from below his right eye after what some of the regulars will forever consider a record toss by Pistol Pete's bouncer.

Welcome to Bakersfield.

Market size: 130.

And falling.

Slug: Newsroom in Fear

Anchor intro:

> *There is a saying in television news that you haven't really made it in the business until you've been fired at least once.*
>
> *Not to worry.*
>
> *News anchors and reporters understand the risk. They live with it, knowing it can change as rapidly as the ratings or the mood of management. Since TV news is also one of the few businesses where being fired is seldom considered a black mark on the resume, there is always another job waiting in another market.*
>
> *Nothing to fear.*
>
> *Unless, of course, your career has been on the downward slide to a podunk town like Bakersfield.*
>
> *If you've reached rock bottom and you're still digging, it's time to panic.*

Roll tape

Snap!

That's the sound of another pencil victimized by Kathy Wright.

Look closely at the pad on her desk. You can see dust particles of several lead points and the minute lines that veered off wildly under the pressure of a heavy hand in mid-sentence. They spell fear and frustration. The F-factor squared has turned Kathy into a serial pencil killer.

Frustration. John Tuttle is history. Fired. Three days after Hunter and Tuttle returned from their trip to L.A., Tuttle walked in on Monday morning to find all of his personal belongings in a box on the floor of his office and a security guard standing by to help him carry it to the car. Kathy has been at KDOA for six years now and has outlasted three station managers and four news directors. Another boss bites the dust.

Fear. A spy over in the sales department says Andrews, the station owner, is talking about pulling a "Birmingham"—as in WBMG-TV in Birmingham, Alabama. WBMG, the CBS affiliate, fired the entire news department two weeks before Christmas because the evening news had fewer viewers than reruns of Sanford & Son. It was in all the trade magazines.

And now this.

Kathy smoothens the crumpled edges of a page from the newsroom fax machine. She had squeezed it like an accordion the first time she read it; now she considers the item again. The UBN stations in Youngstown and Flint, Michigan are cutting their news staffs in half and dropping their early newscasts in favor of the new, expanded network news broadcast with Ryan Billings.

"Are we next?"

The question is scribbled across the top of the page, just below the tiny fax identifier that tells Kathy it came from her friend in the KDOA sales department. Having a spy inside Sales is a lesson Kathy learned when she got her very first job—at KGB radio. It kept her in the loop then, and has paid off a dozen times since KDOA hired her six years ago. The sales slugs always get the inside scoop first.

Kathy rams her pencil into an electric sharpener. It grinds away at the lead and wood. It feels good and, for a moment, she and the appliance are one. Then she takes a yellow sticky-note and writes "UPDATE RESUME" in careful block letters. There is no use in pretending the threat isn't hanging thick in the newsroom air. She pats the note into place just left of the second button on her denim blouse, displaying the little note like a badge of defiance.

The police scanner squawks at her. Kathy locks it on one channel long enough to cut through the jargon and dismiss it as a routine call. She presses another button to send it searching for news across the different emergency channels and turns down the volume a notch so the chatter becomes a chaotic form of white noise in the newsroom air.

Kathy then turns her attention to a larger pad where she draws a line to create two columns. At the top of one, she carefully carves the balance in her savings account one digit at a time. She knows it to the penny. The figure kept her awake all night as she tried to dream it into multiplying. In the other column she adds up rent and the payment on her four-year-old Honda, utilities and groceries. Kathy wonders what kind of severance they'll give her. She studies the numbers. Snap. She kills another pencil. Every time she writes out the numbers, the list for expenses grows and her puny nest egg remains the same. Without a paycheck, she has two months to live.

"Just shoot me now," she thinks.

Her eyes and her thoughts drift. She can see Hunter through the glass wall that separates his office from the rest of them in the newsroom. He is on the phone, leaning in his chair and propped up by the edge of his desk so that his back is to her. The door is shut. Again. Hunter has been holed up in there since Tuttle got the ax.

A low chuckle steals her attention. Kent Abernathy, News-13 anchor, is standing near the bank of TV monitors tuned to each of the different stations in Bakersfield. He is turning up the volume on KDOA. He's watching a sixties sitcom, another retread with poor ratings. With daytime programming like this, Kathy wonders how anyone can expect them to have an audience left for the five o'clock newscast.

"That Jeannie," Kent laughs.

"What's that?"

"I Dream of Jeannie. This is the one where she changes her master into a sultan or something like that."

Kathy watches as the actress Barbara Eden, in her harem outfit, crosses her arms, blinks and performs her hocus-pocus, transporting her and her master to the safety of Jeannie's magic bottle.

Kathy smirks. If only she could blink her own troubles away.

"I picked this up at the front desk." Kent sets down a pack of mail, mostly news releases, government bulletins and letters from citizens with a plea to have their cub scout rodeo or PTA meeting covered—stuff for the file of future stories that may or may not grab Kathy's attention when she decides what will fill the newscast on any given day.

"So what is his honcho-ness up to?" Kent asks.

Kathy shakes her head and shrugs.

Dark and handsome, Kent Abernathy has a strong chin with a dimple deep enough to park a Volvo. A perfect smile and a deep voice, he has all the physical attributes of a top-shelf anchor, except for the hair. Unfortunately for Kent Abernathy, his hair is the first thing people notice about him.

No one really knows just how much hair Abernathy has. He has been cursed with premature baldness so early in life that you would pity Kent if he weren't in such a pathetic state of denial.

Kathy leans back in her chair and, studying Kent, twists one of her dark curls around her index finger without thinking about it. Kent raises his eyebrows as if he can read her mind and brushes the bangs of his cheap but perfectly sculpted wig.

"I got my hair cut," he says nonchalantly, watching Kathy toy with her own thick hair. "I think the barber did a better job than usual."

Kathy stifles a laugh. Everyone knows Kent wears a hairpiece—everyone except Kent. And it's not just a half-plate filler, but a full, over-the-crown, woven rug of cheap nylon or Dacron or StainMaster polyester. They call him Monsanto Head.

What Kent lacks in quality, he makes up for in quantity. He actually owns four wigs, each one progressively longer and a bit more gray, and he wears them in orchestrated progression from short to long to longer. Then, on days like this, he starts over with Wig One and tries to convince you he has just returned from the salon.

Other than that, he's a decent anchor.

"Looks nice, Kent," Kathy says.

"So. Do we still have jobs?" Kent asks. He reaches out and flicks the yellow note on her blouse. Rewrite resume. "Ha. If you haven't done it by now, it's probably too late."

Kathy recoils from his touch. "It's two o'clock, and I'm still trying to cook up enough news to feed the beast. No one has canceled the five o'clock newscast so, yeah, we must still have jobs. But ask me again tomorrow."

"I heard they jettisoned the entire news department at the UBN station in Flint," Kent says.

Kathy waves her crumpled fax at him. "No, just half the staff. Youngstown, too."

"Well, I guess we're next." Kent leans on her desk, lowers his voice and nods toward Hunter's office. "He's known about this all along."

"Hunter?"

"Absolutely. I heard he's a hatchet man. Old man Andrews brought him in to clean house. Or else they'll just give up the news game all together and turn it over to Ryan Billings and the network like they did in Flint."

"And Youngstown." It sticks in Kathy's throat. She hadn't seen Hunter as the grim reaper. His eyes are too… sincere. His smile is too warm, and he uses it often. His manner is reassuring, even if he does come across a bit standoffish. Kathy liked him from the start. How could he come in and fire them all?

"He has been looking at an awful lot of resume tapes since he got here," she says. And she adds hopefully, "Maybe he's going to hire some?"

"But has he even interviewed anyone for the five o'clock co-anchor slot? No." Kent snorts. "Either he's the most deliberate jerk we've had in that office, or he's going to clean house and replace us all. Maybe he's just marking time until they pull the plug and send us all packing. We could be replaced by the *Love Boat,* and I'll bet the viewers wouldn't even notice."

Kathy assumes Kent is just running with the speculation of a worst-case scenario. Still, she hasn't seen any sign of progress for all Hunter's effort. He has been putting a lot of time in front of the computer and the tape machine. And he's been working the phones every day. She scoops up her large notepad and fans her neck and chest. It's getting warm in the newsroom. Don't panic.

Kent continues. "Think about it. Why would someone who has worked in big cities like Chicago and New York come to Bakersfield? Don't you think he could work anywhere else if he wanted?"

"He was an anchor back then," Kathy says. "This is a way to get some experience as a news director."

"Shit. Who'd want *that* job?"

Kathy bites her lip. Kent and everyone else on the staff know she had approached Tuttle about getting the job herself before Hunter was hired. Tuttle's excuse was he wanted someone who could take them in a different direction.

"I'm worried," she says.

"Not me," Kent replies. "It's not my fault the ratings suck, and I've still got another year on my contract. It's good to have a little protection to cover your ass. Whether I do the news or not, they have to pay me."

Kathy swings around in her chair and scoops up the lineup for her five o'clock newscast. It is an excuse to drive the backrest into Kent's hip. That was as close as she could get to slapping his self-absorbed ego.

"Ouch."

"Sorry. Have to get back to work," she says.

Kathy frets. She should have put off getting that brake job on the Honda. Too late now. That's a month's rent she might need. Picking up and starting over isn't as much of an option for Kathy as it is for others in the business. As one of those increasingly rare natives of Bakersfield, she likes it here.

Unlike most of the young people she works with, staffers who appear to be getting younger every day, Kathy is not interested in traipsing across the country chasing a career in larger markets. Getting fired would genuinely be a bad thing.

Something is wrong. Kathy recognizes the signs instantly.

The police scanners have gone quiet. With all the reporters out on assignment, the buzz in the newsroom is calm. Even Kent has turned down the volume on that silly TV show, his attention whiplashed to a tall blond woman standing near the newsroom door. It is as if the silence conspired to announce her arrival.

"Can I help you?" Kathy asks.

"I'm here to see Hunter Riley," she says.

Kathy beckons to the woman. She has Princess Diana's hair. She also has Diana's grace as she glides to Kathy's desk and extends her hand. But too much mascara and a gaudy turquoise necklace that is wide and lies close to her throat betray her royal air. She is wearing a white satin blouse open one button too low with a deep burgundy-colored vest and matching pants. Not a business suit.

"Hi. I'm Sugar Kane. I'm here about the job opening. The news anchor position."

Sugar Cane? Kathy presses her lips together hard in what she hopes will be seen as an accepting smile instead of the effort to choke back a laugh. She nods knowingly at Kent. The woman is obviously another wannabe, someone to be gently but quickly dispatched.

"Is Hunter expecting you?" Kathy asks.

The woman nods. She probably sweet-talked Hunter into a courtesy interview. With the ratings as bad as they are, and with their jobs in jeopardy, they need some experienced talent. Not this. Hunter will never hire her. Well, given the current state of upheaval at KDOA, maybe Sugar Cane will look back at this and be glad.

Kathy leans back to check on Hunter. He's typing at the computer, so she picks up the phone and dials his extension.

"Your two-thirty appointment is here." Kathy turns to the woman. "I'm sorry, your name again?"

Kathy repeats it into the receiver with as much sincerity as she can muster. "Sugar Cane. Is that with a "C" or a "K"? Oh, of course. Sugar Kane—with a K."

A moment later, Hunter emerges from his office-turned-bunker. He doesn't seem worse for the wear considering the pressure they are under right now. If anything, Kathy imagines some previously untapped spring in his step, like an executioner who loves his job. Great.

"You're a little early," Hunter says to the woman.

"Sugar Kane," Kent says, drawing out her name, "is here for the five o'clock anchor job." He's standing right behind her, twitching his eyebrows as if they are all sharing a smug little secret.

Hunter takes that with a smile and makes the introductions.

He says, "Kathy, we need a copy of last night's scripts for Sugar here. They're setting up the studio for an audition."

Right.

She grins at Hunter, but he isn't kidding. "Sure. I'll just print up a copy from last night." Kathy sits down at her computer. "It'll take a couple of minutes."

"Just the first segment stories," Hunter says.

Hunter reaches out to Sugar Kane. "We need to talk a moment before we head upstairs to the studio. Come with me."

As they retreat to Hunter's office, Kathy reaches over and adjusts the volume on the police scanner that has been politely silent for the past five minutes. It responds with a blast of static and jumbled voices from a dozen different departments Kathy monitors. Some forms of confusion are less disturbing than others.

Slug: Holy Bank Loot

Anchor intro:

Still no progress to report in efforts to catch Bakersfield's notorious Senior Bandit. He is now responsible for robberies at seven different branches of South Valley Bank and has bamboozled Bakersfield Police with his bravado.

Witnesses describe him as an older, polite and even sophisticated thief—in every way a perfect gentleman. The Senior Bandit is the kind of suave hoodlum you don't mind giving money to, especially if you're a bank teller and it's someone else's money.

Roll tape

At one time, the Emerald Arms was a crown jewel on the edge of Bakersfield's downtown, a boarding house for high society. Look at her now. Tired and frail, like her current residents. She is like the little old lady in her ancient but barely broken-in Buick, meandering down the center lane of the highway with the constantly blinking left turn signal. With two white-gloved hands on the steering wheel, a pill box hat and cat eye glasses barely visible over the dashboard, the rest of the world speeds by her, rushing to reach the future in lanes on either side of life's highway.

Three blocks east, the tower of Bakersfield's new crown jewel rises from a patchwork of vacant lots and tired buildings. Half-a-million dollars in renovations has turned the historic Fox Movie Theater into a concert hall for big names like Englebert Humperdink and Willie Nelson. The Nile Theater is next. And the fresh look of progress is moving in the Emerald Arms' direction as more lots are developed.

Suddenly land values are soaring. Investors from as far away as Sacramento and Stockton, even some Japanese moneymen are jumping up and taking notice of the Bakersfield land boom. Meanwhile, the Emerald Arms hasn't seen a new coat of paint since the city gave up trying to restore the old gal and turned her into low-rent housing for senior citizens two decades ago.

Across the street, down the street and all around her, the neighborhood is waking up from thirty years of neglect. The newest addition is the Goose Inn. It's a coffee house, the local caffeine dealer with a constant stream of junkies stopping by for their daily fix. To the developers, the lawyers and latte lovers alike, the Emerald Arms is taking up valuable space. To them, she is a holdout in their vision of the shopping and office district the neighborhood could become.

"She has a duty to die," they proclaim.

To others?

"It would be a travesty," the Senior Bandit pronounces.

He bangs the ladle against the side of a large stockpot. He tilts the pot and coaxes the rest of the gravy onto the last food tray.

"'Tis what th'r saying down at the coffee house," Emily persists. Her brogue is as thick as the freckles on her Irish face. "Th'r saying what with the Japanese investors buying up this whole durn block, and wanting to make it into offices, Johnny Davenport—that snake of a property manager—is just looking for any excuse to quit our lease."

"They can't do anything as long as the rent is paid."

"Psh," Emily puffs. "That's never a given around here. I can't go on giving back half me wages like last month."

"Hang in there, woman. Two more months before the city's funding cycle kicks in. The check, as they say, is in the mail."

"'Tis a lie. The biggest lie right up there with 'Of course, darlin', I'll respect you in the mornin'.'" Emily gathers up the unused silverware and inspects a fork. "Besides, what then? We're livin' on borrowed time. If we miss just one payment now, Davenport will give us the boot. And I…" She stops, frowns and nods her head to count each of three trays on the island counter in the middle of the kitchen.

"Jenny!" Emily bellows at the ceiling.

A moment later, her daughter leans into the kitchen, clinging to the edge of the swinging door for balance.

"Jenny, these plates are still here. Who hasn't been served?"

Jenny MacFarlane grabs a stray wisp of red hair and tucks it behind her ear. At twenty-three, she has her mother's robust figure and ready smile. "Mrs. Witherspoon is too sick again to come downstairs. I don't think she's taking her medications."

"Poor woman. She's probably run out again."

"Major Tom is walking around outside," Jenny says. Then she steals a glance at the door on the other side of the kitchen that leads to the building's boiler room and basement. "And Mister Marika is, well, missing."

Emily marches to the basement door and pounds it three times with a meaty fist. "Mr. Marika." She opens the door and pauses to sniff the air, catching evidence of cigar smoke. "Mr. Marika. I know you're down there with the devil."

"No, I'm not." The voice floats up the stairs.

"I can smell that filthy tobacco of yours, Mr. Marika. Must I warn you again? You're not allowed to smoke in this house."

"I'm not here," the voice replies.

Emily looks at the bandit and rolls her eyes. You see what I have to put up with?

She calls out again. "Mr. Marika, supper is getting cold. This pot roast is not going to wait for the likes of you. If you don't come up here in two minutes, I'll feed it to the dog."

"Woof!"

Emily closes the door and mutters a long, rambling plea to all the saints in Ireland for help in straightening out that no-good...

The bandit can't make out the rest of it. He lowers the stockpot into the sink and begins filling it with warm water. "How is Mister MacFarlane, Emily?" he asks.

"I dunno, but I'm certain to find out Sunday," she replies with a chuckle. "He'll be home again fussin' and drinkin' and needin'... attention. Three weeks he's been drillin' on that platform in the ocean." She studies Mr. Marika's cooling pot roast. "I do miss him when he's a-workin' like that."

The Senior Bandit wipes his hands dry on a dishtowel and removes his gravy-splattered green apron. "Will you take some time off?"

"I might be needin' an hour or two here or there."

She moves efficiently across the kitchen. It has held up remarkably well since the Emerald Arms opened her dining room to the public in 1948. Post-war oil money gushed from Bakersfield back then, and the town's petroleum-baptized elite loved the comfort and elegance of the Emerald Arms.

Then came the slow, inevitable decline.

At the height of the neighborhood's deterioration in the 1970s, Reverend Sam Cross lobbied, cajoled, and eventually shamed Bakersfield into making the Emerald Arms a home for needy senior citizens. He waved a rare Carter Administration grant in front of city leaders and converted the suites upstairs into apartments. Now the kitchen serves her two-dozen residents under the culinary command of chef Emily MacFarlane.

The bandit crosses the kitchen to a cork bulletin board behind the door to the dining area. He runs a finger down a schedule of volunteers and assignments for the next week. Nearly a dozen programs are being run out of Reverend Sam's office on the ground floor of the Emerald Arms these days. Meals on Wheels deliveries to the homebound senior citizens are covered. The food pantry, thrift store and other outreach programs seem to be in good shape. His own assignments don't add up to much.

"I will have time in the next week or two, if you need help," he says.

Emily thanks him and shooshes him toward the door. "Go on now. Jenny and I'll clean up. You don't need to be spending your evenings in the kitchen with us women. You've better things to do, I'm sure."

"Ah, but spending time with you, Mrs. MacFarlane, is like lingering with the most beautiful rose in the garden." He watches her blush.

"Now don't go wastin' your charm on me," she smiles. She's known him for nearly five years but never tires of his playful flattery. "You should find a wife of your own, you know."

With a solid thump on the door, Jenny backs her way into the kitchen. She carries an armful of dirty dishes to the sink.

"Jenny," the bandit says. "Your mother says I need a wife. Will you marry me?"

Jenny shakes her head. "Not this Saturday. I've got a date. But I think I'm free next weekend; can I get back to you?"

The bandit lays a hand to his heart and nods. "Until then…"

He slips from the kitchen and out of the dining room along the wall. He keeps his distance from the old folks waiting for Emily's chocolate pudding. Gray heads ring two long tables in the dining room. Some of the residents are already dozing under the weight of Emily's pot roast. Others are chatting with each other or to themselves; it doesn't seem to matter.

On another night, he would have lingered and laughed with them a while. Tonight the bandit moves through the shadows of the foyer quickly to a desk where he picks up a battered tan briefcase. Instead of using the front door, he turns back. Slipping through an exit with a small brass plate marked "chapel", he pushes the door shut behind him.

Light from what's left of the long summer day cuts the chapel in two. It layers the top third of the room with a golden beam that pierces the windows behind the pulpit, while the bandit stands below in the dull, gray film of its wash. As a place of worship, the tiny chapel isn't much, with only three benches and room for a couple of wheelchairs. A large cross and the Star of David stand like sentries on opposite corners behind the pulpit. A wooden collection box hangs waist-high on the far wall next to a small stand of votive candles for the Catholics. Two candles, the prayers of two faithful souls, flicker gently deep inside the colored glass. The bandit steps around the last pew and sits in the bench near them.

He places the briefcase on his lap, opens it silently and pulls out a copy of the *Bakersfield Californian* folded neatly into quarters. The bandit glances at the newspaper's article on the front page. It frames a picture from the security camera at South Valley Bank. The photograph was taken at a cockeyed angle and the reprint is fuzzy. The headline screams about the Senior Bandit. The caption with the picture carries a description that is both fact and fiction. Tall and thin—they got his height and weight right. Even accounting for the ten-year range they guessed for his age, they missed it badly. And as for the collar-length gray hair, well… He scratches an imaginary itch on the back of his head and wonders how much longer the baseball cap and gray wig will fool the authorities. Not much, he suspects.

The news media had paid minimal attention to his first robbery. The second one elevated him to the status of a serial thief. Now he's a cult figure. It took the media three holdups to give him a nickname. He has become the "so-called Senior Bandit" on the evening news and in the papers.

From within the folds of the *Californian,* he pulls out three thousand and seven dollars in what he fervently hopes are unmarked bills. The bandit stands and rocks the collection box. It's fastened loosely to the wall, and he can hear a smattering of coins slide across its bottom. Emily will come in shortly to collect the meager offerings there. It's Wednesday, so the weekly noon service drew the usual handful of ex-cons and others from the Hotel Decatur down the street. Loyal but poor, their donations never add up to much. There may be a couple of dollars from other neighbors who occasionally drop in and pay for the convenience of a spiritual quickie in the local chapel. Prayers on the run. Like with Chinese take-out, you're usually empty again in an hour.

He wedges first one handful and then another through the slot on the top of the collection box until his holy loot is gone. He tosses the newspaper back into his briefcase with a mixture of anger and resignation. A parent forced to make allowances for an errant child knows the feeling.

"Lord, don't make me do this again," he prays. But it is harsh and bounces off the walls of the empty chapel, and it comes back to him sounding like a demand rather than a plea. So be it. This was Your idea, he thinks.

The bandit snaps the briefcase shut and starts for the door at the rear of the chapel, the one that leads directly outside. He pauses long enough to light a candle on the votive stand. After all, he's just paid the rent. It's more than the price of a prayer, and he ought to get his money's worth.

Slug: Sugar's Audition

Anchor intro:

> *The faces come. The faces go. Where they come from, you just never know.*
>
> *When you sit down to watch the nightly news you assume the anchorman or woman inside that box is a knowledgeable, trained journalist with impeccable credentials. That is not always the case.*
>
> *Before we lament the caliber of people shaping and delivering our daily dose of information on the tube, it's important to remember that history is full of geniuses with incomplete or no formal training.*
>
> *Even Einstein flunked math once. And TV news is not rocket science.*

Roll tape

Thwap!

A quarter-inch stack of television news scripts lands on a flat section of the control room panel like rotting fruit falls from a tree.

Look at the way it's marked with red circles and corrections doodled in the margins. It's the stamp of Hunter's twenty-five years of experience, and the stamp clearly indicates, "Return to Sender."

Hunter can't resist. Over those twenty-five years, he has honed his own writing while rejecting the scripts from others he was supposed to read, gutting them of weak sentences, passive verbs, clichés and convoluted dependent clauses. And atrocious grammar! This is the junk they put on their newscast last night. He checks the monitor in the bank of screens on the wall just beyond the control panel. He can see Sugar Kane's face. It's the same script she'll be using for her audition. Poor girl.

He looks down again at the paper in front of him and shakes his head. This is what they teach journalism majors in college, apparently. And once those students graduate, they're thrown into the fire. There is no time and few mentors to help them in TV news. So no one really learns, and you end up with the ignorant leading the blind.

Hunter has spent his twenty-five years in love with words and how they can sing in perfect harmony with video to inform, educate and hold an audience without compromising journalistic integrity. Yes, it can be done in television. You can have high ratings and sound journalism, but that takes time. Hunter doesn't have time; the rumors are true. If they don't improve the ratings quickly, news at KDOA is history. They will all be replaced by *The Brady Bunch*, or some such nonsense.

So as he swings his head from the scripts bleeding red ink from his corrections to the face of Sugar Kane in one of the little black and white monitors on the wall, he says, "Lord, don't make me do this."

"Do what?" The question comes back to him as a shout.

Lee Richards comes up behind Hunter, bobbing spasmodically toward the director's chair to the noise from a Walkman headset. He's rocking out to the Twisted Sisters or Psycho Pixies, no doubt. Maybe it's his favorite local head-banging group, Five Angry Amish.

Richards is the newscast's director. "Chief button pusher," he tells you. He is Captain Kirk, Spock, and Chekov all rolled up into one, and the KDOA control room is the bridge of his Starship Enterprise.

Richards is responsible for making the technical side of the broadcast work. Everything you see at home is in his hands, from the news video and commercials he controls with his panel of Christmas-colored buttons, to the actions of the studio crew who tug and tilt, lug and line up the studio cameras under his command. Hunter looks over the obsolete, battered and duct tape-patched equipment around him and he knows they are light years away from the technology of the twenty-first century, let alone ready for Star Trek. But it is Richards' command, and Kathy swears he's more comfortable at the helm than he seems. Hunter is suspicious.

"Is that your babe?" Richards asks loudly and points to the bank of monitors. He's dancing on the balls of his feet and trying to be heard over the heavy metal music in his headsets. Hunter looks at the monitor labeled "Camera One, Stupid!" and can see Sugar chatting with the studio crew.

"Babe?" Hunter asks.

Knowing what Sugar does for a living makes Hunter more

defensive than he has to be. He reaches out and gently separates the earphones from Richards' head. "Let's just make the tape and…" he lets the words trail off as he releases the headset. It snaps back into place, clapping Richards on each ear like a pair of tiny foam cymbals.

"Right on it, chief. We're buckled in and ready for takeoff. Well, almost."

Hunter hands one copy of the scripts to Richards and scoops up a second for himself. He steals another skeptical look at the director preparing to roll videotape for Sugar's audition. Hunter glances over his shoulder at the audio technician, the ceiling, the walls and then at the door like an inmate casting about for an escape route. Unless he finds one quickly, twenty-five years of journalistic integrity, twenty-five years of fighting the ratings game quick fix, twenty-five years of standing up to consultants with their style-over-substance is about to come to an end.

And for what?

"She's a real hooker," he hears Richards say.

"What was that?" Hunter shoots back.

Richards raises one eyebrow, wary of Hunter's angry tone. "I said she's a looker. Very fine." Richards turns back quickly to his control panel and presses one of the million buttons. Then, deciding that wasn't right, he pokes another. He leans toward a microphone snaking out of the board on the end of a flexible metal rod to his left.

"Roll tape and record, we're going in one minute." Richards tries several combinations of buttons and switches before he's satisfied and then leans toward the microphone again. "Ready on the floor?"

The crew in the studio relays the question. Hunter watches Sugar look up from her scripts, startled. She nods, closes her eyes and draws a deep breath like a diver about to plunge into a cold river.

"Ready camera one and… cue."

Sugar begins reading from the teleprompter.

"Through the roof, bay-bee!" The words ring in Hunter's head. It's John Tuttle's voice he hears, thundering through the booze at Pistol Pete's. Then as the echo fades, Sugar's deeply feminine, almost husky voice replaces it. Hunter catches himself chuckling at her inflection. Sugar has caught the irony in a particular sentence and punched it well. It sounds better than the way their anchor Kent Abernathy delivered it last night.

A telephone behind Hunter's head jangles. Augie, the sound-man stationed at a second panel of buttons and lights, ignores it as long as he can. Finally he answers the call, listens and laughs. "No, really. Who is this? Yeah, right. Whatever." Augie passes the receiver to Hunter. "He says he's Andrews. You think that old fart really has the number down here?"

"That fellow ought to be more respectful, that's what I say," Donald O. Andrews barks at Hunter. "You tell him if he doesn't straighten up, I'm going to fire his ass in the morning."

The station owner's voice sounds as if he's on the other end of a long string and a tin can. From the background noise, Hunter assumes the boss is on the road somewhere, and his cell phone cuts out for a moment. Then it's back.

"Now Riley," the boss says. "I've been reading the report from that consultant we hired to make your job easier."

"What consultant?" What report, Hunter wonders.

"The consultant with the report," Andrews snaps back.

When did they hire a consultant? "I haven't gotten any report."

"You will."

Hunter bites his upper lip. John Tuttle had been his buffer between the news department and the station owner. Now that Tuttle is gone, Andrews calls Hunter three or four times a day.

Sometimes it sounds like Andrews is just blowing off steam, using terms like "dire consequences". Did he really threaten a blood bath in the newsroom? Even in Andrews' more lucid moments, one thing has become abundantly clear—the old man is not happy with the news ratings.

"Fine," Hunter replies. "I'll go over the report and we can meet and…"

"Can't do that right now," Andrews cuts him off.

Hunter leans back in his chair, stumped. Each time he has tried to schedule a meeting with Andrews, the station owner has put him off. Each time he's tried to ambush Andrews in his office upstairs the old man has been missing in action. Hunter couldn't pick Andrews out of a lineup if his life depended on it.

"Damn. Don't do that to me!" Richards is shouting at Sugar in the monitor. "She's not following the script. Ad-libbing at least half of it." He tosses a page over his shoulder. "You want her to start over?"

Hunter shakes his head and motions to mute the volume on the audition.

Andrews finally pauses to reload his rapid-fire repertoire of insults and threats. Hunter jumps in. "Look, Mr. Andrews. If we can meet, I'm sure we could come up with a reasonable plan of action."

"We need to act now. You hear what I'm saying, Riley? If you're not up to the task we'll find someone who is. Don't make me fire you in the morning."

With his eyes on Sugar and his anger on the rise, Hunter could walk away from the job now. They don't need him. Sugar must be reading a lighter story—her dimples are showing. Come-hither dimples, he thinks. Come-hither. That's the message Hunter got, the message that Sugar peddled so well at Pistol Pete's. He's been wondering since that night if Sugar could transfer her magnetism to the TV camera. It has taken him three days to track her down and convince Sugar to try.

Andrews continues his tirade, but Hunter isn't listening; he is watching Sugar Kane.

"I said, what's your plan, Riley?" Andrews' voice finally breaks through.

"My plan?"

"Put up or shut up. That's what I say."

"My plan?" Hunter muses out loud for Andrews' benefit. His plan. Inside, the question reverberates. His plan? He's looking at his plan. She's blond and blue-eyed, speaking to him from the tiny TV screen on the wall.

He raises the telephone receiver to his ear and gets a dial tone in reply. Andrews isn't waiting around for Hunter's plan.

Richards turns up Sugar's microphone just as she wraps up.

"I'm Sugar Kane, and that's more news than you need to know. Have a great afternoon." Hunter watches her lean on the desk and expel an exhausted breath. Then she laughs with the floor crew.

"Not bad," Richards says. "I like her Karma."

She is definitely rough, but this is only Bakersfield. It doesn't have to be network quality.

Sugar meets him in the hallway and they turn toward the newsroom. "I'll get my bag and get going now," she says. "I really do appreciate it." She laughs. "I hope I didn't waste too much of your time, but at least you gave me a chance to perform."

"Audition," he corrects her.

"Audition," she says. "You didn't have to do this, especially after the way I kind of over-reacted the other night. Talk about over-reacting, though? If I had known Rocko was going to toss you into the parking lot like that, I would have thought twice before I splashed you."

"Like I told you, I deserved it—the drink, that is. But Rocko is hardly the type I'd try to settle a score with. We'll just let that be." His mind is working hard, calculating the risks. He is on the verge of something that is either boldly brilliant, or totally bone-headed. It scares him that he can't tell which.

In Hunter's office, she picks up her purse and offers him her hand. . "Thanks again."

Hunter holds it tightly, not letting her get away. "I know it's a little late, but if you haven't had lunch yet, why don't we get a bite to eat?"

Sugar eyes him, first with disappointment and then good humor. She smiles, but a curtain of suspicion drops between them as she shakes her head. "Thanks. But you know, I get that all the time at the club. So just as a matter of principle, I don't date customers. I'll pass."

Hunter takes her gently by the arm and guides her out to the newsroom. "This isn't a date. It's a business lunch. I have a proposition for you."

"Right," she replies. "Always a *proposition*."

"I'm serious. You want a job here? We might work something out."

Static hisses from the police scanner. A photographer cusses at the equipment in one of the editing suites. A reporter on the phone is begging some contact to grant an interview before deadline. It all adds to the jumble of noise as they cross the newsroom. Hunter pantomimes to Kathy that he will be out of the office for a while. He leans closer to Sugar. No sense setting off alarms in the newsroom in case she turns down the offer he is formulating. "This is business," he said.

"Whose business? Your business or my, uh, business?" she whispers back.

"News business."

"Really?" Sugar pauses and searches his face before they reach the door. Satisfied, she answers in a voice a bit too loud. "Okay. But I'll tell you right now. I am not going to bed with you, so don't even think it."

It is a bad time for the scanner to break off its chatter. The phones pick that exact moment to go silent. The editing suites are quiet. Even the constant hum of the air conditioner seems to stop in shock. It is as if all the forces of confusion have conspired so that in a world where different raucous sounds are usually fighting for attention, her words hang in the air like an unwelcomed belch in Sunday prayer service. The others in the newsroom have enough decency, or pity, not to snicker until Hunter leads Sugar quickly from the room.

The laughter follows them down the hall.

And Now A Word From Our Sponsor:

Still to come on Live @ Five...

Ralph Waldo Emerson once suggested if you build a better mousetrap, the world will beat a path to your door. He was wrong.

He obviously couldn't comprehend the demands of competition in the twenty-first century, where multi-level marketing and multi-million dollar ad budgets are rudimentary requirements for getting the public to even acknowledge your work, whether it's a widget, a public policy or something as sweet as Sugar Kane.

But what if you lack the capital to force-feed America a steady diet of your message and get them to "Just Do It" because "It's the Real Thing" and "You Deserve a Break Today"?

Take heart. Every so often circumstances work in harmony to create the perfect word-of-mouth campaign to rival even the best-financed plans of mice and... well, you get the picture.

In this arena, three things are true: Nothing generates interest like word of mouth. Nothing generates word of mouth like a crisis, real or imagined. And no one can exploit a crisis like the news media.

Stay tuned.

Larry Brill

Date: June 28, 1996
Slug: Phase Two

Anchor intro:

> *In the brief history of local TV news there have been a countless number of anchors who arrived in a new town on a campaign of hype designed to generate more anticipation than Jesus' arrival in Jerusalem, only to be sacked when they couldn't produce a ratings miracle. Stations insist they should get their money's worth since the average anchor salary in a major market, even accounting for two thousand years of inflation, is well above the thirty pieces of silver offered for the carpenter from Galilee.*
>
> *What do you suppose Jesus would say about the industry today?*

Roll tape

"Christ, it's a tough business."

Kathy looks skeptically at the tube of Preparation H in her hand. Roy, the KDOA anchor she dated once upon a past, had sworn the cream would solve all kinds of swollen ailments, including the puffy eyes that you can clearly see as Kathy leans closer to the mirror. Roy should know all about Preparation H; he turned out to be a real asshole. He dumped Kathy for a perky nineteen-year-old intern she had taken under her wing. Apparently the intern had been spending a good deal of time under Roy.

The ointment must work. She snitched this tube from Kent Abernathy's makeup kit. It had been tucked away, along with a business card from Polly & Esther's Refurbished Fashion Wigs.

"The right look—It's no hairy deal," the business card proclaims.

You wouldn't think the single light above the mirror in the station's bathroom could be this bad for applying makeup. Kathy never noticed before; nor had she cared. Maybe she should have used the makeup mirror in the studio where the anchors do their faces.

"Grrr." Kathy growls as she dabs the ointment under each eye and begins covering it with makeup. And were those crow's feet there yesterday? Probably, but Kathy has been too busy to notice.

It's been this way since Hunter hired the "News Kitten". It didn't take long for Kathy to come up with that nickname for Hunter's pet project. This one caught on particularly well with the rest of the staff.

Hunter may think it was a good idea to hire Sugar Kane, but he isn't the one being run ragged having to train her. Babysitting might be a better description. Overcoming Sugar's child-like inexperience has turned into a bigger job than Kathy expected.

"Do this," Kathy would direct.

"Why?" Sugar asks.

"Do that."

"Why?"

Kathy's sister has a three-year-old with the same stubborn inquisitiveness. And Kathy has witnessed that conversation too many times. It always ends up with mom frazzled and frustrated. Kathy wonders if this is fate's revenge for not having children of her own. Why bother? She has a newsroom full of them.

If that isn't enough to add saddles to the bags under your eyes, Bakersfield P.D. is making sleep impossible.

The police scanner Kathy keeps near her bed has been squawking every night like a parrot on speed. Most of the calls are false alarms, or breaking news stories that don't live up to their promise. Piddly stuff. Kathy used to sleep through it. Now every night is restless. And you never realize how long and lonely a hot August night in Bakersfield is until you can't find the sleep to escape.

"Don't be a fool," she says to the mirror.

Blaming the scanners won't get her anywhere. She knows Hunter has been on her mind too much, and not only at work. Hunter's face peeks out at her from between the pages of the news magazines she stares at, but doesn't read, in bed at night. His voice sneaks in between those annoying calls on the scanner. Hunter is the one keeping her awake at night. And Hunter is the reason for the Preparation H and the Mary Kay makeover.

Kathy wonders if he'll notice.

Back in the newsroom, bodies are milling about. Day-siders are headed home; night-siders are working on stories for *News at Eleven.*

"Dinner with the boss?" The night-side producer Van Thompson has loaded the question with melodramatic innuendo suggesting a little office hanky-panky.

"Oh, come on," Kathy implores.

Thompson says, "Girlfriend, I just wish this business had more gay news directors. Maybe then I could sleep *my* way to the top. You think?"

Kathy finds it odd the way this white, small-town gay guy could adopt the hip-hop vocabulary so easily. But in reality, their relationship has been close, and it has evolved over the past four years to the point where "girlfriend" describes him perfectly.

"Maybe *you* should hit on Hunter," Kathy suggests with a sly smile. "He could be gay, too. Just not so flaming obvious about it."

"Uh-uh! Everyone knows he's cuddling the News Kitten."

"Sugar?" Kathy makes a weak attempt to hide the disappointment in her voice. She stares at Thompson for all of two seconds before he breaks.

Thompson laughs, "I knew it. You have the hots for him. It's about time."

Kathy wants to protest, but Thompson raises a bony finger to his lips. Her secret is safe. Except that she knows a secret in a newsroom is about as safe as a piñata at a party. Everybody will take a whack at it until the candy flows.

Over Thompson's shoulder Kathy can see Hunter in his office, switching off the computer and shuffling papers. It's the end of the day.

"Talk him into dinner at Uricchio's," Thompson says. "Nice and romantic. Good foreplay."

"Stop that," Kathy hisses.

"Or The Wool Growers."

The Wool Growers is not only Bakersfield's favorite Basque restaurant, but it has the distinction of being the bistro where Barbra Streisand and James Brolin dined on their honeymoon. Babs had the pork chops. No one seems to remember or care what J.B. ate.

Twenty minutes later, Kathy thinks Hunter actually looks a bit like James Brolin—the younger *Marcus Welby M.D.* vintage Brolin—as they drive 24th Street and across north Bakersfield. It's just after seven o'clock, but the day hasn't cooled enough to enjoy riding in Hunter's aging convertible. The BMW looks in good shape for a twelve-year-old car. Kathy would have preferred to put the top up and the air conditioner on high, but Hunter explains the AC is on the fritz.

"How did the Five O'clock Report go?" Hunter asks.

"It went okay, considering the live van was hemorrhaging parts all over California Avenue this afternoon. They say it's the transmission. But Hunter, I can't believe you hired a tow truck to haul it half-way across town just so Valerie could do her live shot."

"But it worked. You see what I was saying about not giving up so easily? We just need to be more creative. Think positive."

"But it's embarrassing that we have to tow our equipment around just to get on the air."

"Well, a new live truck isn't in the budget, and Santa doesn't live here. I'll see what I can do." After a pause, Hunter asks, "How did they do tonight?"

"Who?" As if Kathy didn't know.

"Kent and the News Kitten. How'd they do?"

Kathy uses both hands to adjust her sunglasses. "News Kitten?"

"I know what you call her," Hunter replied. "All of you."

Kathy squirms. It hadn't been nasty. Not much, anyway. It's just… just typical newsroom humor.

Her eyes hurt from the strain of trying to look at Hunter and judge his reaction without actually turning her head in that direction. Funny. Hunter doesn't look angry at all.

She begins to wonder if he ever gets angry. Maybe Hunter is one of those festering slow-burners who will just go postal some day. How does he stay so cool? In the four months since Hunter arrived at KDOA, his friend the station manager has been fired and everyone in the news department has their jobs on the line. The ratings in May were another disaster and, speaking of disasters, two words: Sugar Kane. She is floundering on the *Five O'clock Report*. Kathy is panicked, and Hunter doesn't flinch. He's either the coolest customer Kathy has ever known or a complete idiot. In the news business, you never know.

"Kent and Sugar? It was another mess." Kathy says. "Sugar still isn't following her scripts very well. She throws everybody else off, and Kent is ready to kill her because she steps on his lines when they're on camera together."

"They're not clicking," Hunter says flatly.

Kathy sighs. She's getting used to Hunter understating the obvious. "Well, if you thought pairing them on the newscast was going to bring up the ratings, we're all going to be looking for jobs in the morning."

Hunter doesn't answer. He looks at her, but all she can see is the sun's glare as it bounces off the metal frame of his RayBans.

"We're not all going to be looking for a job in the morning, are we?" Kathy asks again with fear rising.

Oh no. That's what this is all about. Hunter wants to get her away from the newsroom to break the bad news. They're all fired. She's fired. She should never have nicknamed Sugar the News Kitten. It's as clear to Kathy as the crude, hand-painted sign in front of Dave's Tacos where Hunter pulls the Beemer to a stop. Dave's Tacos? Not even a decent last meal before the execution.

"Everyone is looking for a job," Hunter says as he climbs from the car. "But no one is going to be fired. Not yet, anyway. We're golden. No worries. At least through the November ratings period. After that…" Hunter leaves her hanging with a shrug.

"You're not making me feel much better," Kathy says. She matches Hunter step for step across the gravel lot. The crunching beneath their feet adds urgency to her voice. "How can you stay so… so disconnected? So calm. We are going to lose our jobs and you're not worried?"

"Of course I'm worried," Hunter replies. He reaches to his collar, unbuttons it and loosens his tie with one hand.

Like everything else, Hunter does it with ease. Kathy's never seen Hunter with a hair out of place or his tie askew before. He tempers this relaxed look by adjusting his tie clip so the material lays flat and orderly against his shirt.

"To be honest, I'm flat-out scared," he says.

"Scared?" she asks, surprised. "You don't look it."

"Scared enough to do something I never thought I could."

Kathy thinks for a moment. "You hired the News Kitten."

Hunter takes off his sunglasses and looks at her. Damn that look. He's given Kathy that look once or twice before, sly and full of amusement. It's as if he has just shared a naughty secret with her, and the look says they understand one another perfectly.

"I hired the News Kitten," he confirms.

Kathy looks at Hunter with new admiration. It's an amazingly candid admission. And admitting it was a desperate move proves Hunter isn't as clueless as she had feared.

"It didn't work," she says.

"It will, trust me." Hunter says. "I'm not as clueless as you think."

Oops. If he thinks Sugar will work out in the end, Kathy is back to questioning Hunter's sanity. This is getting too confusing.

Hunter says, "It isn't working, but that's just phase one. What do you want?"

"What do *I* want?"

Hunter points to the tiny stucco kitchen that serves Dave's Tacos. "What do you want?"

Dave only offers three items on the menu. Beef. Beef tongue. And chicken. Take your pick for a buck and a half. Kathy shudders at the thought of beef tongue.

"Chicken," she says quickly.

Since both of Dave's plastic patio tables are taken, Hunter and Kathy dine while leaning against the fender of his BMW. He becomes evasive when Kathy presses him about phase two of his plan to save the newsroom. Hunter changes the subject.

"Is this great, or what? Only in Bakersfield can someone drop that shack on a vacant lot and have people lined up to buy tacos. Is there a real Dave?"

She inspects the chicken wrapped in tortilla. Disappointed, she wonders what lamb from The Wool Growers would taste like in a tortilla like this. She would even settle for the Basque pickled-beef tongue. So much for a romantic dinner. Well, at least she still has a job—until November.

"I'm not sure about Dave," she says. "But the building is new. He used to sell out of one of those mobile kitchens. You know, a roach coach. And worse. For years, Dave—if there is a real Dave— used to park in any vacant lot he could find. So you'd have to drive all over town to find him."

"I guess he's settled down," Hunter muses.

Kathy still can't get much from Hunter as they stroll north along Chester Avenue sipping diet Coke. The sun is setting, and a light breeze carries the promise of a nighttime temperature that might drop all the way into the eighties.

"If hiring Sugar was just phase one," she says, "then I assume you do have a phase two?"

Hunter nods but doesn't offer any more. It's as if he's still formulating the plan. They stop walking across from a traffic circle that sits in the shadow of an elevated highway. A statue, about twenty feet tall, stands in the middle of that round patch of green on Chester Avenue. It waves to the motorists who barely slow down enough to negotiate the circle, let alone acknowledge the monument. Hunter asks her about it.

"That's Padre Garces. He was the first white man in this part of the valley. Taught the Indians. Martyred, naturally. That's how you get a statue."

"Either that, or you have a good PR machine," Hunter says.

He takes advantage of a break in the traffic to jog across to the traffic circle. Hunter stands at Padre Garces' feet and looks down Chester Avenue toward downtown. When Kathy catches up to him, Hunter is nodding like someone who has just wrestled a decision and won. The light has returned to his eyes.

"What?"

"Phase two," Hunter replies. "You want to know about phase two?" He pauses as a big truck on the highway above them downshifts and fills the air with a loud, depressing moan.

"Crack babies," Hunter says.

"That's phase two?"

"You were right about Sugar. She's not the answer. Sugar alone isn't going to be enough to pull us out of this hole. Give me crack babies."

Slug: Crack Babies

Anchor intro:

> Polls indicate that Americans don't trust the media. Journalists rank with bottom dwellers like insurance agents and used car salesmen, and only slightly ahead of politicians.
>
> This lack of respect clearly comes from the over-emphasis on titillating stories and flashy pictures. The problem is that sexy stories draw ratings.
>
> Now, what if you attract viewers with the promise of sex and sensationalism, but deliver insightful, quality reporting of the news instead? You'd be guilty of a kind of bait and switch tactic—the likes of which in any other business might get you two-to-seven in the county jail.
>
> If such a thing is possible, start raising bail. KDOA is about to commit intellectual fraud.

Roll tape

Kathy's eyes are so wide you can almost see your reflection in them.

"Crack babies?"

Hunter nods. "Crack babies, abandoned by their mothers who happen to be nuns. They can't abort their poor little drug-addicted fetuses because of the church, so they've been dumping them on the community and we need to find homes to adopt them."

"I've never heard that story. Do we have nuns with crack babies here?"

"Probably not. This is only Bakersfield," Hunter says with a wry smile.

He watches the idea take root. Kathy's dark eyebrows are furrowed. Then they relax as she tilts her head and the confusion clears.

"You mean something controversial," she says. "Anything?"

"Controversy is good. Scandal. But something with zing to it that is more than just a story. I want to find that perfect story that we can turn into a cause. Mix outrage with empathy, and we can build a story we can ride for a month or more."

Hunter throws an arm around Kathy's shoulders. He waves his other hand across the city's skyline and, with his anchor voice says, "Exclusive. See it only on News 13."

It had only been an act of showmanship, perfect for the moment. Hunter hugged Kathy without thinking of the implications. When he realizes how bad it looks to be fondling your employee in the middle of traffic, Hunter pulls back. The notion of a sexual harassment suit collides with the pleasure he feels in having been that close to her, if only for a moment. And he draws his hand softly against the small of her back as he moves away.

Kathy stares down Chester Avenue. Hunter can't tell if he's frozen her with his touch, or with his grand scheme for a quick fix to save their jobs.

"Sure. We all dream about it, but those big scandals aren't exactly a dime-a-dozen. We hardly scare up teeny-tiny scandals. Not here in Bakersfield, anyway. Where are you going to get us a story like that?" she asks. "Don't make that my job, I've got enough to do just feeding the beast each night."

Hunter cranes his neck to look at the statue of Padre Garces. The idea has been with him for a couple of days. Maybe he's been thinking about it too much, and it's starting to bug him. Preoccupied by the problems at KDOA, it took an extra three days before he could get an audition tape in the mail to Denver. By the time he followed up with a phone call he had missed the cut. He could have nailed down that job if he had been quicker. He'll do better next time.

"What's the story that everyone is talking about right now? Not necessarily the most important, but the one that everybody wants to know about?"

Kathy shrugs. "The Senior Bandit. When you go to the grocery store or the mall, that's all people talk about."

"Right. Because he's not some run-of-the-mill punk. Why does he do it? Is he destitute? Is it for the thrill of it? An *old* guy like that. Very weird. It's a mystery, and people love mysteries. You never hear of a geriatric gunman like this."

"I don't think he carries a gun," Kathy says.

"Why? Another mystery."

Kathy says she doesn't see how they can turn a couple of robberies into the Big Story, but she is starting to catch Hunter's infectious energy. As much as Hunter wants her support, unadulterated and enthusiastic for this to work, he wonders if that could be too much of a good thing. Kathy doesn't spend much time in the middle ground between delight and despair. One or the other, her ability to feel both so deeply is one of the things that attracts him. But the power of their combined excitement could send Kathy over the edge to some kind of spontaneous combustion.

"But he's just a pathetic robber. Where's all this heart-tugging sympathy you want? We don't know anything about him."

Hunter agrees. "That's where Reverend Sam comes in."

Kathy's enthusiasm turns into a whine. "Aw, not Sam. He's been after us to do a story again. He's out of money. The senior citizens are poor. Nobody cares. I've heard it all a million times. And every time we do a story with him it's never enough."

"Yeah. I talked with him the other day. He says you don't like him and won't give him coverage."

Color rises in her cheeks. "That guy is a pain in my backside, pardon my French. Maybe he's great to have around when you need to do a story; he has contacts and he plays the game. Oh, how he plays the game! I think he uses us more than we use him."

"Is he trustworthy?" Hunter asks. The question makes Kathy pause.

"Trustworthy? That's an odd question. Yeah, I guess so. But what does that have to do with the bandit story?"

Hunter starts across the street and back to the car. He holds his palms up. "On one hand, we have this Senior Bandit. The mystery man everyone wants to know about. On the other hand, we have the poor seniors who—assuming Reverend Sam is telling the truth—could lose their home if the community doesn't do something. Evil bandit? Poor honest seniors. Two contrasting pictures of old folks."

"But there's no real connection, is there?"

"Only the big 'W'," Hunter replies. "As long as we keep asking why this is going on in our community, there is a link."

They talk about different angles the story might take. Health and housing issues, hospice and nursing homes, food and welfare. It's a long list.

"That's a pretty big horse to beat to death," Kathy says.

"Exactly. But here's the catch. We'll give the viewers what they want to know about the bandit and then make them care about Reverend Sam's poor people." Hunter smiles. He's all teeth and hair and practically glowing. "And if we do this right… if we really do this right, we might actually do some good."

Hunter pauses and composes a time line in his head. "We'll start a file of stories now and start running them in September. Way ahead of the November ratings."

"Why?" Kathy asks. "Why not do special reports for the sweeps period like usual?"

"Because we need to grab their attention before the Nielsen folks start counting noses. Do it while all the other stations are on auto-pilot ahead of the ratings period and hope to hell the audience will stay with us afterwards. And they will. We're that good. The audience just doesn't know it. Yet."

A win-win situation. Marvelous.

Hunter adds, "And we'll put Sugar on it first thing tomorrow."

Not so marvelous. Kathy's face tells him so.

"Not Sugar," she says. "Let me put Andy on it. Or Valerie. Anyone but the News Kitten."

Hunter is firm. "No. It has to be Sugar. First, we need to raise her profile. We need to showcase her with the Big Story. This way, not only will we see her at the anchor desk with Kent, but we'll also see her out in the community covering the news. Not just any news story, mind you, but something with impact."

"Impact." Kathy says it in a way that leaves no doubt she needs much more convincing.

"Impact. For the benefit of the community. Another thing is that she won't cover it like any typical reporter. She's not jaded yet. I want someone who will look at this story the way any old Jane on the street would see it. Fresh eyes. Sympathetic heart. It's perfect for her."

"So, what? Are you going to try and make a serious journalist out of her? You've already put her on the air because she's pretty, and okay, maybe she can talk a little. But serious is not what she does."

"I'm not looking for serious journalism, per se. I just want it honest. Let's just report what she hears and what she sees and, most of all, what she feels. Let's quit pretending to be objective twenty four-seven. I'll bet it's exactly what everyone at home feels. I can work with her and the other reporters on that. But you're the key, Kathy."

"Me?"

"We have to get the whole crew behind this project. Not only will they have their share of special assignments, but we can't neglect the rest of the news entirely. You're the one who will have to manage it all."

Kathy gives one of those Elizabeth Montgomery twitches of the nose you used to watch on *Bewitched*. "Do I have much of a choice?"

"Sure. You can make it happen. Or we'll fail."

"Well, since you put it that way. You know, I've always said the stories I like best are the ones where we can make a difference. This could do that. I suppose."

"And we just might have some fun doing it."

Kathy agrees. The lights from the used car lot next to Dave's Tacos casts a soft, flattering glow on her cheeks. Her skin is moist. Standing in the twilight heat of another Bakersfield scorching summer day, Hunter can't help but notice the way Kathy's light cotton dress clings to her body. She wears perspiration well.

He suggests, "Let's find someplace quiet. This wasn't much of a dinner. The least I can do is buy you a drink."

She shrugs. "I'd like that. But I don't drink."

"Not at all?"

"I'll share a club soda with you. Is that all right?"

"Of course. Just a bit surprising."

Hunter moves closer to her. He says, "You don't drink. I know you don't smoke. And I'd be shocked if you did drugs or kicked little puppies. And yet...yet you seem to live with such," and he pauses for effect while moving a step closer, "passion. Don't you have any vices?"

Kathy blushes but doesn't shy away. "Wellll… I do have one vice. Just a tiny excess, really. But it feels so good when I do it that I just lose control. Does that make you feel better?"

"Tell me," he says.

"Mmmm, I'd rather show you."

Throw caution to the wind. Bring it on, baby. Hunter says, "Sure."

Thirty minutes later, Hunter watches as Kathy bounces up and down and then rocks her hips. With her eyes closed and her head tilted back, she raises both hands and runs them sensually through her long brown locks. She is a woman in the throes of passion.

No one else in this country line dance can match her fluid moves and perfect timing with the music. She gives a whoop as the entire line turns on its heels and begins a choreographed three-step move to the left.

From his seat at the edge of the dance floor, Hunter laughs. Kathy is the only one he knows who could find passion at Buck Owens' Crystal Palace.

He thinks it's funny that Bakersfield's pride and joy, its claim to fame, is this combination dance hall and temple to the country western singer whose name is synonymous with the TV show *Hee Haw!*

Thinking further, he decides it's a good match. Buck Owens, the Buckaroos and Bakersfield. Fun-loving, simple music for fun-loving, simple folks. Simple, yes. But hardly stupid.

Hunter will have to shepherd KDOA's news coverage very carefully over the next few weeks to make sure they don't patronize, and ultimately alienate, the audience. They may have to tease the sleaze to attract the viewers, but it will take simple and honest reporting to keep them. No one in the world is better suited for that kind of message than the good folks in Bakersfield.

The wild card is Reverend Sam. It only took two minutes of Sam's preaching over the phone for Hunter to recognize that the reverend is a volatile character. Sitting in the old west saloon atmosphere of the Crystal Palace with his drink in hand, it's easy for Hunter to summon the nerve of a riverboat gambler. Now it's Reverend Sam's turn to deal.

Hunter ponders that a bit more before his attention is drawn back to the line of dancers as they twirl and move to the right. Kathy catches his eye and smiles broadly. She points to the floor beneath him.

Hunter realizes he has been tapping one foot with the beat. This country music would be easier to hate if it wasn't so damned catchy. As he watches Kathy shimmy her backside toward him in line with all the other dancers, even Bakersfield seems a tolerable little town.

Or maybe, he thinks, it's the company we keep.

Slug: Seniors in Fear

Anchor intro:

> *Experts tell us there are as many as seven million impoverished seniors in America. Seven million who are too poor to live on their own, but too rich or too healthy for a government-subsidized nursing home. Financially abandoned by family and friends, they are orphans of age.*
>
> *It's sad. It's deplorable. But it's not news. For seasoned journalists, it's an issue flogged so often by the whip of their pens that it has been buried in a file of stories to be resurrected only as a last resort. It is a story of desperate people for people in a desperate situation. In other words, a story tailor-made for KDOA.*

Roll tape

"If I don't have this place, I don't have nothing. I'm too old and too cranky to go some place new."

Louisa Witherspoon's face is dark and sagging. Look at the way it's etched with the wrinkles of a hard life that has left her nothing to live on but a meager monthly social security check. That money barely covers rent, utilities and cat food for her only companion. After that, nothing is left over for Louisa.

A single, harsh spotlight mounted on the camera behind Sugar adds shadows to the creases, deepening them in Louisa's face, and it brings out the gray in the old woman's hair for the videotape.

Had Sugar and her photographer been more experienced, or creative, or manipulative, they might have deliberately used the light and shadows to make Louisa look this utterly pathetic. It just works. They don't know why.

"I keeps the shades down full all day," Louisa says. She stops and smacks her lips, works her tongue and resets her jaw between sentences as if chewing the words before offering a thought. They come slowly. "Keep that heat out."

Sugar realizes the TV light is turning Louisa's apartment on the second floor of the Emerald Arms into a sauna. She hopes the interview won't take long. Louisa is sitting in a large, green easy chair in front of Sugar, fanning herself with the cover torn from the front of a cheap romance novel.

Sugar leans forward. The kitchen chair they have placed at the old woman's knee wobbles. "How old are you?" she asks. "How long have you lived here? Do you have any family?" They are elementary questions, and Sugar scribbles the answers in a narrow, white notepad.

Louisa ambles down memory's lane of marriage and children, divorce and death. She's ninety-one now. The offspring she hasn't already outlived are too busy struggling with their own lives and families to pay any mind to Louisa. "I don't see them much."

Sugar's attention wanders to the corner of the room where the television set is tuned to a talk show. Dysfunctional characters are leaping out of their chairs and trying to get a piece of each other. The picture is snowy with poor reception from the bent antenna growing like a weed out of a patch of family photographs on top of the TV set.

Louisa continues, "I gets by all right. Don't know how sometimes. Likewise, all the folk in the building. It just wasn't supposed to be this hard after all these years. It just wasn't supposed to be this hard. Maybe I lived too long."

The words tear at Sugar's heart. She waits, hoping an intelligent question will come. It doesn't. In its place is the realization that she has just recorded the perfect sound bite for her story. She smiles inwardly, not for eliciting that nugget of emotion from the old woman, but for recognizing it so quickly. She is learning.

"Make her cry if you can." Those were the last words of advice the producer Van Thompson gave Sugar as she left on this assignment. She laughed a little. He was kidding, of course. Maybe.

Behind Sugar, behind the camera and her photographer Raul, Reverend Sam Cross is leaning against the wall. He is nodding, with one arm across his chest and the other propped on it to rest an index finger against his lips. He isn't watching the interview so much as he is absorbing it, digesting Louisa's words like a politician's debate coach, looking for anything that may need further clarification.

"That's it. Exactly," he interrupts. He leaps in at every pause in the interview to add, correct or otherwise place a spin on the old woman's story. Sugar lets him. After all, it was Reverend Sam who set up the interview.

"Absolutely wonderful, Louisa," Reverend Sam says when they are through.

Raul says, "We can turn the air conditioner back on." His brow is beaded with sweat as he transfers the camera from its rickety tripod to his shoulder. He asks Louisa to pick up the photo album on the floor at her feet. Sugar grabs it first and lays it gently in the old woman's lap.

"Just flip through the pictures slowly," she directs Louisa. Raul begins rolling video again.

Reverend Sam moves to an air conditioner mounted in the window near Louisa's easy chair. It rattles and growls like a small outboard motor. "I'll set it on low," he says. "We can't afford to run up the utility bill."

Sugar steps back into a shadow near the door where she can juggle her emotions away from the camera's glare in case one gets away from her. She sniffs, touched by Louisa's tale. On one hand, her heart aches for the hard life Louisa is living. On the other, Louisa's hapless situation thrills Sugar. Not only will it make great television, but it's an important story that needs to be exposed. And somewhere between her joy and her pity, Sugar has her personal agenda. She wants to earn some respect.

She knows what the newsroom is saying about her. Hunter has stayed close by, mentoring her with tips and long chats while reviewing videotapes in the editing room. It has helped her confidence, but all that attention has chapped the general morale at News-13. Classic teacher's pet envy, she sighs. People are so judgmental. Sugar wouldn't kick any of them off the stage at Pistol Pete's. She's the only one in the newsroom with three—albeit widely diverse and relatively useless—college degrees on her resume. Maybe the others will look at her differently after this. Maybe this assignment will make Sugar one of them. After all, this job's not so hard. It's a kick.

"How many residents do you have here, Reverend?" she asks. "And how much is the rent?"

"Thirty-one residents. Twenty-four apartments," Reverend Sam replies. He sidles next to Sugar and steals a look at the old woman. Louisa is wrapped up in a world of memories, reminiscing out loud to no one in particular as she touches the photos in her album. Raul is squatting on the floor with his camera, recording the monologue.

"The rent varies," Reverend Sam says softly.

"Oh?"

"We use a sliding scale based on what they can afford. But even at the top end, it's well below what the Land Pirates are getting on apartments anywhere else in Bakersfield."

"Land Pirates?"

Reverend Sam nods and crosses the line into Sugar's personal space. His face is stern and his eyes flash with fire and brimstone. Sugar holds her ground and prepares for a sermon.

"They don't like to be called slumlords. There is a shameful dearth of nonprofit housing in this town. In this country. Why? Because what we take in rent here isn't nearly enough to pay the lease on the building. That's why our federal grants are so vital. Do you realize the government will pay to put people in a nursing home, but can't spare a dime to provide assistance so they can live at home?"

"I didn't..."

"We're bridging the gap for a handful of clients. But a handful is all we can handle. Did you know Bakersfield has one of the fastest-growing senior citizen populations in the country?"

"I didn't..."

"And these aren't rich retirees. These are working class. Many of them are farm workers and migrants who never had enough to begin with, let alone plan for retirement. There is so much to do. And we spend so much time trying to wring dollars out of Washington, Sacramento and the city council that we scarcely have time for the ministry.

"Miss Kane, as I told you on the phone, this story will generate contributions, but this is not just about raising money." His voice is rising now. "The threat that we could lose all this is very real."

Amen.

Sugar feels the reverend's passion. After two years at Pistol Pete's where she sold sex and passion to drunken customers night after night, emotions she learned to turn on at will, Sugar knows the difference between make-believe and the genuine article. The truth is in Reverend Sam.

Sugar takes him by the arm. "I'd like to see the rest of the place, and right now I'll bet Louisa would like us to get out of her hair." She turns to say good-bye to the old woman.

Louisa is standing in front of her chair now, the photo album flopped open at her feet. Clicking her tongue against her gums, she wavers. "You're not going to lose our home, are you Sam?"

The reverend tries to assure her they are doing everything possible. "That's why we asked Miss Kane here today. You knew that, Louisa. We hope she can help."

Sugar reaches out to shake Louisa Weatherspoon's hand. It isn't really a fair fight. Instead of taking Sugar's hand, the frail ninety-pound woman with failing eyesight and arthritic movement goes for the knockout. She places both hands on Sugar's arms, then steps closer to give her a gentle hug.

"Bless you, dear."

Hugging is not a subject that comes up in journalism class, and Sugar has the notion that seasoned news reporters don't wrap up a story in the arms of their interviewee. Imagine Mike Wallace getting warm and fuzzy after grilling Mohamar Ghadaffi. Or Andrea Mitchell giving Bill Clinton… well, some things are better left to the imagination. But if it's in the headlines tomorrow, remember we broke the story here first.

To Sugar, it doesn't seem fair. Reporters are told to be objective; they aren't allowed to be human. She wants to believe doing a story on Reverend Sam's project will save Louisa's tiny rent-subsidized apartment. Maybe it will be no help at all. But she knows that what Louisa needs right now is hope. So she holds the old woman firmly with one arm and strokes a wandering wisp of gray hair back into place with the other. She thinks more stories should end with hugs.

Slug: Seniors in Fear—Part II

Anchor intro:

> *The golden years have lost their luster for two-dozen senior citizens in Bakersfield. They could be turned out onto the street if the agency which provides them with shelter doesn't raise the capital to stay afloat. The Emerald Arms can't pay the rent and the wolf, in landlord's clothing, is at the door.*
>
> *So the organization is using the media in an attempt to save its hide at a time when, oddly enough, the media turns to the seniors with the same desperate agenda of self-preservation. And in the middle is an emotionally pliant stripper-turned-reporter who holds the key to their success.*
>
> *If you thought politics makes strange bedfellows, imagine the peculiar offspring this ménage à trois would produce. Some call it news.*

Roll Tape

"Cat food?"

Sugar raises a hand to her throat, as if that will stop the

revolting taste she imagines. Sympathy and sadness clutch her voice. It sounds tiny. She's eating cat food?

Reverend Sam nods. "If we don't keep a close eye on her, Louisa will skip the meals here in the dining room. We know that she and her cat Lester share the same fondness for Tender Vittles. We do our best."

"But why?"

"That's the way she lived for several years before we brought her here. She simply can't let go of that last shred of independence even if cat food is all she can afford. At least Lester eats well."

Reverend Sam is standing in the common area on the first floor of the Emerald Arms. It's not large, only a portion of the original lobby. But it is comfortable in a drab sort of way, with half a dozen potted plants, three easy chairs, a checkerboard in one corner and a television set in the other. The walls are decorated with old photographs of the building at different stages of its youth and the notable characters who haunt its history. It smells of dusty lace and Old Spice aftershave.

Raul is backed into the corner near the door with his video camera rolling.

"We are caught in the confluence of opposing currents," Reverend Sam is telling Sugar. With his arms crossed, you can see several tattoos on his left forearm. The most prominent is a bible with a cross and the words, "Born To Preach".

He continues, "On one side, Congress cut COPE funding again last year. That was a major portion of the matching funds we used to get in a grant from the state. We could almost survive that until the Wrightwell Foundation, one of our leading donors, rejected our funding request this year."

Sugar is scribbling only key words in her narrow reporter's notebook. "Why?"

Reverend Sam scowls. "The money interests in this town are all in bed with one another. They blackmailed those weaker, soulless members of the foundation's board. The developers who control this block are trying to force us to move. And the quickest way to do that is to cut off our funding."

Reverend Sam is tall and lean with a hawkish nose. His hair is white, and closely cropped where it hasn't gone bald. His eyes are dark with flecks of gray that swirl like clouds before a storm as the passion once again rises in his voice.

"They want us out, plain and simple," he says. "Ha. It won't be as easy as they think."

"You really think the developers are plotting against you. Is that what you're saying?"

"Most definitely," he replies.

Sugar motions to her photographer. "Will you go on camera to say that? I mean, accusations and all?"

Reverend Sam pauses. Sugar is convinced it is more for show than deliberation. "Our attorney has advised us not to tell the truth so bluntly." Sugar can see in his face the reverend has no intention of following the advice.

Raul sets up his camera in the center of the lobby. Sugar has barely begun the interview with Reverend Sam when the front door swings open. A barrel-chested man with a tan military uniform and a ramrod bearing swaggers across the lobby, passing between Sugar and the camera. He nods crisply to her and salutes the reverend.

"Chaplain."

"Major." Reverend Sam salutes back.

The soldier moves directly to the elevator. "I have finished my rounds. The perimeter is secure," he announces to the elevator doors. They slide open slowly as if responding to his words with the same age related ailments of the Emerald Arms tenants. The major steps inside without looking back, and then he's gone.

"That's Tom Sheeley," Reverend Sam explains. "Forty years with the Marines."

Sam taps his temple. "Eighty-two. They diagnosed psychotic depression after his wife died two years ago. He thinks he's back in the service, and he's become our unofficial watchman. Just like clockwork, he comes out twice a day."

The words dredge up something from Sugar's psychology courses. Something about old age and being delusional. It sure looks different when you see it in person.

"Is he dangerous? He had a holster. Was that a gun?"

Reverend Sam smiles for the first time. "It's not loaded. I checked. He doesn't have any bullets, as far as I know."

As Sugar picks up the thread of their interview, she begins to understand the anger and frustration driving Reverend Sam. No wonder, she thinks. It sounds like they really are out to get him.

When the interview is over, Reverend Sam escorts Sugar and Raul through the chapel, the kitchen and day room. He introduces them to residents who shuffle in and out of Raul's camera range.

The photographer stops, chats briefly and charms them into picking up a book, putting down a book, walking in or walking out, taking up a game of checkers or any other activity he can think of to stage action for the video. They respond cautiously at first, and then warm to the task like children on stage for the school pageant.

"Can you do that again?" he asks. Raul then records it from a different angle. Wide shots and close-ups. Sugar thinks they have adjusted well to life inside the dull gray-green interior of the Emerald Arms. She looks at the cracked walls, dark melancholy rooms barely warmed by cheap lamps and wonders if she could ever feel comfortable here without a daily dose of Prozac.

"Poor things."

Back in the lobby, Reverend Sam points to an apartment sandwiched between the front door and the chapel. "That's my humble little home," he says. "No need to see that."

Across from his apartment, Reverend Sam leads them through a heavy wooden door. "This is my son. Sam Junior," he announces.

A younger version of the reverend is seated at a scratched brown desk that takes up most of a small office. He rises to greet them. Sugar guesses Junior is about forty-five. He has more hair than his father; it's gray and sits like a pair of nappy bookends on either side of Sam Junior's face. He has Reverend Sam's narrow eyes and sharp nose, but unlike the sour-faced preacher, Sam Junior smiles easily.

"We're glad you could come by today," he says. He leans on the desk and stretches awkwardly out to take Sugar's hand rather than risk tripping over boxes and plastic wrapping he has discarded on the floor.

Reverend Sam says, "Junior is the administrative officer of the housing program. He's really the one who should be giving you the tour."

But Sam Junior shakes his head. "Not me. I don't get along with cameras very well. Dad, here, is the official spokesman."

Like the rest of the Emerald Arms, the office is not large and every bit of available space is utilized to capacity. The walls are decorated with old black and white photos in dark frames, yellowed newspaper clippings and posters from long forgotten charity events, and certificates of appreciation from various civic groups. Over Sugar's right shoulder next to the door, a faded red and black United Farm Workers Union banner hangs from the ceiling.

Sugar sneezes. The smell is musty, and dust seems to have settled in the few spaces not covered with important paperwork. She takes a step back toward the door. "You look busy. We'll just..."

"Actually, I'm playing—sort of," he laughs. Sam, Jr. waves an upturned palm across a clutter of computer gadgets and cables on his desk. "Chuck and Ginny Barton's son up in San Jose sent this video email kit. You can hook up this little web camera, plug it into our computer and send video messages. Jerry Barton asked us to set it up for him so he can check in on his mom and dad."

Reverend Sam shakes his head. "Don't do it."

All three heads turned to the reverend in disbelief.

"Jerry Barton can't be bothered to come down and visit his parents. And he thinks this is good enough. It's not, and we shouldn't make it easy on him."

Reverend Sam steps between the desk and cabinet and nudges his son aside. With one hand, he flips quickly through a Roledex next to the telephone. With the other, he picks up the box from Jerry Barton's gift. Holding it at arm's length to focus his eyes, Reverend Sam smirks and then waves the box in front of the others. "This is Jerry's company. He didn't even have to buy it."

Reverend Sam finds the number he wants and has Jerry Barton on the telephone in no time. "Yes, Jerry it *is* an emergency. Your parents haven't seen you in nearly six months," he says. He rolls his eyes in exasperation, not so much for what has already transpired in the short conversation, but for what he expects will come.

"Yes, we received the equipment, Jerry. But you know what I'm going to do? I'm going to send it back. C.O.D., Jerry. We don't want it."

Reverend Sam turns and faces the general direction of San Jose and jabs his finger as if his antagonist is just on the other side of the wall instead of three hundred miles away. "No. Don't make excuses, Jerry," he says.

"Then I will throw this gadget out with the trash. Sorry. I won't help you with that. I will not let you shirk your responsibility with some high-tech pacifier for your guilt."

Sugar looks at Sam, Jr. His head is down as he pinches the bridge of his nose and shudders with a quiet laughter. Then he looks up at Sugar and nods. Yes, he's seen this all before.

Sugar bites her lower lip as Reverend Sam raises the level of intimidation. If he takes it up one more notch he'll be shouting into the phone. He has spun back around and faces them; the telephone cord spirals around him like a snake. He becomes more animated. Then Reverend Sam ends the conversation with an exclamation point by slamming down the receiver and thrusting out his chin.

"He'll be here Saturday. With the grandkids."

Sam Junior picks up the computer camera. "Fine. I was looking forward to fiddling around with this to see if I could make it work. Or maybe we can sell it to pay the rent this month."

No one laughs with him.

Reverend Sam rubs his hands together. "That was interesting. Now let's stop chasing bunnies and get back to the problem at hand."

He launches into a litany of under-funded programs for senior citizens in Bakersfield when a large, Irish-red freckled woman raps on the doorframe.

"What is it, Emily?" the reverend asks.

Sugar gasps as she turns. And then she shoots a confused look at Sam and his son. No one else seems bothered by the figure of Death who follows the woman into the office. He's wearing a chocolate sackcloth cloak and carrying a scythe. In the shadow of his hood, Sugar can see a powdered face with dark eyes rimmed in black. It's as if Halloween has come early to the Emerald Arms.

Emily says, "Reverend Sam, would you kindly come and do soomthin' about Mr. Marika? He's in the basement with his foul smellin' cigar again. Mrs. Henderson and some of the other ladies are complainin'. If they go to the fire marshal, well, we just c'not afford another citation."

The reverend nods and looks from Sugar to Emily and back. Then excuses himself. "Give me just a moment." He pats Death on the shoulder as he squeezes through the doorway. "J.B."

"How did opening night go?" Sam Junior asks.

"That sniveling hack Jonathan has taken his character to new extremes of mediocrity," the hooded figure replies. "They should have given me the part of Willie Loman."

Sam Junior waves a hand toward the man and makes introductions. "Sugar Kane, Channel 13 reporter, this is J.B. Hickok, our Meals-on-Wheels driver, number one volunteer and resident actor with the Bakersfield Community Theater."

Sugar inspects him from head to toe. "That's very convincing."

J.B. pulls the scythe to his chest and gives her a slight bow.

"J.B. has another performance tonight," Sam Junior explains.

"I don't like to stray too far from my character at times like this," the actor finishes. "*Death of a Salesman.*"

"And you are?"

"Death, of course."

English Lit—Drama 121, Sugar thinks. She can't remember any mention of Death as an actual character in the play when she studied it in school. She mentions that to J.B.

The actor sniffs. "It's not a speaking role. But as a visual clue to the audience it is the most important character of the play, hovering ever-present in the background. How can you possibly have *Death of a Salesman* without Death?" He says it as if lecturing a third grader.

The lesson over, Sam Junior asks J.B. what he came for.

"The garage called and says we need to replace the brakes on the blue van. They want you to call them back and okay the work."

Sam Junior tilts his head and scrunches his nose. "Did he say how much?"

"Three hundred-something."

Junior pulls a ledger to the edge of his desk, mumbles and makes a notation. "Do you have lunch deliveries today?"

The actor sweeps his hand slowly past the doorframe and replays with an affirmative bow.

"Then please wear something else for your rounds," Sam Junior says. "You're liable to scare the bejeezes out of the folks if you show up on their doorstep like that."

The actor bows again and floats away.

"That was quite a show," Sugar says.

"He's a character all right. He and his mother moved in just a few months ago."

"He doesn't look old enough to be here," Sugar says.

"Mmm. He's probably a few years older than I am. His mother is pretty spry. Seventy something. But it was an emergency case. We hope it isn't a permanent situation." Then Sam Junior sighs. "She can barely afford the rent, so J.B. makes up the difference by doing maintenance work, deliveries and errands for us."

Sugar bites her lip.

"That's only half of it," Junior says. "The reason she's here is because she was cheated by a con artist posing as a loan officer from her bank. He convinced her to sign over the mortgage to her home. A reverse mortgage. She was supposed to stay there rent-free and get a guaranteed monthly payment as long as she lived. Of course, he took out a second on the house and then sold it out from under her and disappeared with the money."

"That's horrible," Sugar says.

"J.B. was out on the road with a touring company at the time. The musical version of *Schindler's List*, I think. By the time he got home, the bank had foreclosed on his mother's house and it's been trying to garnish her monthly pension. He's still fighting South Valley Bank over that."

Sugar's eyes mist. She searches the floor and the walls of the office for something appropriate to add. Nothing comes.

"Not every story in this building is so tragic," Sam Junior says to lighten the mood. "We're really not all pathetic. Take the Bartons, for instance. They're in pretty good shape. And I think their son, Jerry, is used to having my father harass him about coming to visit." He holds a hand to one ear with his thumb and pinky extended to mimic Reverend Sam's phone call.

"That was quite a display your father put on."

"You should see him when he's really riled," Sam Junior replies. Sugar's attention wanders to the photos on the wall. She points to one, a newspaper clipping with a picture of a bearded man in a clerical collar, handcuffed between two very large and very stern police officers. He is waving the handcuffs proudly for the photographer.

Sam Junior says, "That was at the city hall in San Francisco, about 1967."

"That's your father?"

"Just one more entry on his arrest record. The picture next to that one is Father with Cesar Chavez just before they were arrested in Watsonville."

"He must have stayed busy."

"That's where he began the ministry," Sam Junior says.

"Watsonville?"

"No. Prison. That's where he answered God's call. He spent so much time in and out of prison that he developed quite a following of inmates when he was preaching in the cellblock. He was a natural at it, so he decided to get his degree from divinity school."

"Did he get all those tattoos in prison?" Sugar asks.

"You have to do that in prison. But it was also a way to score points with the inmates, to really become one of them. He's done something similar, becoming one of the pack, with the senior citizens since he's gotten older."

"I can see he means well."

"Yeah, but he never outgrew his rabble-rouser phase. That's why the city council and some of the other town leaders hate him. He's always in their face, rousing rabble."

"What about you?" Sugar asks. "You're in the middle of it, too."

Sam Junior's gentle smile turns tight, thin-lipped and tough. He looks more like his father now. "The work we need to do is important, very important. But I'm not like him."

"So what will you do?" Sugar asks. "About your financial problems, that is?"

"Honestly? I think we're sunk."

Sugar is surprised by his frankness.

Sam, Jr. says, "Dad's been fighting this battle for fifteen years, but he hasn't really looked at our books lately. I guess that's my job," he smirks. "And I have the ulcer to prove it."

"You met Louisa and some of the other residents." He raises his hand and squints at Sugar through a tiny gap between his thumb and forefinger. "They are this far away from the nursing home. This place. This ugly, rundown, bug-infested—don't tell the health inspector I said that—money pit of a boarding house is all that stands between Louisa and an institution. And there is one thing that I am absolutely convinced of, something I've learned in my years with these wonderful people." Sugar waits. Sam, Jr. radiates empathy the way his father stews of anger and outrage. And he obviously inherited the reverend's gift of words.

"Old people who are sick and frail and in pain will suffer anything to hide it, anything to avoid being put in an institution."

"Like eating cat food?" Sugar feels that taste in her throat again.

"Dad told you about that. He shouldn't have. It's… it's not something that belongs on TV."

Between Reverend Sam's burning indignation and Junior's warm compassion, Sugar is overwhelmed by a need to stir the fire. Something should be done. This is a major story that needs to be exposed. Where is Mike Wallace when you need him? This is a story worthy of *Sixty Minutes*. The network needs to know. Hunter must have known.

Then she stops her mental rant. Hunter must have known this is a big story. Of course. And since he made a point of handing the assignment to her instead of one of the other reporters, he must think she's the best person for the job. Ha. Let the other reporters laugh; Hunter has faith. Somewhere deep inside, the News Kitten is purring.

Slug: Newsroom Revolt

Anchor intro:

> *Total objectivity in news reporting is a lie. Total objectivity is humanly impossible. All reporters enter the game with the biases of their upbringing, their training and their experience (or lack of it). The media have no choice but to perpetuate the lie, if for no other reason than out of self-preservation. Or do they?*
>
> *What if we strip TV news to its very bone? Cut away its fancy sets, the eye-grabbing graphics, and stop requiring reporters to be something more than human. What if we just offer what we see and hear, with all of our passion and none of the pretense, and give viewers credit for being intelligent enough to distinguish between the two?*
>
> *It would be unthinkable.*
> *It could mean anarchy.*
> *It might draw ratings.*

Take Live Shot

Sugar is standing in front of a charred patch of oak trees. Fire has scorched a hundred acres at the Ming Lake Recreation Area, and Sugar is there. The fire sent families scampering for their lives when it consumed their campground. The wind that whipped flames across the area earlier in the day now tugs at Sugar's hair and swirls smoke in front of the camera lens to take us there, too, involving us so much we can almost taste the dry ash in the air. It is great TV.

Hunter's eyes narrow. He is watching Sugar on the newsroom's monitor. He's watching her closely, defensively. He knows the others are standing behind him; they are also watching her with a critical eye. He can almost feel their knives in his back.

As an anchor, Sugar has been a big bust—which, anatomically speaking, is her best asset. In contrast, her delivery is flat. Her chemistry with her co-anchor Kent Abernathy fizzled—if it had any sizzle to begin with. Maybe separating them, by putting Sugar in the field more often, will help.

Sugar had only been on the air three days before the newsroom jury had tried and convicted Hunter of all kinds of executive misdemeanors and management felonies, the least of which is simple incompetence. He can't blame them. The evidence appears to be overwhelming.

Even the most ratings-hungry consultants who push eye candy—strong visuals like sexy anchors and titillating video—would shake their heads and have Hunter locked away for this one. What was he thinking when he hired this big-breasted nightclub stripper who can ooze sex appeal through a GorTex parka in an Alaskan winter?

"She looks good."

No, that's not it.

Hunter realizes the voice came from outside his own head, so he shifts his eyes without turning and measures the voice for sarcasm. He gives it only a three on a scale of ten. One of the reporters, Andy Blackman, is standing at Hunter's elbow. Andy reaches out and turns up the volume a notch on the monitor. Hunter likes that.

Sugar bends momentarily out of your view and picks up a metal pot, scorched in the fire and abandoned at one campsite. She talks with compelling simplicity about the families who had their vacations cut short by the emergency, and how they escaped just ahead of the flames.

This is why he hired her, Hunter thinks. It had been a snap decision under pressure, but based on instinct. It was an impulse purchase to buy them time before the station owner shuts down the news operation.

But whatever Hunter saw in Sugar's audition has been missing until tonight. It has stayed just out of reach as he worked with her through her first rocky month at KDOA. Watching her now, Hunter sees the spark again. It's a relief to know he isn't crazy after all. Now he needs a way to capture this lightning and put it in a bottle.

Unfettered by scripts and teleprompters, Sugar is golden. When she is set free to talk with you one-on-one like this, you forget how beautiful Sugar is, and that is no easy task. She sets aside the pot and introduces Andy's report on the campers who have taken refuge in an emergency shelter. The videotape rolls.

"Nice piece," Hunter says when Andy's story is done. He raps the reporter softly on the arm. "Very nice."

Together they watch Sugar talk her way through three more stories related to the fire before she takes them into a commercial break. Hunter is pleased. That worked.

Sports.

Weather.

Kicker.

When the newscast is over, Hunter sits at his desk and follows the second hand as it sweeps around the dial on his wristwatch. Thirty seconds. He looks over at the tiny television set near his desk where Ryan Billings is doing the national news. Hunter wrinkles his nose at the sight of Billings, and listens for the sounds of remote controls clicking, imagining everyone in Bakersfield switches to Tom Brokaw on NBC. He turns his attention back to his watch. Ten seconds. Five. Cue the anchor.

Kent Abernathy storms into Hunter's office exactly one minute and twenty seconds after the final credits. It is as quick as a dignified march down the hallway could get him here.

"Did you see that 'cast?" He flings a pile of scripts toward the wastebasket. The pages bounce off the side of Hunter's desk; half of them slip off the trashcan and onto the floor. Hunter leans to his left to judge the effort. Kent's aim has improved decidedly in the five post-newscast trips he has made to Hunter's office since being partnered with Sugar. "Did you see what she did? She had the entire first segment to herself. What was I there for? I'll bet I didn't have thirty seconds of T.U. in the whole first half of the show."

"T.U.?" Hunter asks.

"Talent units. Never mind," Kent blusters.

"What is that? Like measuring face time?"

"Forget that," Kent says. "The point is she stole the entire show."

"Interesting," Hunter says. "T.U. I've never heard it put that way before. Talent units. Hmm."

Kent responds in a grating singsong. "You're not listening. She is just a co-anchor."

"No," Hunter corrects him. "Tonight she is the T.A."

"T.A.?"

"Top Anchor."

Kent scowls. "Who calls it that?"

"Nobody. I just made it up."

"First you put this nobody, this inexperienced college intern, on the air to embarrass the rest of us. Then she grabs control of the news and thinks she can get away with it because she's pretty and has big…" Kent coughs into his fist. "A big smile."

Hunter scratches his head. Looking at Kent's wig makes him itch. The anchor must really be riled because even his synthetic hair appears more ruffled, a bit scruffier than usual. Hunter wonders if Kent is wearing his third-week wig. Maybe it's Number Four. He doesn't get to ask.

Cue the director.

Lee Richards bounces into the office, tapping Kent on the right shoulder and slipping behind him to the left before he plops into the chair across from Hunter.

"Did you see that 'cast?"

"That's the question of the day," Hunter replies.

"That was so cool," Lee moans like a teenager falling in love with his first car.

"It was a fiasco," Kent growls.

"It was so out of control, so out there! I didn't know what we were doing next. Sugar said this, and I punched that. I punched this, and she said that. She rocked. I rolled." Lee drums his palms on Hunter's desk.

"It was chaos," Kent says. "She didn't even follow her scripts."

Lee nods. "He's right. Totally awesome. Totally, uhm, live." He bounces to his feet and then steadies himself. "Yo. Head rush."

There is no doubt Sugar had a good night. It's as if Sugar has two personalities. Hunter thinks of Patty Duke on that old TV show where she plays identical cousins. One is formal and boring, and the other is a shining free spirit. Maybe Sugar has a twin.

The formal Sugar is a stiff in the studio where the format is tightly controlled and she's committed to the teleprompter scripts with their words etched in...well, paper. The free-spirited twin Sugar is a dream in the field. Sugar can't read a lick, but she can communicate like the dickens.

"I'm jazzed," Lee says.

"I'm not," Kent grumps.

Hunter nods and ignores them. An idea is sprouting. He leans back in his chair and relaxes, coaxing the notion to grow.

"We've got to let her do more live stuff at five." Lee says. "Even though she didn't follow the script. And she changed our cues to roll the video—shit, she even dropped a story entirely and drove everyone in the booth crazy. It was like she was talking right to me." Lee sways with his eyes closed. He floats into a dream, waving his hands rhythmically like a conductor carried away by his symphony's music. "She knew what I had, and I knew what she wanted. The timing was so good between us..."

Lee pops his eyes open wide. His shoulders slump. "God. I need a cigarette."

He bounces out of the office, bumping into Kathy Wright on the way.

Cue the producer.

"Did you see the 'cast?"

"Doesn't anyone think I watch what goes on around here?" Hunter asks.

"No." Kathy and Kent reply in unison.

Kent scratches his wig and tries to reclaim the conversation. "Now, if you want to demote Sugar to, say, featured reporter, I can handle the anchor desk just fine without her. But all I got tonight was table scraps from the producer." He jerks his thumb at Kathy. In response, Kathy flips a defiant hand through her thick and—unlike Monsanto Head's wig—obviously natural hair.

Kent continues, "Sugar got all the meat. But my contract strictly spells out..."

Hunter is doubtful Kent's contract spells out any such thing. "Kent, your nose looks a bit shiny, your hair is crooked, and you have the Six O'clock Report coming up in a few minutes. You'd better get ready."

"But…"

"Trust me. Sugar's barely in the show at six. You'll get more than your share of T.U.s or whatever."

Kent tries to protest, but Hunter isn't going to let him get another word out.

Activity is picking up in the newsroom. We are now ten minutes away from the six o'clock newscast. A controlled panic has set in as Van Thompson, the producer, screams for a missing script. Someone launches a fresh videotape of the campground fire across the newsroom into waiting hands in hopes of getting it edited before deadline. Kathy closes the door as Kent retreats, to block out the noise of the news machine as it gears up for the next broadcast.

"What took you so long to get down here?" Hunter asks her.

"I wanted to review the tape of the show. Get a more objective look at how it came across, since it was utter chaos in the control booth."

"How did it look?"

"The show looked smooth."

Hunter waits. "You know what I mean."

"SHE," Kathy emphasizes, "did fine, I guess." It is a major concession on her part, and Hunter is gratified.

Kathy nearly had kittens when Hunter had first suggested putting so much of the newscast into Sugar's hands. The *Five O'clock Report* was, after all, Kathy's baby. In light of Sugar's dismal performance so far, it seemed suicidal and they fought over it. They both knew it was a desperate attempt at damage control, an effort to put some distance between Kent and Sugar. And Hunter won out only after he admitted to her that pairing those two on the newscast was a mistake of Chernobyl proportions.

Hunter looks at Kathy. He wants to take a gentle hand to the wave of hair in the limp last days of a long-forgotten perm. It is hiding one side of Kathy's face, and he wants to see her eyes. Kathy must be reading him. She combs her fingers through the offending bangs in a drawn out, sensual motion. But then she looks away.

"Yes, she did a lot better tonight," Kathy says. She puffs up her cheeks and releases a slow breath. It turns into a whistle with the last wisp of air. "It wasn't easy, but it was fun. It was certainly different."

"Good. I think we learned something. Do you want to try it again?"

Kathy shrugs. "We can."

"It's obvious it was a mistake to put her at the anchor desk with Kent. I can see that now."

"The rest of us saw it a couple of weeks ago," she says.

Hunter shoots her dead with a glance.

"Sorry," Kathy replies without a trace of contrition.

Hunter continues, "Watching the newscast tonight, though, I think I've settled on the best way to use her strengths. But that means expanding Sugar's role even more. And…" he squares his shoulders. "It's going to take some faith. No. A lot of faith on your part."

"Haven't you done enough for her?" Kathy asks. She is biting her lower lip softly.

"This isn't about Sugar and what we can do for her."

"Isn't it?"

Hunter tries to ignore the question. Kathy isn't as immature as the others in the newsroom. She should understand. He plucks one of several pencils growing out of a coffee cup on his desk and winces at the sight of the stack of his own audition tapes sitting there. Damn. Hunter had promised a station manager in Seattle he would get an audition tape in the mail on Monday. Last Monday. All this work is getting in the way of his job search. He'll just have to deal with that tomorrow.

"Sugar has a talent unlike anything else in this market. It's a rare thing that I've only seen once or twice before."

Exasperated, Kathy says, "You're the only one who can see it, Hunter."

"No. You've seen it. I can tell by the way you watch her."

Kathy shakes her head. "You're just trying to justify this scheme of yours to build everything around her. You have it all dialed in, don't you? This nice, neat little plan."

Hunter studies the pencil in his hand. "Nah. I really don't have a clue; I'm making this up as we go along. Total ad-lib."

There. He said it. Kathy has been trying to get him to loosen up, and there it is. It is more truth than he cares to admit to himself but, strangely, there is comfort in confessing it to Kathy.

She returns his honesty with a withering look. Kathy doesn't buy it.

They stare at each other for a moment before Hunter continues. "If we find the right way to tap into Sugar's talent, the audience will see it, too—that is, if we can grab their eyeballs long enough to give us a try in the first place." He looks straight at Kathy and leans forward. He speaks softly and smiles slyly. "But I can't do it without you."

"Sorry. This window is closed. You've already used that line enough," Kathy says. "Hunter, the only thing Sugar has going for her right now is sex appeal. She has you and the other men standing around with your tongues hanging out. *That's* what you see. And I can't believe you're going to risk everything on such a...a cheesy, obvious attempt to sell sex and call it news. Why not just have her anchor the newscast in the nude?"

"It's not that far-fetched," he says. The more he weighs the idea, the more sharply it comes into focus and the more he likes it. Kathy's eyes are wide and cold, but as she studies Hunter's face, they melt into puddles of uncertainty.

"Tell me you're not thinking what I think you're thinking. That's it. J.K. Just kidding, right?"

Hunter shakes his head. He extends his palm and stares into the distance. "Live. Live. Live. Live at Five," he says. "That's what we'll call it. Live at Five with Sugar Kane. No better still, @ Five."

"At Five? Live At Five?"

"No, Live @ Five."

"That's what I said. Live At Five."

"Yeah, but you're not seeing it. We'll use an @ symbol." Hunter holds up his hand, fingers circled over his thumb, not quite making a fist. "This says we're hip. We're modern. We're with the times. Everything is going to the internet today, right? They keep telling us that not too long after we hit 2000, maybe by 2005 or so, most people will be getting their news from their computers. That's what this whole MS-UBN thing is leading up to. Cable TV is just the first stop. We'll be ahead of the game." Hunter's mental engine was leaving the station and picking up speed. He is talking faster now.

"But Hunter, it sounds the same. Live At Five. Live @ Five. You can't hear any difference. And besides, it's only a title." Kathy mimics his hand gesture. "*This*," she says, "hardly makes it cutting edge."

"Is anybody else doing this? Not a chance. And yeah, it's only the perception. But I keep tellin' ya, in our business perception is reality."

"I know, and reality is what we say it is. I wish you'd stop saying that," Kathy sighs.

"We'll plaster the city with billboards. Nothing but a big @ on them. Create some mystery, some buzz. And then, when people are talking about it, asking what is it with the @ thing, we launch Live @ Five with Sugar Kane. Five o'clock is the place to be—@."

"I think you're being an @ss," Kathy mumbles.

"I heard that."

"Either way, you're getting ahead of yourself, don't you think? I mean, this is stuff for the promotions department to worry about."

"The promotions department doesn't have the balls to do something like this."

"I think Becky Drake might be offended by that."

"You're probably right. I stand corrected. She doesn't have the ovaries for it. Whatever." There is no stopping Hunter now. "But's what I'm thinking here is that it's got to be more than just a name change. If we're going to build this thing around Sugar, we've got to tap into her strengths. We've got to let her do it in a way that only she can do."

"Right. So you're going to have Sugar do the news…"

"Naked."

Slug: Naked News

Voice intro:

> *Now, from the heart of the Golden Empire, with News 13 Anchor Sugar Kane, Meteorologist Bob Moorman, and Boog Powers on sports:*
> *This.*
> *Is.*
> *Live @ Five.*

Take live report from scene

The deep thunder of the announcer's voice is rolling into the distance as Sugar's image fills your screen. She is on the steps of City Hall. Not standing, mind you, and certainly not posturing with serious attitude, as journalists tend to do when they want you to think what they have to say is important.

Sugar is sitting casually on the steps like someone who's been waiting for you and you are right on time for an after-work drink at the tavern around the corner and a few stories. Sugar just wants to tell you about her day.

She points over her shoulder. "The city council just finished a work session,"—she checks her watch—"about an hour ago. They're trying to come up with the money to shorten the amount of time it takes to get a fire truck to your home. It means buying some new communications equipment, and it looks like they'll have to raise our taxes to do it."

A September breeze ruffles the pages of the notepad in her hand. It promises a quick cool down from the eighty-nine degrees weatherman Bob Moorman recorded as the high temperature of the day. It peaked just before the broadcast, but Sugar doesn't appear affected by the heat. She's wearing a conservative cream silk blouse and dark pants. Not overtly sexy, but stylish in a way that accentuates Sugar's curves. She looks good.

She ought to look good. Kathy and Sugar spent the entire weekend chasing after just the right look at stores all across Bakersfield. Armed with the station's credit card, a modest clothing budget and a handful of examples Hunter had ripped and clipped from fashion magazines, they negotiated the jungle of sales racks on a two-day safari and came away with an impressive collection.

This is Naked News. Are you impressed?

It's the first night of their new format, and Sugar's outfit is the least of Kathy's worries. She is nervous, fumbling with her terrifyingly thin stack of scripts in the control booth back at the station. Each one is marked with video commands for the director and nothing but the words "ad lib" on the anchor's portion of the page. Kathy feels as if she is the one Hunter has left undressed.

This is not at all what she had in mind when he proposed revamping the newscast. Kathy doesn't think about her hand as it moves unconsciously, bashfully, to cover her breast. It is the reflex of a woman who perhaps suddenly became aware that she leaned a bit too low, exposing too much to be tasteful in public. Her fingers brush a yellow sticky note Hunter handed her as she headed to the control booth ten minutes earlier. Kathy peels it from her blouse and reads it again.

"Have fun." Hunter's last piece of advice.

Richard Lee is sitting next to her in the director's chair, wearing a crash helmet. His hand is hovering over the control panel, shaking from hyper-anxiety and fueled by the caffeine rush of a twenty-ounce Mountain Dew he had slammed just before the broadcast.

"Roll tape?" he asks.

"Not yet," Kathy answers.

"Shit. I just hit the button. I didn't mean to. We're in black. Wait." He pokes at the control panel, a white button. "No, this one." A red button this time.

Kathy holds her breath as the largest monitor on the wall in front of her—the one to indicate what the viewers at home are watching—goes dark. Then it cycles through quick glimpses of an empty anchor chair in the studio, a dog food commercial, (or maybe that was the Taco Bell Chihuahua), Bob Moorman picking his nose in front of the camera mounted in his weather office before it finally lands back on Sugar.

"Sorry," Lee apologizes. He blows on his index finger like a gunslinger cooling his weapon.

Out at City Hall, Sugar scratches her chin and points off camera, presumably to her own TV monitor a few feet away. "Just like that, it's been confusing and tense during the budget meeting today." She smiles.

Kathy smiles with her. Smooth. A true professional would have ignored the video chaos, but somehow Sugar manages not only to make it acceptable, but comfortable. How did she get to be so cool in front of the camera with so little experience? The question has dogged Kathy, and Kathy has clamped on to it like a pup with a Milk Bone.

She peppered Sugar with questions over the course of their two days together building a news wardrobe. The answers didn't satisfy. Sugar told Kathy about her life as a career college student, but said little about the jobs she took to pay the rent and nearly ten years of tuition. After all that education, Sugar has certainly shown she is bright. And while she can be captivatingly descriptive about some parts of her life, Sugar has been maddeningly vague about others. And Kathy feels she still knows very little about her.

She won't give up easily, but right now she can't help smiling as Sugar delivers the one line that was actually written into the script for her.

"Roll tape. NOW!" Kathy calls out. Video of firefighters performing CPR on a young boy fills the screen. Sugar explains the budget battle and the need for better communications equipment as she watches the video on her monitor at City Hall. The hour Sugar spent cramming for the newscast like it was one of her college midterms is paying off.

While you and the rest of Bakersfield are watching the videotape of firefighters in action, Kathy watches a second TV set where she can monitor Sugar. The anchor makes a yakity-yak motion with her hand, a signal Hunter taught her.

"She wants the sound bite," Kathy says.

"Roll tape." Lee punches another button and, presto, Councilman Deleno is there, and talking about the size of the tax increase he has proposed. Kathy checks the script in front of her; at least this part is on paper. She reads along with the councilman. When the sound bite ends, Lee puts Sugar back up on your screen to wrap up the story.

And if you want to know more about this story, read about it in tomorrow's newspaper. Kathy slides the top page of her stack and drops it into the trashcan at her foot.

That is how you do the news naked.

Hunter swears it's been done before in various forms in Chicago, Miami and even on PBS. It wasn't until they had rehearsed it for a week that Kathy gave her grudging support for the idea. In fact, a week of rehearsal for anything new at KDOA is a novelty. Former news directors made changes without consulting the staff, implemented them immediately and expected everyone to work out the bugs on the air.

Hunter has her off balance. He seems to change course and make these risky decisions as if he's just flying by the seat of his pants, but then becomes methodical in final preparation.

More troublesome to her is that Hunter, like Sugar, is holding back a part of him. Kathy mopes. Maybe those two were meant for each other.

The day after that wonderful evening Kathy spent line dancing with Hunter—okay, she danced and he smiled—Hunter cinched his tie and put some distance between them again. He has been spending a lot of time mentoring Sugar. Private chats to review videotapes in the editing bays. True, he has been working with all the reporters, especially on the stories involving Reverend Sam and his poor senior citizens. But Hunter seems to reserve special time for Sugar.

She fans out the remaining pages of her script on the console like a poker player revealing a weak hand, and she wonders how they will fill the time.

Kathy slides another script into the trashcan as Sugar gives minimal attention to the crime stories. Three of them. On a normal day, Kathy would have led the newscast with the shooting at Pinky's Bar. Not any more. Hunter won't allow it. Violence and car crashes on Highway 99 get buried in the newscast unless it means more than a random act to the rest of you at home.

Stories like this:

"Two customers got into a fight at Pinky's Bar on Seventeenth Street," Sugar says. "One had a gun, and he used it. Now one is dead, one is in jail, and that's a waste of two human lives. That's all we need to know."

Kathy turns to her director. He's staring wide-eyed at the monitor with his mouth agape. The front of his crash helmet rises, pushed up by his eyebrows. "Did she really say that?"

"Well, I guess we won't be using *that* video," Kathy replies.

Lee whines, "What was that, a seven second story? I didn't even have time to roll."

"Never mind, keep moving. She's on the next one already." This is madness. The pace is picking up. Kathy scribbles on one of the scripts a reminder to tell Sugar to stretch those stories with video.

Sugar mows through several more stories on their rundown for the day without any more surprises for the crew. Kathy barely absorbs a word she says. She checks off each item on her list, eyes the clock on the wall with suspicion, plots ahead and tries to reconcile the number of stories left with the time remaining.

"I don't know about this," she says a bit too loudly. She wonders why Hunter couldn't just change the color of the news set or the graphics and leave it at that. What will they have when he's gone? Not much, if he's like all the other bosses Kathy has seen pass through the revolving door on the news director's office—five of them in her six years at Channel 13.

As she watches the monitor, Kathy wonders how Sugar is being affected by her new celebrity status. Three times during their weekend together at the malls, Sugar was recognized and endured a bit of fawning. The ratings have always been so bad at KDOA that a News 13 anchor could dance naked in the street without raising a single eyebrow from some passerby who might recognize them. They were as anonymous as anyone else. But three viewers in one weekend perked up when Sugar passed by. Kathy sees that as a sign that things are changing. It didn't hurt that Kathy was able to call in a long-forgotten chit with the lifestyles reporter from the newspaper. At least the reporter had long forgotten the favor Kathy provided a few years back.

"That's not fair," Amanda Suarez says when Kathy finally gets around to the reason for her call.

"C'mon Mandy. This has sex and it's entertainment. It really is something different. And…" wait for it, here comes the hard part. Kathy shivered when she adds, "The boss say you can even rip us a new one—up one side and down the other if you want. Write whatever."

"Whatever I want? Not pitch some puff piece?"

"Anything. Trust me, though, it's a decent story on a slow day. Just don't bury it on Saturday, okay?"

By gosh, by golly and what the fuck. The paper actually runs with it. The angle is more about Hunter's vision for a strictly ad lib format, and vague on the News Kitten's qualifications to handle the role of trusted news anchor, Hunter is actually disappointed that the article was so, so…"objective." Hunter is making a star out of Sugar. He designed this new *Live @ Five* format around her to let Sugar anchor alone. He pushes her for the best stories and the special assignments. Sugar is pretty, Hunter is charming, and Kathy is jealous. She can't help wondering when the two started sleeping together.

"Don't go there," she says to herself.

"Where?" Lee is looking at her. "The package is already rolling." He nods at the monitor.

Andy Blackman's report on the new classroom computers at Baker Elementary is on the screen. "Oh? Geez, we have only one more news segment to go." Kathy pushes the intercom button on her side of the control panel, the communication lifeline connecting her to Sugar.

"You're doing great, Sugar," she says into the microphone. "We need to pay the bills. Toss to the commercial when we get out of this story." She lets up on the button and tries to relax.

Lee leans forward against the control panel. "Okay, she's wrapping up the school story," he says. "Dominique, VTR one. Roll the tease video."

The first segment has been a blur, but with a little finagling and Sugar's long piece on the senior citizen's center coming up, they just might make it after all.

"You know, it's freaking hairy but I like it," Lee says.

Kathy crumples another page from the script and tosses it at him. "Well, just don't get too used to it."

Slug: Bandit Arrested

Anchor intro:

> *Scoop.*
> *On the battlefield of commercial journal-*
> *ism, nothing is more honored or voraciously*
> *coveted than the exclusive story. Beating the*
> *competition by mere seconds is cause for cel-*
> *ebration in the deadline-warped, compressed*
> *universe of TV news. Ratings can be built, for-*
> *tunes can be made, and careers catapulted*
> *by the scoop.*
> *Here's one for you: Reverend Sam Cross*
> *is Bakersfield's infamous Senior Bandit.*
> *He was arrested by officers at the Emerald*
> *Arms. And Sugar Kane was the only reporter*
> *at the scene when officers swarmed in to cuff*
> *the criminal cleric.*
> *That is a scoop with a cherry on top.*

Roll tape

You can see the inspiration for those crimes on one wall of
Reverend Sam's apartment at the Emerald Arms. He's turned the
wall into a shrine to dissidents and dreamers, reformers and rivals

of the status quo. Half a dozen portraits hang there. Some are icons like Martin Luther King, Jr., and Abraham Lincoln.

In the center, a small piece of embroidered cloth quotes Ghandi.

"*It is better to be violent, if there is violence in our hearts, than to put on the cloak of nonviolence to cover impotence.*"

The room is dark and dusty. It is unquestionably a man's den with a musky scent and a neat but worn attitude suggesting female callers are few and far between.

Sugar is recording it all with the camera on her shoulder. There was no photographer in the newsroom when she got Reverend Sam's urgent phone call, so she grabbed a camera and was out the door before anyone could protest. Now she tries to remember what they taught her about framing and focus, and how the hell to make the camera work in general. It would be a shame to ruin this story with rotten video.

Reverend Sam is standing by the window. Light slices past the curtain and creates a shadow, cutting him right down the middle into two separate beings, one dark and one light.

The reverend's attorney, Charles Meade, is sitting calmly in a deep green Lazy-Boy in the corner where two crammed bookcases meet. He's a fifty-year-old cherub with a button nose and thin-lid eyes squeezed between fat cheeks and a thick brow.

Sugar lowers the camera and holds it at her waist. "Are you sure the police are on their way?"

"Oh yes. A colleague of mine downtown—he's with the jail ministries—he told me they were marshaling the troops."

Meade looks up from his magazine. "We could be here forever.

The FBI is in on it. They'll spend half the day just blundering through the red tape and jurisdiction squabbles before they actually show up. The Feds will want to run the damned show. Bakersfield P.D. will be tripping all over the place like slobbering puppies. Then the paperwork will be all wrong." Meade sighs. "I'll have to hold their hands and make sure the bust goes down legally."

Reverend Sam turns from the window and nods. "That would be appreciated, Charlie."

"On the other hand, let them fuck up the arrest, and we can get you off without having to go to trial. That would be the way to go. Especially since you're not paying for the privilege."

"Come now, Charlie. You love the fight. And a little pro bono work is good for your radical soul."

The attorney scratches his whiskers. "Pro bono doesn't feed my dog."

"Then I'll have Emily bake him a pie or two."

"He likes chocolate. Lots of it," Meade says.

Sugar frowns, "Don't feed him that. Chocolate will kill your dog."

Reverend Sam laughs. "That's all right, Miss Kane. Charlie doesn't have a dog," He turns again to the window. "I'm sorry this is taking so long, but I wanted to make sure you didn't miss it."

"Why?"

"For all the work you've done recently. All those stories about what we're trying to do here have helped increase donations." He sighs, "Unfortunately, it's still not enough."

"So, then, you *are* the Senior Bandit?"

Reverend Sam attempts to answer, but Meade coughs loudly and then feigns a sneeze that sounds roughly like "Bullshit."

Reverend Sam moves closer to the window, still shielded from the street outside by the heavy curtain. "Am I the Senior Bandit? The police certainly seem to think so," he says. He stands at the window and rocks gently back and forth. Sugar thinks he's at the center of a tug of war, a decision-making battle going on inside his soul.

Then Sam turns and walks toward her. He bends and peers into the lens of her camera as if it was a peephole to the rest of the world. "That isn't on at the moment, I take it?"

Sugar struggles to raise it to her shoulder, but the Reverend stops her. "No," he says. "It's not time yet. But it's important for you to know that I…"

"Sam!" The attorney barks at the preacher. He snarls like the dog he hasn't got, and warns Reverend Sam to stop. Sugar watches the attorney shake his head with exasperation as Sam turns his back on Meade.

"Yes, Miss Kane. Isn't it obvious that I must be your 'Senior Bandit'? But it would be premature to confess at this moment. At some point you will get to tell the world. It's comforting to know you'll be the one to do it. Tell them I'm the bandit. And it's important for them to learn that. People will hear your story and they're going to wonder why the bandit would steal that money. But I also want them to ask why this community is stealing the quality of life from our senior citizens. The bandit isn't a thief—he's a messenger."

Sam stops. Something has caught his attention. He moves to the window while Meade drops back into his chair and pinches the bridge of his nose between his fat fingers.

Sam draws a breath and throws his shoulders back. Sugar swears she can see him grow an inch taller. "Ah, that looks like an advance scout out there now. Charlie, they just pulled up across the street," he says.

He turns and looks at Sugar. "I promised you the story, and you'll have it in full. Right now, it would be better for both of us if you leave it all to speculation. Far be it from me to tell you how to do your job, but I've seen the way the media will cover a story over and over again while there is still anticipation and speculation. Once the cat is out of the bag? Nothing. Nada. I don't want this to become yesterday's news today. So let's just let it simmer for a while. It will come out and when it does, we will talk with you first."

What? Why? Stunned by Reverend Sam's admission, there are so many things she wants to ask. She presses him but he won't give her more.

Sam says, "Charlie, come look at this. It appears Bakersfield's finest has responded in their usual overly enthusiastic manner."

Meade pops up from his chair and moves to the opposite side of the window from Reverend Sam. "I see two cars on this side, half a block away. And they're pulling weapons out of the trunk."

"I can't quite tell from here," Reverend Sam says. "But I think I see riot gear on this side."

Sugar sets her camera on a coffee table, forgetting for the moment the job she came to do. She steps tentatively toward the reverend and peers out the window. Reverend Sam pulls her protectively behind him. Sugar can see four men standing at the rear of a nondescript Ford across the street. One of the men is in uniform, and he's arguing with the others.

"Are we in danger?" Sugar asks.

"Not much," Reverend Sam says. Then he adds, "I pray."

But a shriek from beyond the door to Reverend Sam's apartment kills the confidence he offers. "Sam! Reverend? There are men in the street. They have guns. Oh my!"

"Calm yourself, Mrs. Henderson," he calls out. "It will be all right."

Meade moves quickly to the door and swings it open. "Give me five minutes, Sam. And Miss Kane, it's been nice meeting you." With a raised eyebrow, he looks at the camera on the table. "I hope you'll get the pictures you came for."

Sugar hoists the camera and balances it on her shoulder, feeling as if she were caught with her journalistic slip showing.

Sugar follows Reverend Sam to the lobby of the Emerald Arms. Three women are in a huddle and wringing their hands. The elevator pings, and four more residents spill out. The collision of excitement and fear creates such a ruckus in the room, it feels to Sugar like feeding time at the zoo when all the monkeys and lions and birds compete for attention. She swings her camera from one face to the next, holding out a microphone to capture each roar and every squawk. It is making her dizzy.

"Good gracious. What is going on?"

"Is this a raid?" someone else croaks. Her voice was filled with fright.

"How exciting," another voice adds. This old lady is more amused than concerned.

Major Tom steps forward. He's added a helmet to his Marine uniform today. "Chaplain, we've had a breach of security." He draws the gun from his holster and holds it with both hands above the group. "I'll find Sergeant Collins," he says before marching off.

Mrs. Henderson cackles, "I saw police officers from my window."

"With guns," another voice chimes in.

"What are they doing? What are they here for?" The questions bounce around the room.

From out of nowhere, the feisty little Mr. Marika shuffles up behind Sugar. "Hide your stash, ladies," he announces. "It's the cops."

"Why are they here?" someone asks again.

"It's simple," Marika croaks. "They're here to bust Mrs. Henderson. She's been slipping Viagra mickies into the drinks of her dates."

"Really?"

"Oh hush, Mr. Marika. Don't be silly."

A tussle in the elevator draws everyone's attention. Major Tom and another man tumble into the lobby, wrestling one another in a feeble battle. The old soldier's adversary is dressed in pantaloons and a bright and multi-colored tunic. He looks every bit the court jester, a fool from a Shakespearean comedy who has just stepped off the stage. His head is shaved and he is has painted his upper lip and chin black in a child-like attempt to give himself a goatee. Suddenly aware of the crowd in the lobby he turns.

"You knave," he swears at the soldier. Then he crosses his chest with one arm and gives his audience a short bow. J.B. Hickok, the Emerald Arm's resident actor, is in the spotlight.

"Everyone, listen to me. Just calm down." Reverend Sam shouts. He is in the center of them now, with both hands raised and explains in a deep, forceful voice that everything will be all right. The police have come for him.

"There is no reason for alarm if you all remain calm and stay inside. Go back to your apartments. This will all be over soon. And Junior will explain it all when we're done."

For the first time, Sugar notices Sam Junior standing like a sentry near the lobby's front door. He's staring past one of the narrow, frosted glass columns that frame the portal as if he can really see more than just light and shadow on the other side. Sam Junior turns at the mention of his name. A sour look of despair has replaced the cheerful compassion Sugar had admired. It adds age to his face, once again making Junior look more like his father.

"What are we going to do?" someone asks.

"Lock the doors."

"Be reasonable."

"Can't you go out and talk to them, Sam?"

"We must not surrender!" Major Tom shouts. He has moved to the edge of the circle. He is holding his revolver above his right eye, as if saluting with the weapon.

Then a hand reaches from behind him and snatches the gun. J.B. Hickok dances backwards three steps and laughs. He twirls the pistol around his index finger.

"You silly, impotent old man. What are you going to do with this? Scare them to death? It's not even loaded, you stupid fool." He flings the gun. It skitters across the floor past Major Tom's feet. The soldier bends, but he's too slow to intercept the weapon. He chases it down from his stooped position, a groveling, demeaning act. Sugar thinks a dog, going after scraps tossed from the master's table, would have more dignity.

"And the rest of you," Hickok says. "What choice do we really have? They hold all the cards. They have all the guns. They call all the shots. Just go out and give them what they want, Sam. They're going to get it anyway. They always do."

The actor's shoulders are slumped and his face is deeply lined. Sugar guesses he can't be too far into his fifties. Sam Junior had said, on that first day, that J.B. and his mother wouldn't even be here if not for the bank's foreclosure on her home. She wonders if it is the stress of his mother's financial collapse, or the hard life of a two-bit actor that has worn down J.B. Hickok. But right now he looks as tired and old as any of the Emerald Arm's residents.

"Please! I'm imploring you all to be calm. There is nothing to be afraid of if you just stay here, inside, with Sam Junior," Sam shouts.

The preacher motions to Sugar. She follows him, hugging the camera to her chest like a favorite, albeit heavy, child's toy. Outside the Emerald Arms, Meade and four men dressed in navy blue police windbreakers appear to be on the verge of exchanging blows. There is disagreement about how to proceed with the arrest. One of them, a stern and obviously superior officer, points at Sugar. More to the point, at her camera.

"What is that doing here? Who let her in on this? Get that camera out of here."

He starts up the walkway, but Meade cuts him off before the commander takes more than a few steps. "Come on, Bob. This will be good publicity for you guys. Who knows? You may wind up on *Incredible Capers Of Cops In Action* or one of those other badass-whupping TV shows. If you want, we'll even go back inside so you can crash down the door and make you look macho doing it." Then Meade stops the other officers with a wave. Sugar watches through the eyepiece of her camera as she records the scene. Meade turns serious and peddles persuasion to the senior officer in a hushed tone. The commander finally nods, and the group moves toward them again.

"This will be quick," Reverend Sam whispers to Sugar.

"Will you be all right?"

"Certainly. But if you really want the story on this, find out where the money is. It won't be difficult, but that's the real story."

"Samuel Raymond Cross?" the commander demands. Reverend Sam nods. The officer asks him to step inside the old hotel, but the reverend refuses.

"Lieutenant," he says. "It is Lieutenant, isn't it? There are a lot of people inside who have absolutely nothing to do with all this. If you are here to make an arrest, get on with it." Reverend Sam assumes a martyred look and thrusts his wrists forward.

Sugar steps back to get a better picture. After the commander exchanges shrugs with Meade, he signals to one of the officers. Bank robbery suspect Sam Cross is handcuffed, and they march him to the curb as a Bakersfield P.D. patrol car pulls up.

Sugar stumbles behind them, trying to negotiate the path while balancing the camera on her shoulder with one hand and the microphone thrust out in front of her with the other. Sam exchanges a brief word with his lawyer at the patrol car door before the officer places a firm hand on the reverend's head, forcing him down and into the back of the vehicle.

Sugar pans her camera along with the patrol car as it pulls away from the curb and picks up speed down the street. It swerves to avoid a television news camera crew running to the scene from the opposite direction. Sugar zooms in and records the cameraman's frustration as he hoists his equipment too late to get anything more than a rapidly receding government license plate.

"Gotcha," she smiles. It's golden, as Hunter would say. Not only has she scooped the competition, she's scooped the other reporters in her own newsroom. For those who refuse to admit she could be a real newswoman, just watch this and kiss my...

She sets her camera on the sidewalk and tries to catch her breath. Now what? People. Hunter keeps saying the news is about people. Reverend Sam is one, obviously. Who else? The residents, of course. What do they think? What is the mood? How is this affecting them? Most of all, why is this happening?

Before she can finish her line of thought, Reverend Sam's attorney steps up beside her. "Did you get everything you need?" Meade asks.

"Most of it, I think."

"I can issue a statement now. My client is innocent and all that."

"Innocent?"

"It's best to forget anything he said inside for now. If the camera is on, I say he's innocent. Did Sam say anything else to you before the arrest?" Meade asks.

Sugar stops to think. "He said to find the money. Find the money. What did he mean by that?"

Meade blinks and rolls his lips inward. His anger is obvious and it has the effect of causing his mouth to disappear into the hair that forms his moustache and beard. Then he says, "It's nothing sinister, I can assure you. But I suspect that is the real story here."

"I don't understand," Sugar says.

"You will. Your boss says you are very perceptive."

Hunter? "What does Hunter Riley have to do with this?"

"That is why you're here, isn't it? Sam. Your boss. Even the police, though they don't realize it. They are all part of it. This has all been arranged, or hasn't Mr. Riley explained that yet?"

Sugar raises a hand and bites hard on her pinkie. It's a small distraction from the pain and confusion of Meade's words. It's been a conspiracy all along. Made for TV news, and Hunter has been part of it. He has been using her, just like he used those poor old, pitiful seniors huddling in fear inside the Emerald Arms.

Sugar wants to press Meade for more information. But before she can say anything, she is bumped from behind. A microphone with the Channel 29 logo on it leaps out toward Meade. Another darts between them, this one with a radio station's call letters attached. She can hear the swearing and jostling, and the clank of camera tripods setting up. News crews are invading, circling the attorney. Talk. What's going on? The questions come quickly.

Sugar has questions of her own, but the most pressing ones won't be answered on the street in front of the Emerald Arms. She'll save those for Hunter Riley.

Slug: Preacher Thug

Anchor intro:

> *There is something profoundly unsettling about a respected leader's fall from grace. Their sins seem larger, even in those cases when their motivation is worthy of the pedestal on which we've placed them.*
>
> *So reaction is swift, and rejection is strong. In an instant, they can drag a hero down to the level of a common thug.*
>
> *And if you think this about Reverend Sam Cross, think again.*

Roll tape

"It is unthinkable that such a highly respected member of our community would do this. I don't believe it. If you say Reverend Sam is capable of robbing banks, you're saying Reverend Sam Cross is on the same level as a crack smoking, welfare leeching, gun toting common thug."

Tap the pause button on the videotape machine. Look at the way the mayor's face freezes in the monitor with his eyes half-closed and mouth cockeyed, like the snapshot of a boxer taking a hard right to the jaw from his opponent.

"Crack smoking? Welfare leeching?" Hunter asks. He's standing over his reporter Andy Blackman in the converted coat closet that now serves as a video editing room.

Andy doesn't look up as he scribbles some notes. "Mayor's up for reelection. He's a sound bite machine."

"Works for me. Let's put him on TV. Who else can we get to talk about the arrest?"

Andy ticks off the names of Bakersfield's best. "I have calls in to several of them, but they're kind of reluctant to go on camera."

"That's easy," Hunter says smoothly. "Call them back and say, if they won't comment, we'll just make up something and attribute it to them."

Andy's eyes narrow, and then he dutifully makes a note in the pad on his knee.

"Just kidding," Hunter says.

The young reporter smiles weakly, relieved. He crosses out the scribbles he had made.

Hunter continues, "Figure out if they're a friend or foe. Friend? If they like the guy, stress that Reverend Sam needs their support. Foe? If they think he's a jerk, tell them someone needs to stand up against this kind of criminal activity. Beg. Threaten. Offer them your first-born child if necessary. Just get them on TV."

Andy's smile widens. "Kidding, right?"

"Nope. Serious. Get on it."

Hunter checks his watch as he glides across the newsroom. Two o'clock. His skin nearly tingles as if the big story of the day has charged the air with electricity. This is fun.

The producers and anchors are clustered around Kathy's desk for the afternoon planning session. Round up the usual suspects: Kathy is going over a list of all the stories she plans to put in the five o'clock show. Van Thompson is arguing with her. He has one particular angle he wants to hold back for six o'clock. Sugar is taking notes. Kent is staring off into space. And the director, Lee Richards, is sitting behind him, focused on the back of Kent's head and surreptitiously inching forward with fingers poised as if to pluck a flea from the anchor's wig. Or maybe he's after the whole wig. Who knows?

Hunter pulls up a chair and reaches for a rundown of the day's stories. Everyone stops. An alien being has landed among them.

"What?" Hunter asks.

"Nothing," Kathy replies. "Thought you'd be busy, as usual, so we started without you."

Hunter knows he deserves it. He must have seemed disinterested in the day-to-day operation until now. Hell, he *was* disinterested and never dropped by the afternoon meeting before. So it's not surprising they would cringe when he swoops in on the biggest story to come down in a long while. They must expect him to offer little and probably hope that he has the good sense to stay out of their way.

"I want to start with video of the arrest right out of the commercial. Bang!" Thompson says. "Did you see it? It's exclusive. And it is so good, I nearly wet myself."

"Catch the viewer before they can switch channels," Hunter offers. "Good."

The back door slams and, like a blast of Arctic air, Valerie Watson blows into the newsroom. "I heard they caught the Senior Bandit," she says. She drops her handbag on her chair and tosses her notebook on the desk as carelessly as she tosses her strawberry blond hair away from her face. "What do we have?"

Valerie Watson is one of those reporters with the striking looks and bearing that command attention when she walks into a room. If for some unfathomable reason attention isn't deflected her way, she will grab it by the throat until natural order is restored.

Thompson describes the arrest. "The sweetest part? Sugar was the only one out there when they busted the preacher's butt. A golden moment. Drama. Pathos. Exclusive."

Valerie's eyes light up. Emboldened by her self-anointed status as the newsroom's top dog and smelling the lead story, she demands, "Where are the tapes?"

Thompson holds them up like an auctioneer waiting for the highest bid.

Valerie reaches for them. "I'll build my report around this stuff." She checks her watch. "But if I don't have the sound bite from the cops I need, I'll zip on over to headquarters and get something fresh from the chief."

Sugar looks at Hunter for support but doesn't waste a moment waiting for his response. "I don't *think* so!" she says curtly. "I can do all that."

Valerie shakes her head like an amused schoolmaster. She turns to the others for affirmation. "Of course, this is my story," she says. "I was covering the Senior Bandit from the very first robbery. Duh!

I'm the one who named him the Senior Bandit. It's been my story from the start, and it's my story now."

"Then where were you when they made the arrest? I was there."

Nonplused, Valerie responds, "I was out on another exclusive. Something that takes real investigative work." Then she turns to the producers to reassure them. "Don't worry, it'll hold for another day."

Thompson wavers. He throws his palms up and says, "This is Valerie's kind of thing. She has more experience."

Kathy's head is down, pretending to read the page in front of her. The reporters pick up the battle again, with more intensity. It is Sugar's passion versus Valerie's conviction. Hunter steps in before either can draw blood.

"We can sit here and argue all afternoon about this and nothing will get on the air at all." He points to Kathy and hopes she makes the right decision. "What do you want to do?"

Kathy reflects for a moment and then raises her eyes. She doesn't search any of their faces for validation as the others had. She says, "Looking at the big picture, I say we go with our strengths. Valerie's right. She's been on this since the beginning."

Hunter watches the triumphant look in the ball-busting reporter's face. But from the tone of Kathy's voice, he knows what is coming next.

"That's why we'll have Valerie concentrate on the background story. We'll use her experience on the history of the robberies to do a 'town-breathes-a-sigh-of-relief-the-suspect-is-caught' piece."

"That's not a lead story," Valerie says.

"You don't get it."

"Get it?"

"The lead story. You don't get it. Sugar has worked her tail off building contacts with Reverend Sam and the seniors there. That gave us an exclusive on the arrest, so I'd say she's earned it."

Valerie storms off in one direction while Sugar skips away in the other. Hunter sits with amused admiration. Whether she realizes it or not, Kathy has just put her stamp of approval on his scheme to reinvent *Live @ Five*. But more importantly, she did it at the risk of alienating their most experienced, potentially trouble-some reporter because it was simply the fair thing to do. That Kathy. She's all right.

Hunter watches Kathy punctuate her comments with a waggle of her finger or a comic scowl leading into a laugh. She is pretty, and she is passionate about news. It's an alluring combination for Hunter. Her vitality captivates him. Kathy catches Hunter's eye. It's as if she is reading his mind, and it leaves him feeling exposed, but he resists the temptation to look away.

Sugar is back and asking questions. Andy Blackman is on her heels. Give and take, the exchange is charged with good-natured energy. Everyone has something to add. Hunter drops his head and rests his chin thoughtfully, embarrassed to see it working so well. He's about to make a suggestion, but someone beats him to it. The news engine is hitting on all cylinders. Despite the dubious way they scored the exclusive story, and the shameless way they are going to hype it, the newscast itself is coming to life and Hunter is proud. They have approached every angle intelligently and with respect to all sides. It's growing into a solid piece of journalism.

Hunter hasn't felt this alive in years. The team—his team—is coming together into a real news operation. Tonight, he finally feels comfortable with his decision to hire the stripper. That was a desperate roll of the dice, betting on his instincts and her potential. A stripper!

And then the sell-out. The deal with Reverend Sam for an exclusive story is a gray area. Okay, so maybe it is a deep and dark-charcoal kind of gray. But when he raises his eyes and catches pride lighting up the newsroom, his newsroom, the distinction between right and wrong is fuzzy. If it gives them even one day's reprieve from the ratings ax, one more day on the airwaves to do the job they were born to do, then principles be damned—let's do news.

The afternoon strategy session is over, and Hunter retreats to his office. As he drops into the chair at his desk, he's surprised to find Kathy leaning on the doorframe.

"Nice, the way you handled Valerie," Hunter says.

"She's pissed off, but she'll get over it." Kathy moves gracefully to the edge of his desk. Dressed in a blouse and a skirt shorter than her normal style, Kathy looks like she's been sharing fashion tips with Sugar. Business-sexy, Hunter calls it.

"Well, it's time to admit this is working better than I expected," Kathy says. "And I'll tell you, I wanted you to fail."

"Thanks. That's reassuring."

"Seriously. I wanted to be able to say 'I told you so,' but I can't."

"No, I guess you can't."

Kathy sighs. "It turns out your bimbo isn't a total bimbo at all.

Sugar's okay. Totally raw and all, but I think she'll be okay. And we've had a lot of calls from people wanting to help those poor old folks. So, I mean, it's having worked in those bigger markets. You had a clue, and the rest of us are just... clueless."

Hunter says, "It's not quite what you seem to think. Hell, I don't have all the answers—but you didn't hear that from me," he grins. "We did this on a wing and a prayer." And we sold our soul to the devil, he adds to himself.

"But it's gotten us this great exclusive story."

Exactly.

Kathy goes on, but Hunter switches to some internal channel. It's a mystery, isn't it? For the first time in his career, he has stopped listening to the consultants and the research, the networks and the station managers and all the time-honored theories about the way journalism "ought to be done". He is operating on instinct, and instinct is winning.

After living his entire adult life in front of the camera and never risking a thought—let alone some deed—that might offend anyone, he can finally relax. He can finally have fun. He looks at Kathy. Maybe he can finally get a date.

"Not on your life," Kathy says.

"What was that?" Hunter asks. He tunes back in.

"Never," Kathy says. "I simply wouldn't have guessed this strange vision of news you have could work." She rolls her eyes, and all her fingers dance on the air as if to suggest something mystical is going on.

Kathy smiles at him and repeats the motion. This time her

fingers dance to the beat of three raps on the door. They turn, and Sugar is standing there.

"I'm glad you're both here," Sugar says. "I wanted to thank you guys. You know, for that show of support out there."

Kathy simply nods.

"Me?" Hunter asks. "I didn't do much."

"You only did everything," Sugar is almost breathless. "I wouldn't have gotten the story without you. And you could have given it to Valerie or Andy, but you gave it to me. That touches me right here," Sugar places a finger beside her left breast.

"Your heart?" Hunter asks just to be sure.

Sugar nods.

She folds her lower lip beneath her perfect white teeth and adds, "Reverend Sam's lawyer said to thank you for all the news coverage. It did help them raise some money like you said it would, and he says we can have another exclusive when the Rev gets out of jail."

Kathy turns to Hunter. Her eyes narrow and shift left, then right. Her internal computer is processing this new information.

A shout from the other side of the newsroom snatches Sugar away. Kathy stretches a foot out to catch the corner of the door and swings it shut behind her. She leans against it, facing Hunter with her arms crossed. "Okay, cowboy. 'Fess up." She is not smiling.

"There's nothing to 'fess."

"You cut a deal with the Reverend, didn't you, Hunter? That's why we had to do all those stories about his poor little organization."

"It's a good cause," Hunter replies. It's a lame response. Surely, he can do better.

Kathy shoots first. "It was worth one or two stories, max. But not nine or ten. That's how many stories we've done in the past month. And let's not be coy, most of them were manufactured just to make Reverend Sam and his group look good. All that coverage translates into donations, and you knew it would. You forced us to go over the line just to pay off the Reverend."

Hunter leans forward. He desperately wants to give her every excuse, every rationalization, every argument he has already exhausted within himself for what he has done. In the end, he focuses on her with a cold, unflinching stare.

"I did what I had to do." He says it with steel in his voice. Ben Cartwright couldn't have been more stoic facing down a lynch mob on the Ponderosa.

Kathy steps forward and leans on the desk until their noses are no more than a foot apart. "So you went to him and said something like, 'We'll get you money, Rev. Now go get arrested in front of our camera'. What kind of journalism is that? Why didn't you just write Reverend Sam a check and get it over with?"

"Because we don't have the money to buy an exclusive story like this."

"We don't *buy* news stories," Kathy says. "That's what separates us from the Jerry Springers of the world. That's what separates us from trash TV and those scuzzy, grocery store, tabloid newspapers." Her voice is rising. It grabs the attention of Van Thompson and several others beyond the glass wall between them and the newsroom. Heads are turning.

Hunter knows he should stop to reload his arguments, but wounded by the obvious, he says, "Wrong. You do buy the news, if that's the only way to get anyone in this wretched little town of yours to sit up and tune in to a fourth-rate operation like this."

Kathy whirls and reaches for the door. One parting shot. "If this is such a miserable little newsroom, then what are you doing here? And yeah, our ratings suck. But at least we got them honestly."

Only when Kathy is gone, Hunter hears his phone ringing.

"What?"

Phoebe from the promotions department is on the line. Did Hunter see it? She asks if Hunter is near a television.

The first promotional spot hit the airwaves just a minute ago. Exclusive video. Exclusive story. Tonight, only on News 13—*Live @ Five*. Hunter had to admit he had been too busy. Phoebe rattles off the list of times during the day the promotion will run again on KDOA. She has also bought time on half a dozen radio stations in town, as well as thirty-second commercials on CNN and two other cable-TV channels.

"Just like you wanted," she says. "Ray the WebGuy even put it on the Internet already."

They've blanketed all of Bakersfield with the promise that something very special is happening only on *Live @ Five* and only tonight. If he thought it would help, Hunter would shout it from the rooftop. This may be the only time some viewers will sample KDOA's brand of news, ever.

Hunter sets down the phone. He scratches his chin. He's paid a heavy price to grab their eyeballs for this one moment. It may turn out to be nothing more than a one-shot audition for the long-term relationship KDOA needs to go on living. If Kathy, Sugar and the rest do their jobs as well as Hunter expects, maybe—just maybe—they can keep those eyeballs coming back.

It's show time.

The phone is ringing again. Hunter expects to hear Phoebe, with some forgotten detail.

"Riley," the voice snaps. "I hear you caught yourself a bank robber today."

Hunter pumps his fist. It's good old Donald Andrews, the station owner. Donnie. Don. Don-o-rama, the old man himself. Hunter is bursting to tell D.O.A. the highlights of their coverage. Even a pinhead like Andrews will appreciate the scoop. They are going to own this story, and they are going to tell it with depth and style unlike anything Bakersfield has ever seen. This is just the beginning.

"Yeah," Hunter replies as he plops down smugly into his rickety chair, and then has to steady himself to keep from tipping over. "They arrested Sam Cross this morning, and we were there."

"Good for you," Andrews replies. "Now I want you to kill the story."

Hunter stops cold. Nah, he didn't really hear that.

Andrews repeats, "I want you to kill the story."

Slug: Bandit-cast

Anchor intro:

> *If you're getting the impression that agendas, large and small, all too often dictate the content of a local TV newscast, you're absolutely right. Some are the issues of the community while others are intensely personal.*
>
> *But if it is a journalistic crime to manufacture news where none exists, a greater crime is to bury a story even at the risk of burying one's own career. And on the eve of KDOA's big scoop, the message is: Kill the story or face the firing squad.*

Roll tape

"Ready...

"Aim...

"Fire!"

Lee Richards roars. He drives a bony finger onto the control panel button, putting *Live @ Five* on the air.

Back in the newsroom, Hunter's throat is dry, his stomach is nervous, but his spirit is steeped in anger and steeled by determination. Hunter never committed to killing the big story before

Andrews hung up on him this afternoon.

He marched from that phone call to the producer's desk and threw himself into helping Kathy and Thompson each plan their entire newscasts around Reverend Sam's arrest. Start with Sugar's exclusive, add reaction from the poor seniors at the Emerald Arms and a dash of reflection from city leaders, stir in some background about the Senior Bandit's crime spree along with government statistics on issues of the elderly, and you have a recipe for news.

The news team responded like a finely tuned orchestra as it conceived, arranged and prepared for this performance of *Live @ Five*. He never told them about his argument with the station owner. He'll face that music alone. He stands in front of the bank of TV monitors on the wall near Kathy's assignment desk. Each one assigned to a different newscast and, at that moment, competing for Hunter's undivided attention.

Kent Abernathy is a distraction. He strolls past Hunter, breathing deeply and humming a full range of pitch from his highest, most ridiculous falsetto to the bottom of his bass. Hunter isn't sure if Kent is warming up his vocal cords for the six o'clock newscast or trying to clear his sinuses. High pitch slides to bass; he does it again. They say Kent used to reverse it, practicing from bottom to top of his vocal range, but gave that up when the staff complained he sounded too much like a bull moose in heat.

Hunter takes a moment away from the monitors. He is certain Kent's wig is different. There is less gray, the fiber is matted, and the length… Hunter swears it's shorter. "Your hair," he says.

Kent smiles and rolls his head in a circle to stretch his neck muscles. It's either a nervous quirk or another pre-performance warm up—Hunter isn't sure. "Yeah. I got my hair cut today."

It's a freaking wig. "Looks nice," is all Hunter says.

Kent walks away with a John Wayne swagger, and Hunter turns his attention back to the bank of monitors. He uses a remote control to pump up the volume on *Live @ Five*. Sugar is in front of the Emerald Arms. Investigators are inside Reverend Sam's apartment right now, searching for more evidence. That's a big bonus for the newscast, validation for being live from the scene. Something is actually going on as she gives her report.

He mutes the sound. He triggers the remote control to boost the volume on the next monitor. Channel 17's reporter is also at the Emerald Arms. Judging from the angle, Bob Priddy is droning away only a few feet from where Sugar is standing.

Click. His attention switches to Channel 23. "Eye-witless News" is live from police headquarters.

Click. Hunter sneers. Best of all, the Ken and Barbie anchors on 29 are rambling and flustered, chained to their anchor desk. Their video isn't rolling on cue, and they are hung out to dry.

Click. Sound up. Hunter is back to focusing on KDOA.

"You have the right to remain silent." You can hear the voice of the arresting officer. It's punctuated by the ratcheting of handcuffs on Reverend Sam's wrists. Turn it up. Oh that sound! Clear and isolated, it grabs you by the ears and pulls you in. Hunter wants to stomp his feet with the joy of a child getting the toy he so desperately wants.

Sugar's exclusive video is rolling. From somewhere off camera you hear the sound of a woman wailing as officers march Sam down the sidewalk. The scene cuts to four weathered and worried faces peeking through a narrow opening in the door of the hotel. One woman is sobbing. Hunter strokes the remote control in his hand. This is great television.

He had previewed the video with Sugar an hour before the newscast, but he is touched again. The video speaks for itself—a point Hunter tried to impress on Sugar. She took the coaching well. Out there, reporting live from the Emerald Arms now, she ignores every reporter's natural temptation to keep talking. Talking. Talking over compelling pictures and sapping their impact.

Hunter back-pedals across the newsroom with his eyes on the monitor until he reaches the door to his office. He sneaks a glance at the telephone. How long is D.O.A. going to wait before he's seen enough and calls down here to ream Hunter's ass for the coverage? Surely he's watching from his lair.

This afternoon, the station owner had tried to rationalize his reasons for holding back on the story. He talked of character. "Look at all the good Reverend Sam Cross has done. No need to drag him through the mud."

He talked of civic pride. "What do you think folks are going to say when they hear one of the most prominent—I'd go so far as to say heroic—members of our community is caught up in this sordid sort of thing?"

He talked of fairness. "Nothing's been proven. It could be a lie. No sense making much of it until we know more."

But eventually he talked of money. "Frank Elderberry is on the local board of the United Charities. United Charities pays for a quarter of Reverend Sam's yearly budget. Frank suggested to me today this is an embarrassment to them all and that we should play this story down for now. I agree with him, and you should too."

"Frank Elderberry? As in Elderberry Ford? Elderberry Toyota and Elderberry Chrysler/Jeep/Eagle/Dodge/Oldsmobile/Yugo?"— Wait. They don't make the Yugo anymore.

So that was it. The owner of Bakersfield's largest car dealership, and consumer of ungodly amounts of advertising on TV, put the squeeze on D.O.A. over lunch at the Rotary.

"Did he threaten to pull his commercials?"

In a roundabout way, D.O.A.'s answer was yes.

Hunter has seen it before. He's even caved to the reality of it all a time or two. Or three. It is naïve to believe the business end of the TV business doesn't occasionally stick its nose in the news department's business. It happens at all levels, from the smallest market to the network towers. And for many people in both camps, it is hardly a shock when someone violates the separation of powers between sales and news. At worst, it's a bee sting that, if it can't be ignored, is soothed with an antiseptic-strength dose of alcohol at the nearest tavern at the end of the day.

But Andrews has picked the wrong day, the wrong story and the wrong person on which to push his agenda. Hunter has already bent the rules too far to get this story.

The old man had spit out a final warning before hanging up. He did it with a loud slam of the phone that has Hunter wincing even now, three hours later—and four and a half minutes into their coverage of the story on *Live @ Five*.

Hunter retreats into his office. A photographer has flicked on a bright light in the newsroom. Valerie Watson is up next with her live report. She is at her desk. It's a surreal scene from this angle. Live and in color, all Hunter can see is her profile as she faces the camera. In the small black-and-white TV on his desk, she is talking directly to him. She is giving her report now on the history of the robberies and the investigation of the Senior Bandit.

He pushes aside a stack of paperwork and sits on the edge of the desk. Hunter checks his watch. Six minutes into the newscast, and the station owner still hasn't called. Maybe he's actually impressed. He should be. Their work has been fair and as complete as it can be in a superficial medium. No one is out to "hang" Reverend Sam, as D.O.A. had put it, no matter how guilty the preacher may be.

"As far as reaction from city leaders," Valerie says to the camera. "The mayor had this to say:"

Head and shoulders, the mayor fills your screen. "Reverend Sam Cross is on the same level as a crack smoking, welfare leaching, gun toting common thug."

No!

The phone on Hunter's desk jangles like a fire alarm. Hunter is sure it's the urgent ring of an angry boss. D.O.A. will have to wait. Hunter reaches Valerie Watson's desk before the spotlight from above the camera has faded. Her report is over; the damage is done.

"What the…" Hunter roars. Then he pulls back to finish in a

low tone as every head in the newsroom turns his way, "…fuck are you doing?"

Like a bad actress in an amateur melodrama, Valerie takes on the role of a scheming virgin. "What do you mean?"

Imagine Scarlet O'Hara batting her green eyes, and you get the picture.

Hunter places a firm hand on her elbow and helps Valerie out of the chair as she rises. He increases the pressure and guides her through the newsroom to the editing closet in back. He closes the door behind them.

"I saw that entire sound bite with the Mayor this afternoon," he tells her.

"You did?" Valerie is surprised, and definitely busted, but not in the least bit remorseful.

Hunter swats aside several videotapes piled carelessly on the editing machine, searching labels until he finds the right one. "You took that sentence out of context. That's not at all what the mayor said."

He feeds the machine and punches a button. The tape is still cued to the interview with the mayor Valerie had plundered.

He rolls the tape. "*I don't believe it. It's just not true. If you say Reverend Sam is capable of robbing banks, you're saying Reverend Sam Cross is on the same level as…*."

Hunter waits for an explanation.

"I was trying to keep the piece under a minute and a half. I couldn't run the entire interview," she tells him.

"You distorted what the mayor had to say."

"Not entirely," Valerie says with her usual conviction. "I mean, it captures the real mood of the folks at city hall."

"You turned it completely around. He said one thing, and you gave it the opposite meaning," Hunter snaps.

Valerie sniffs. "The people I talked with downtown say they're not at all happy with Sam Cross. Let's face it, he's guilty. They know that." She crosses her arms, smug and defiant like a playground bully, almost challenging Hunter to take a swing at her. "Isn't that what you've been preaching around here? Be human. Be honest. Just tell it like it is, and let the viewers decide what to make of it."

"You forgot the most important part," Hunter replies. "I said, above all, be fair. You've tried and convicted the guy on television. You rammed your own warped judgment into the story. That's not fair."

"Fair?" Valerie appears shocked. "You want to talk about fair? What's fair about giving this story to that... that slut. She has no business being here. If I fuck you, will you give me a big scoop too?"

Hunter lashes out with his palm flat. He misses her face by inches, but hits his intended target—the wall behind her. He leans into it, bringing his face close to Valerie's and the first hint of fear to her eyes. "Get out of here. Go home. You are suspended until I say otherwise. And I may not get around to saying otherwise."

Valerie appears lost for only a moment before she recovers. "Okay. My purse."

"What?"

She drops her eyes to the floor behind Hunter. "My purse is

still on the floor there. Will you get it for me?"

Hunter leans back and opens the door to the little room. "Get it yourself, and then get out."

Valerie nods. "I just want to show you something I found before I go." She grabs the straps of a large black leather bag. Valerie pulls out a glossy booklet and hands it to Hunter.

"What's this?" he asks, even though it doesn't take more than one look for the answer to register.

"It's last year's calendar from Pistol Pete's."

The quality of the calendar is cheap, and the photography is amateurish. It's a piece of promotional fluff to help patrons commemorate their visit to the exotic land Pistol Pete offers, and remind them of why they must return some day. It proudly features the twelve hottest dancers from the nightclub, and there is no mistaking the identity of Miss October. In her wig and a pumpkin-colored bikini not much bigger than three postage stamps strung together and strategically placed, Sugar Kane is giving Hunter a come-hither look from the page in front of him.

Valerie taps the photograph. "Everyone was wondering if she had the boob job before or after you hired her. I guess now we know."

Hunter seethes, "Who else knows about this?"

"Right now? Not many. Tomorrow? Everybody."

Slug: Bandit Follow-up

Anchor intro:

> *It can be argued the world's first journal-ist was a caveman. We don't know his name; there were no bylines back then. He painted his lead story on the wall of his cave. It was a story of the day's successful mastodon hunt and, maybe, the fertility dance that followed. It was a noble effort.*
>
> *So through the millennia reporters have considered themselves privileged to carry his journalistic torch. To this day, the media consid-ers itself an elite and exclusive club with the sacred job of writing history as it happens. It is also a seductive job. It has a special status in society, which is difficult for a reporter to relin-quish even if she admits she won it—not with her brains, but with beauty and a big bust.*

Roll tape:

Ka-ching!

The cash register rings at the Golden Key Thrift Store. The drawer slides out, and you see a smattering of well-worn bills in its belly. This is one of several locations where money ended up from the South Valley Bank robberies. The cops matched the serial numbers.

"I don't remember what day it was. Not exactly. But I remember it was strange. Mister and Mizz Shurman never had any money. Old folks who shop here, they don't have money."

Margaret Barse is a clerk at the thrift store. She's been here for twenty years. With a face tanned too dark from a bottle and deeply etched like driftwood, she leans on the cash register and looks straight into the TV camera. Her voice is ravaged by years of cigarette smoke. "Coming here all those years, and they never bought anything that would amount to anything," she says. "But that day, Mr. Shurman had a big bunch of cash. This thick."

Sugar is standing across the counter from Margaret Barse. It's the day after their "Bandit-cast", as the newsroom dubbed their exclusive reports on Reverend Sam's arrest. It's a day to act on the preacher's advice to Sugar and follow the money.

After a short tussle, Sugar is able to wrestle the microphone away from the camera-struck clerk. "What did Mr. and Mrs. Shurman buy with that money?" she asks.

"They bought a 'frigerator," Mrs. Barse replies.

"A refrigerator?"

"Mr. Shurman said they needed a 'frigerator. Said theirs broke down more than a month ago. Said he heard we got one in the store here. Said he wanted it."

"They came here to buy a used refrigerator because they had no where else to go?"

"That's what he said."

Sugar nods.

Hunter is standing behind her with a camera on his shoulder. He hears it whir softly and holds it gently in return. It's been a while since he's handled a camera and Hunter is cautious to the edge of paranoia that he will do something stupid, like stick a thumb in front of the lens or hit the eject button and send videotape spilling all over the floor. He had never worried about handling a camera until Des Moine. He got a crash course when a flu bug spread among the photography staff at the station and was pressed into service. That's when he realized he had hit rock bottom. And then he kept on digging.

He could have let Kathy assign a photographer for Sugar, and she certainly didn't need his help reporting this, not after the way she covered Reverend Sam's arrest. But Hunter wanted an excuse to escape the newsroom and lay low.

He had successfully dodged D.O.A.'s calls after last night's newscast, and he ignored the urgent messages from the station owner this morning. Even if he can only escape being fired for one more day, fine. The story is still too hot and too important to fall victim to D.O.A.'s meddling.

Hunter knows that if he can stall the station owner long enough to get this on the air tonight, they will have wrapped up the loose ends of the biggest story to hit Bakersfield this year. And they will have done it with intelligence and depth—a masterful two days of journalism that could make a news junkie's heart skip a beat. The news team deserves it. The audience deserves it.

"You think Reverend Sam gave them the money, don't you?" Sugar asks.

Tsk. Tsk. Margaret Barse shakes her head slowly. But she says, "It's all I can figure. And it's just like Reverend Sam to give them the money like that. And that's what I told them."

"The Shurmans?" Hunter asks.

"The police," Mrs. Barse answers. "They wanted to know. So that's what I told them."

The police, in turn, passed that tidbit along to News 13 ace reporter Valerie Watson. And Valerie coughed it up in a plea bargain with Hunter. Hunter knocked two days off her suspension in return.

"Sources close to the investigation" tipped them off to a series of suspiciously coincidental acts of charity following each holdup by the Senior Bandit.

The Shurmans got their refrigerator. Mrs. Alberta Diaz paid her utility bill—three months delinquent—with cash on the night before P.G. & E. would have turned off her electricity. She doesn't know who left an electric company envelope full of money in her mailbox. She didn't think too much about it. She just praised the Lord and cranked up her air conditioner for the first time in a month.

There are others. Sugar's interview with Robert Hall will break your heart. 82 years old. Mr. Hall buried his wife Matilda last week. They were married fifty-eight years when she passed on. His last gift to her was a casket and a decent headstone. And he couldn't have done it without the help of a three thousand dollar gift from an anonymous, kind-hearted Robin Hood. It turns out that money, too, had been "withdrawn" by the Senior Bandit from a suburban branch of South Valley Bank.

But the biggest beneficiary of the Senior Bandit's donations appears to have been Reverend Sam's housing project at the Emerald Arms. Large cash contributions had helped pay the rent.

The pattern is clear as Hunter and Sugar step out of the thrift shop. Hunter breathes deeply. The air is fresh and has lost the thick, oppressive heat of summer. October is almost here.

Sugar checks her watch. They are in a hurry now. "Sam Junior said his dad would be released on bond about one o'clock," she says.

They drop the camera gear into the back of their news vehicle. It's a military style Humvee painted in the station's colors, blue and orange. Battered and battle-tested by first the army and then too many joy rides by D.O.A.'s teenage grandson, it has two hundred and ten thousand miles on it. But the all-terrain Hummer can still haul tail across scorching deserts, gallop up rocky mountain roads, and crush most commuters in its path on a California freeway. Nothing can come between it and a good story.

Hunter steers it down H Street with an iron grip on the wheel. The big metal military beast responds as it would to a superior officer, and Hunter has no doubt they'll get to the jail on time.

Sugar is navigating from the passenger seat. "Next light, turn left. I don't believe it. Four blocks, turn right and then right again," she says. "I don't think Reverend Sam did it."

Hunter brakes to a stop within inches of a yellow VW Beetle at the intersection. The Humvee responds with a low, impatient rumble as it idles. Hunter steals a glance across at Sugar. Her as-yet uncorrupted faith in the goodness of men like Reverend Sam is charming, to a point. Sugar scribbles something on her notepad and looks out at the street over granny sunglasses perched at the point where the tip of her nose turns up. She's having fun. She smiles that full-lipped, thick-toothed grin that always seems fresh like the first light of day.

"Valerie Watson knows about your job at Pistol Pete's," he says.

"So?"

"So if she knows, everybody knows."

"Oh."

"We knew it was just a matter of time."

"I guess it's time, then." Sugar sighs. She lowers her chin to ask, "Is there any way we can, you know, derail this thing?"

Hunter shakes his head. "Not much longer. Do you still think you're up to it?"

Sugar peers at him over her sunglasses, disgusted with the question. "We can hardly quit now. That would ruin your plan, wouldn't it?"

"I'm not sure it was much of a plan," Hunter says.

"Come on, Hunter." She draws out his name like a whine. "You said it would happen. But I assumed you would be the one to make a big, public deal out of it. I thought you wanted to create a fuss and get people to tune in. You know, check out the naked lady on Channel 13?"

"You make it sound like some kind of freak show."

"You're the one who wanted a freak show," she replies without animosity. "You got it. Hey, remember me? I'm used to dancing naked, dip...head! I'm so long past apologizing for who I am and what I do. And I'm not going to apologize for the past, either. You could learn a thing or two, buddy.

"So, I took off my clothes and danced in a club. I made good money doing it. And in case you've forgotten, I made a lot more money dancing than you're paying me. I've had worse jobs. A lot of times it was fun."

Hunter grins. There may not have been any animosity in her voice, but Valerie would have a field day editing the tape, parsing the words into a full-throated rage.

Sugar continues, "You know what the big difference is? I actually have people who recognize me in public now who are not ashamed of it. They don't have to turn the other way because they're with their wives."

Sugar taps her notebook thoughtfully against her knee. "The point is, I'm still the same person I was before. I've just traded one stage for another. That one is behind me. I like this better. Way better. I don't want it to end yet, and that's what hurts."

Hunter doesn't want it to end either. His eyes linger on Sugar as he swings his head to check traffic to his right. Unashamed and unbowed, Sugar has never used any pretense either in front of the camera, or behind it. Maybe that's the secret to her success. Love her or hate her, she's genuine all the time.

He swerves at the last minute into the first open space in a no-parking zone near the courthouse, bouncing the Humvee's front wheel over the curb so that it sits cockeyed and listing to the street.

Hunter says, "Maybe I'll be wrong, and no one will make a big deal out of it. Maybe no one will even notice."

"I'd like that."

"But don't count on it," he continues. "The key is to ride it out for just a little while. A year from now you'll be in L.A. or Chicago. I know these things. You have something special. You won't be in Bakersfield long, and this won't be an issue in your next town."

"Why do I want to go to L.A.?" she asks.

Hunter makes a face and stops short of a snort. "Because anybody who is anybody in the business is in L.A. or New York. Certainly a top-ten market. That's how we measure success."

"That's what they say, I guess." Sugar sounds unconvinced.

"Don't worry. You'll make it. You were born to do this. And as soon as I can get this newsroom on its feet—by hook or by crook," he adds with a wink, "I'll get back on the anchor track to the big time, too."

"You?"

"Sure. You've found your calling. When I finish what I have to do here, I'll get back to mine."

Sugar starts to respond but pauses to push her sunglasses to the bridge of her nose, hiding her eyes. Hunter isn't sure what is making her choose her words carefully.

"What?" he demands.

Before Sugar says anything, a cameraman from Channel 17 thumps the hood of the Humvee as he dashes past and flashes them a thumbs up. He quicksteps as much as his camera equipment will allow toward the growing mob of media near the door.

Sugar's eyes follow him. "Oh," she says, as if pricked by the sight of Sam Junior standing at the edge of the crowd. She scrambles from the Humvee as gracefully as one can in a short skirt and drops two feet from the Humvee's door to the pavement.

Hunter squints through the glare on the windshield and catches sight of Sam Junior, too. "Try to get him aside for an interview. I'll get the camera. Hey, maybe he'll tell us why his dad has been robbing those banks."

"I still think the old man is innocent," Sugar counters.

"And we're going to hammer on his innocence every night at five o'clock until they take him away to Folsom Prison."

"But if he didn't really do it..."

"That's right. We have to be objective and fair. He's innocent until proven guilty."

"It's easier to report it like that if you believe he is."

"Oh, you have so much to learn about being cynical," Hunter laughs over his shoulder as he climbs from the Humvee. But Sugar is already gone. He pulls the camera equipment from the back of the vehicle and tries to gauge the energy of the media cluster near the courthouse doors. He rates it low enough to know they haven't missed anything yet.

Sugar is talking earnestly with Sam Junior on the fringe of the group. They share a laugh, and she touches Junior's elbow. He brushes a stray strand of hair away from her face. It's unprofessional. So it isn't just Sugar's naiveté. She must be too caught up in Reverend Sam's plight—and Junior's charms—to stay objective about the story. It troubles Hunter.

Then he stops. If Sugar has crossed that line, it's his fault. "You've smudged that line so badly," he mutters to himself. "It's a friggin' wonder anyone can find it."

He picks up the camera and hoists the tripod onto his shoulder as he watches Sugar and Junior at the top of the steps, oblivious to the news at hand. Well, at least this should give them a lock on a sincere and heart-wrenching interview. It may be golden.

Slug: Stripper News Breaks

Anchor intro:

> *Critics of the news media seem to delight in disparaging reporters as a scandal-thirsty pack of wolves. They may believe reporters are piranhas without a conscience or concern for the consequences of their feeding frenzy.*
>
> *Always the predator and seldom the prey, reporters can't understand why they can be cursed as vultures. But now, in Bakersfield, California, the news hounds at KDOA-TV are about to find out how it feels to be the media's roadkill.*

Roll tape

Red on white, signifying a hot story. The tip of Kathy's felt marker races along the plastic-coated assignment board on the wall. She finishes the final word with a flourish so that the last letter carries like a stylistic wave into the next column. Kathy steps back.

Since Moses came down from the Mount, newsrooms have had assignment boards like this. She is making a list of all the stories for the day. She pauses to consider the weight of each item feeding the news beast, although if you back up and look at this from a wider angle, you might think she's an artist casting a critical eye on some masterpiece she has created.

Kathy waves the red-tipped pen under her nose like smelling salts, and it stimulates a quick psychedelic buzz. She wrinkles her nose and worries that her brain is rotting from accumulative over-exposure to its toxic fumes. And she wonders. Twenty years from now, will her friends and co-workers mourn Kathy Wright's pre-mature death from the newly recognized ailment known as Toxic Marker Shock Syndrome? Probably not. No, when her time comes, she won't even rate a twenty-second story on the evening news. No producer will call for a respectful fade to black to punctuate the end of her life as they go to commercial. Oh well.

She caps the pen. It must be having an effect because, for the first time in two weeks, Hunter's obsession with those pathetically poor, putout senior citizens seems to have merit. Given the way the story is taking on a life of its own today, even the deal Hunter cut to get the exclusive seems palatable.

Damn him. She can't hate Hunter if he keeps making them look good.

She shouts across the newsroom. "Andy! Are you going down to City Hall or not? Don't leave us hanging."

Andy Blackman is standing at his desk, pressing a phone between his shoulder and his ear as he takes notes. He points to the phone receiver with a big smile and nods.

After the exclusive reports on Reverend Sam's arrest two days ago, and the strategy Hunter laid out for them to continue cover-age since, the reporters, producers and photographers have been feeding off each other. The synergy is amazing. Everyone has a story idea. Everyone has an angle to cover. Two weeks ago they were whining about covering so many "geezer stories", but today they can't get enough.

Andy's story may top them all.

"I've got it confirmed," he tells her as he stops at her desk. "You know how Reverend Sam says their funding was cut off by the Wrightwell Foundation this year? And that's why they're having all the financial trouble?"

"Give me the thirty-second version," Kathy replies.

"Geez. You sound like Hunter."

Yes, she does. That's not a bad thing. She considers it a moment more. "Okay then, Andy. Pretend this is a live shot. Give it to me straight and quick. Go. Twenty-nine. Twenty-eight. Twenty…"

Andy draws a breath, as if sucking his report from the air. "Wrightwell Foundation cut off funding for Reverend Sam's organization after some serious strong-arming from a member on the board. A guy named Davenport. Davenport owns a property management and development company and apparently has a sweetheart deal with a group of Japanese investors who bought up the entire block that the Emerald Arms sits on. The other three pieces of property are ready for development. So he's under the gun from the investment group to get rolling. Follow me so far?"

Kathy nods. Andy continues.

"Hello! Reverend Sam has an open-ended lease that lets him stay there as long as he makes the rent. But without the funding from the Wrightwell Foundation, where can he raise that kind of money? He's shit-out-of-luck."

"He can always rob a bank. And you can't say shit-out-of-luck on the air," Kathy chuckles.

"I'm not on the air, and Reverend Sam is screwed. Did I make my thirty seconds?"

"Uhm, two seconds over," Kathy guesses. "But it was worth it."

"Ah. You say the nicest things. So can I have fifteen more?"

"Dazzle me."

"The only real source of funding left for the Emerald Arms is the annual city grant which, of course, is up for renewal."

"Yeah. Hunter thinks the Sam-ster is just trying to keep them afloat until they can get the next installment."

Andy agrees. "Here's the kicker, though. Davenport has been a recent and major contributor to the election campaigns of three members on the city council."

Naturally.

"Since Reverend Sam got his butt busted, Davenport's turned up the heat on them. Now they've got this emergency ordinance thing happening, and the council is going to take it up for a vote next week." They're going to cut off funding for the program immediately, and Reverend Sam will be broke by the end of the month."

Kathy doesn't know whether to laugh or cry. The Senior Bandit's efforts to save the old folks may turn out to be the final nail in the Emerald Arms' coffin. Those poor residents.

Andy starts toward the door. He's on his way to get reaction from any city council member willing to talk. "Davenport has already contacted the County Constable's office. When they miss the rent payment next week, they'll post an eviction notice. All those senior citizens living there? They'll have thirty days to get out."

"Be prepared to go live at five tonight," Kathy says. "You got it. Lead story."

Andy puts a hand over his heart and feigns a stagger. "You mean we're not going to give this to the News Kitten?" he asks. "Cool. Can I at least get a photographer to shoot this for me?"

Kathy hates to disappoint him but shakes her head. "Sorry. Raul called in sick. You'll have to be a one-man band. I'm fresh out of shooters."

Andy replies, "No shooters? Again? I guess that's why Hunter is out there in the field playing with Sugar these days. Photographer, I mean."

From the smile on Andy's face, Kathy knows he never intended that little dart to hurt. "You," she drawls, "can handle it on your own. You don't need someone looking over your shoulder."

"Neither does Sugar."

Andy is right. In spite of all their misgivings about the News Kitten, Sugar has done well. Hunter doesn't need to be out on the story with her. He weaseled his way into the assignment because he wants to be with Sugar.

Damn him.

Why do they always slobber at the feet of the News Kittens of the world? Kathy knows she is pretty enough, and smarter than most. After two tough lessons in office romance, Kathy is

convinced she's learned enough to avoid falling for the good looking news gypsies, the reporters and anchors who consider Bakersfield and its women only temporary relationships until their heart
is stolen by a larger TV market.

But Hunter is different. He has already been there. He talks
about going back, but if he is so intent on getting back to the
larger markets, why is he spending so much time and energy on
this place?

His experience, and the way he helps the reporters and producers, has made them all better news people. He's even managed
to sell them on his crazy vision of keeping the news simple, yet
intelligent—a combination the consultants and cynics believe is
incompatible in TV. He's the best news director Kathy has ever
worked with. And she's had, Lord, how many now?

It's even better when they're alone, working on a story or hatch-
ing a plan to cover some future event. Hunter really listens to her,
as if nothing else matters. And the way he looks at Kathy still has
her losing sleep at nights. She sighs now. Just when she allows herself to believe Hunter's attention is real, the news gets in the way.
Or worse, Sugar steals him from her.

Damn him.

That is what she ponders as her phone rings.

"News," Kathy growls.

It's a reporter from the local paper, the *Bakersfield Califor-
nian*. Interesting. He's not a Lifestyle reporter, but a beat reporter
Kathy has met a few times. City beat, if she remembers correctly.
Investigative stuff like Valerie Watson. The reporter launches into

a lengthy explanation about why he wants to do an article on the news staff, and Sugar in particular.

Of course. They all slobber over the News Kittens of the world.

"No, Hunter Riley is the news director," Kathy tells him. "You need to talk with him, but he's not in at the moment."

He presses for general information about Sugar. It's a red flag that forces Kathy to grab her yellow pad. She scribbles notes on each question. Most of them are vague; the reporter is fishing for something. Kathy puts him off. She doesn't know much about Sugar's background. "You really need to get this information from the news director," Kathy repeats.

The reporter relents, with just one parting question—if she can verify it, that is. He wants to know if it's true Sugar's last job was at a place called Pistol Pete's.

"Pistol Pete's?" Kathy asks.

Pistol Pete's.

Kathy hooks a finger thoughtfully over the teeth of her dropping jaw as the reporter explains in rather colorful terms how Pistol Pete's offers its customers only two products: alcohol and feminine flesh. It isn't necessary. Everyone knows Pistol Pete's. He must mistake her silence for ignorance.

"Where did you get this story?" she asks.

She can feel her face flush, as he naturally refuses to tell her the source of his information. But the reporter seems certain of its accuracy.

"I don't know anything about that," Kathy swears.

She hangs up the phone with the same mixture of dread and

titillation that ignites her adrenaline like a first call over the police scanner. Those calls have to be acted on immediately, but with a healthy dose of skepticism. More often than not, they deteriorate into non-news events by the time the cops and the reporters get to the scene. This is the same.

She knows instinctively that the reporter isn't chasing any old rumor down a useless bunny trail. He has something solid. She heard it in his voice and she needs to act on this like that first call on the scanner. But still, it could be a false alarm. Nope. It's a crisis in the making. A big story. Only this time, KDOA is the story for others to tell. If what the *Californian* reporter says is true, they have become the news.

Kathy swallows hard. Hunter hasn't hired a News Kitten, he's hired a Sex Kitten. An "Exotic Dancer." A cheap, bump-and-grind, topless showgirl. He's hired a stripper to be their respected news anchor. They are going to be the laughing stock of Bakersfield.

Damn him!

Slug: Stripper Fallout

Anchor intro:

> Code Three.
>
> That is the standard designation for an emergency that requires police, fire or ambulance to respond with full lights-and-sirens, ninety miles an hour if necessary. It is the emergency dispatcher telling those responders we have a life or death situation going on.
>
> Code Three.
>
> There is no equivalent for it in a TV newsroom, but maybe there ought to be. Especially when it's your own news operation whose reputation is shot and bleeding credibility. For KDOA, it is time to dial 911.
>
> And hope someone will respond to the call.

Roll tape

The chant is clear.

"Boycott porno news!"

The newspaper broke the story yesterday. Today? A young man, gaunt and far too stern looking for his age, screams to a passing car. The cardboard sign he carries reads: "Live @ Five. Sex at Six. Boycott Porn News 13."

He's not alone. Half a dozen other demonstrators shuffle along the sidewalk in a never-ending circle, each with a placard of their own.

"Stop the Smut."

"News, not Nudes."

Hunter leans against the tall window in the station's lobby and looks across a narrow parking lot to where the self-appointed Porn Police have taken up their position.

Just behind and towering over Hunter, an imposing, muscular, black security guard in uniform rocks back and forth from his heels to the balls of his feet. "You want me to run them off?"

Hunter shakes his head. "No. Let them go as long as they don't do any harm." Hunter doesn't expect trouble, but feels better about hiring extra security. "Just keep an eye on them, Joe."

"Good. They don't look dangerous. In fact, you gotta admire their sense of humor." He wags his finger at the edge of the protesters' circle near the station's driveway, where someone had blown up one of those inflatable sex dolls. They propped her up behind a large brown box that resembles the news desk, complete with a crude but close replica of the KDOA-TV News-13 logo on front.

Joe the security guard raises the Metro section of Monday morning's paper to eye level and compares Sugar's picture on the page with the scene outside.

The *Bakersfield Californian* anchored its story about Sugar in a box at the bottom of the page and framed it with two photographs. Left: a picture of a television set with Sugar the news anchor on the screen. Right: last year's calendar from Pistol Pete's with Sugar the stripper in her pumpkin-flavored bikini.

"Except for the blond hair and that sexy little beauty spot up there, you know the one above her lips on the right side, that doll don't look much like Miss Kane at all. You sure you don't want me to run them off, Mr. Riley?"

Hunter shakes his head again. He hadn't counted on a demonstration, but the threat of real harm seems minimal as long as Sugar follows orders and uses the back entrance to the station. No, he's not worried about the mob in front. The natives in the newsroom are restless, and that's a much bigger concern.

If you can't stand the heat, get out of the sauna. Not only has the staff been really steamed, but since the *Californian*'s exposé on Sugar hit the news stands, the tension in the air is thick enough to squeeze the breath right out of you.

Hunter didn't have the patience to sweat it out in his office, where he would have had to endure so many snide comments and dirty looks from the staff. Instead, he has spent most of the morning camped out on D.O.A.'s doorstep, where he has endured snide comments and dirty looks from the sales team, bean-counters and paper-pushers who wandered past.

More than anything, Hunter had wanted a face-to-face confrontation with the station owner. Just get it over with. If D.O.A. is going to fire Hunter for not killing the Reverend Sam story, Hunter was ready. And now? Shit! He hoped to make his own execution convenient. But, as usual, D.O.A.'s office was as empty as his secretary's head, and she has no clue as to the station owner's whereabouts.

Hunter hadn't planned on still being employed this morning. So instead of spending the day cleaning out his desk, Hunter has time to clear the air. Now he moves quickly and reaches out to a pizza deliveryman struggling to get through the door with a half a dozen boxes on one arm and waving a receipt with his free hand. The hand-off is tricky, but the timing is good.

Armed for battle, Hunter delivers the pizza to the newsroom and sets down the stack of boxes with a noticeable thump on Kathy's desk, disrupting her doodles. She has been lost in thought that spilled on to the yellow pad in front of her. Hunter catches a glimpse of the page before she can whisk it into a drawer and out of sight. Her drawings are filled with sharp edges and wicked-looking souls. On the desk top, Hunter counts at least half a dozen pencils, each one with points that have been mashed into useless stumps.

"Everyone," Hunter sings out.

They are all here, the producers and photographers, anchors and reporters. Even Valerie the witch has decided to grace them with an appearance. She is supposed to be at home—still suspended from work. Hunter will deal with Valerie later for siccing the newspaper on Sugar. Everyone is here but Sugar, and that is by design.

"What I have here, folks," he begins, "is a blatant attempt to bribe you all."

Hunter lifts the lid on one pizza box and lets the aroma of pepperoni escape. He pulls out the first slice, a generous one, deep dish and expensive from an upscale family-run operation over on Broadway. This is too important to trust to Domino's. "I want to buy your understanding. If I can't get that, at least some cooperation."

One of Hunter's mostly benign but lethal fantasies is that if he ever wants revenge on a news operation, he will spike a modest quantity of food and set it out in the center of the newsroom. Cookies and cakes, popcorn and pizza left unguarded are consumed with no questions asked. No one cares where it comes from, or why. As long as it's free and digestible, it won't last long. While Hunter presumes free food is a good way to poison a newsroom, now he hopes it is a way to medicate one. He has always believed that pizza and chocolate are good for whatever ails you.

He carefully places one slice on a paper plate and hands it to Kathy, pausing as their hands touch. He searches her face for the slightest sign of support. Hunter takes heart that, while there is no respect in her gaze, a gaze steady and focused like a tennis opponent returning his serve, it comes at him lacking any vicious intensity. It isn't the lob he hoped for, but it's an opening. He needs her support to sway the others.

Hunter turns and looks over the young and the ignorant. He doesn't blame them for being angry and confused. "Right now I know a lot of you think I'm an idiot. And if I were in your shoes, I'd probably think so too.

"I see by the morning paper that we have a former stripper working for us these days. Yes, it's true. Does anyone have a problem with that?"

Hunter raises his hand and waits. He watches them exchange puzzled looks, too timid to challenge him yet. Give them time.

Hunter pauses on the tightrope between being their boss and approaching them on an equal level. "Look, I've been in your position plenty of times before and put up with lousy, arbitrary, or just plain fucked-up ideas from news directors just like me. I know exactly how you feel right now. Exactly how you feel. But let me tell you, this idea—hiring Sugar and knowing this town would get its panties in a bundle over it—this idea may be crazy. It may be unconventional, but it's not fucked up."

"We're not here to practice journalism for the ethically challenged," Valerie says. Of course, it would be Valerie.

"What's unethical about putting someone in front of the camera who has sex appeal? Do you think you got a job on TV because you're ugly?" Hunter asks. "Any of you?"

"We are here to report the news and inform the public. But how do you expect to do that if nobody is watching? People, we are a tree falling in the forest. If no one is there to hear it, we don't make a sound."

Hunter points to one of the reporters. "Andy! When you work so hard and turn out that kick-ass story on the transit authority's cost over-runs, doesn't it bother you that more people are watching Gomer Pyle reruns than our newscast? And Valerie, and Kent. And that goes for everyone in this room. We've done a lot of great work here, and I'm proud of you all. In all the years I've been in the business, I've never seen better, more honest and comprehensive TV journalism than what you have produced. But it's going to waste. It's going to waste every night because—I hate to tell you, folks—there ain't nobody on the other end to see it."

Kathy raises a finger. "Hunter. The sales department says some of their clients are pulling commercials out of our newscast already. They're ready to hang us."

"We're only a week away from the next ratings period," Hunter replies. "When they get a look at how many more people are tuning in, and how much more they'll be able to sell that commercial time for, they'll be kissing our... toes."

Someone behind Hunter giggles. It's a good sign. Andy Blackman ventures near enough to take a slice of pizza. One of the photographers steps up behind him. Hunter's not sure if it's hunger or acceptance that lured them to the table, but either way, he's glad to see it.

"I don't like it," Valerie Watson declares. Brusque and uncompromising, she tosses her reporter's notebook on to the desk in front of her. Overacting again. "This is a joke. And we're the laughing stock of Bakersfield. Probably the whole country by now."

Someone else adds, "I hear Sally Jesse Raphael is planning to do an interview with Sugar. And they're going to have an entire show on 'Shady Lives of TV News Anchors'."

"'Sluts on TV'," Valerie says.

"It's not true," Kathy says. "And it's not like Sugar's still working at that club."

"Does anyone know where Sugar was last night?" One of the photogs asks. Hunter hopes the question is rhetorical.

"I mean, if her paycheck looks anything like mine, she'd have to keep her night job just to get by."

Hunter can hear grumbling from each corner. Don't even open that can of worms, though he's tempted to suggest that this stunt may be the only thing keeping those paychecks coming until the dust is settled and the ratings are in.

Kent Abernathy steps forward. "This is just like when WMAQ in Chicago hired Jerry Springer to do the commentary on their newscast."

"This is entirely different." Hunter protests.

"Not far off," Van Thompson says. "One night on the air was all it took in Chicago. That's the kind of shit that just splashes all over everyone else. And that's kind of how it smells around here."

Kent says, "The anchor at WMAQ was so disgusted she resigned."

"She was a hero. Everyone says so."

"Yeah," someone else chimes in.

This is not going well. Hunter asks, "Are you a hero, Kent?"

"If that's what it takes," he replies without confidence.

"I am." Valerie says. "If *that woman*, and I won't even say her name, stays on the air here, then I quit."

They turn to Kent. He nods.

"Van?" Hunter asks.

The lanky producer shrugs. "Got to. It'd be bad form to stick around."

The other reporters and the photographers, the youngest and most impressionable ones in the room, exchange looks waiting to see how the story plays before committing.

Hunter turns to Kathy. Her look is unflinching, and he knows which side she will take if he drags an answer from her. He decides to leave bad enough alone.

Instead he rubs his hands together and smiles. "Okay, then. That will just save us all some time and trouble, won't it? You've all heard the rumors that D.O.A. is going to cancel the newscast and fire everyone after November. Quit now or be fired later? Might as well do it now."

"Those are just rumors. He wouldn't really do it," someone mumbles.

"You think not? If the numbers stink in November, we'll get the same treatment as... as..." Hunter snaps his fingers and squeezes his eyes shut. He knows the answer but asks, "Kathy, what CBS station was that last Christmas?"

"Birmingham," she replies.

"Right. They fired the whole staff and replaced the news with reruns of *Sanford and Son*. The reruns got higher ratings."

Van Thompson is looking at the ground. "An anchor-chick friend of mine got it in Winston-Salem a few months ago. Same deal. Only the weather guy survived. The rest of the staff? Gone. Replaced by *The Match Game*."

"I can give you five more examples," Hunter says. "They're pulling the trigger faster than ever before right now. We're next. Even if our numbers are golden in November, I can't guarantee you'll have a job the day after the ratings book hits D.O.A.'s desk. So I'll make you a deal."

Hunter points to the pizza. "Eat up. We have to get back to work. The city council is going to vote tonight to cut off funding for the old folks home. Right, Andy?"

Andy Blackman nods.

"It's the nail-in-the-coffin story. It's a big story. Sugar is already over at City Hall getting ready to do her part. So here's my deal." Hunter pauses, letting his words hang in the air with the aroma of cheese and tomato sauce.

"I hired Sugar to grab the viewers' eyes. But you are the ones I'm trusting to grab their hearts and their minds. That's what will make us a success, and that's what I've been counting on from the start. Do your jobs for just a few more weeks and, when the November ratings are up, add that to your resume and get the hell out of here. You are all good enough to find jobs in a bigger market. Isn't that what you want? Give me just a few more weeks of your life, and I'll press every contact I have to help you move up to the network or New York, Chicago, all those places I've worked."

A murmur works its way around the room in the same uneven fashion the "wave" ripples through the crowd at a baseball game. Now they remember Hunter's big market pedigree. And the prospect of riding that influence seems significantly more intriguing than the game at hand.

Hunter knows he has scored points. Before he can find out whether he's won them over, he scoops up the ringing phone everyone has ignored.

"Mr. Riley? It's Joe. Out in the lobby. I think you may want to come out here and see this."

A small crowd of sales and administrative staff is squeezed into the doorway of the station when Hunter reaches the lobby.

"Will you look at that?"

Hunter can barely believe it. A Channel 29 news unit has stopped across the street. A photographer and reporter are setting up to interview the leader of the Porn Police, while his followers continue their march along the sidewalk.

"Channel 17 was here a while ago," Joe Security Guard says.

Hunter clasps his hands and looks to the sky. "Thank God for slow news days."

"Do you really want them here?"

Hunter nods. "Freedom of the press."

He won't admit it, but Hunter knows if the other stations in town cover this story with any gusto at all, it will generate more publicity than Hunter could ever get with his own paltry promotional budget. Numbers. Numbers. It's all about numbers. And despite what he told the staff from his soapbox in the newsroom, the numbers are climbing; he can feel it. He's heard it from the Sales Slugs on the other side of the building who spend their days pounding the pavement and schmoozing clients over expense-account lunches. He's overheard it in the checkout line at the grocery store and down at Jelly's Tavern. More people are watching.

If he can keep people watching KDOA for one more month, just through the November ratings period, and if the numbers come back strong enough, the station's owner, Don Andrews, won't dare pull the plug. They just might still be doing news when Christmas rolls around.

One of the staffers leans too heavily on the front door, and the crowd spills into the October sunshine. From the other side of the parking lot, the Channel 29 photographer swings his camera lens in their direction.

"Hey look! Wave, everybody. We're on TV!"

Slug: Council Riot

Anchor intro:

> Given the fact that a TV newscast is usually produced amid a cacophony of both noise and visuals hitting your senses from every direction, where stories are juggled and egos are tamed, the comparison to a three-ring circus is inevitable.

> If so, reporting live from the scene is the high-wire act of journalism, requiring equal parts of showmanship and balance to get the story right.

> That's how it was on one night in the final week of October when KDOA turned its spotlight on the death-defying performance by Reverend Sam and his geriatric troupe under the big top we call City Hall.

> And then fate sent in the clowns.

Roll tape

Focus on the lens. It stares back at you, glassy-eyed.

Block out everything else, Sugar reminds herself.

All she wants to see now is her reflection in the camera's round lens three feet away. She tries to ignore the laughing, leering faces on either side of the camera and filling her peripheral vision. They are the faces of frat boys and other curious bodies who jostle her photographer and his equipment, and they stumble over the cables that snake from the vestibule of City Hall to the live remote truck parked on the street. Inspired by the newspaper article about Sugar, the frat boys are obviously drawn to City Hall out of raunchy curiosity instead of civic duty.

The city council has already begun plowing through the day's agenda. Reverend Sam and funding for the Emerald Arms won't come up for another hour.

Sugar has never had more than one or two curious onlookers at one of her live reports before. News had been her refuge from the gawking, groping and drooling mobs, the kind that filled Pistol Pete's tables, sending dirty dollar bills and even filthier thoughts her way. At least Pete's customers liked her. Rising above the heads, she can see a cardboard sign, something about nudes and news. A couple of mean-spirited protesters have wandered off the street, hurling cruel comments her way and striking up a chant. The protest eventually dies for lack of support.

All the chaos will disappear if she can just stay focused on the camera's eye.

Focus on the lens.

As for her personal story, Hunter was right. She had to say something. So at the end of Tuesday's newscast she confirmed the newspaper story in one minute's worth of airtime with neither shame nor defiance. She was a student. It was a job. A girl's got to eat, right? She never believed her past—her employment at Pistol Pete's—would remain a secret. The story hit the newspaper and it's been featured on the radio. The other TV stations, with their tiny prick-sized attention spans, covered the day of protest outside KDOA and then moved on. Hunter says she couldn't avoid it. He's right. Sugar just never thought the reaction would be so strong and so… public. She feels exposed in a way dancing naked never embarrassed her.

Sugar realizes she has been on the air and talking for thirty seconds or more while her mind had wandered away. She doesn't know what she said; she hopes it was coherent. She needs to focus, to set aside her own story and concentrate on Reverend Sam, the city council, and the moment at hand.

The senior housing issue is well down on the agenda, but it has already packed the house. Sugar says so to the camera, and points to the filled auditorium behind her.

"And if you look at the front row, you'll see Reverend Sam Cross sitting there. It appears he is making notes, probably editing and rewriting the remarks he plans to make to the council this evening. What he has to say tonight could save—or sink— the senior housing project."

Sugar glances down at the tiny black-and-white monitor at her feet. The picture is snowy, but she can tell Lanny has zoomed past her for a close-up on Reverend Sam. Now she's free from making eye contact with the camera and checks her notes. Sugar recounts Reverend Sam's alleged crimes and the pending trial in as few words as possible, keeping it simple and direct, the way Hunter taught her. Who. Where. What. When. Why.

"But why bank robbery? That is the question we haven't been able to answer." She thinks the question is in her head. But in the pause that punctuates it, Sugar realizes she has laid it out there, on camera, uncensored. She's committed now.

"Reverend Sam Cross has pleaded not guilty in court, but he refuses to deny in public any connection to the robberies. In our exclusive report…" Use that phrase again. And again. Hunter told her to hammer it into the viewers' consciousness. We may never have this opportunity again. So she says, "In our exclusive report on Live at Five last night, we explained how many senior citizens touched by the reverend's agency have received money—charity or acts of kindness, if you will—from the Senior Bandit. But that still doesn't answer the question: why did he turn to robbery?"

Sugar reiterates that Sam and the bandit may not be one and the same. "But earlier this evening, he shared his anger with us over what he called a conspiracy to close the Emerald Arms. And he said he would welcome any action to keep the program going. Even an illegal one."

A close up of Reverend Sam's face fills the little monitor at Sugar's feet. The videotape of the latest sound bite is rolling back at the station. Sam is raising his anger and his rhetoric to a new level, railing against a conspiracy he believes is out to destroy the seniors. Sugar has already seen this video. Still, it disturbs her.

Since the arrest, Reverend Sam has become a hot news property—not only for the local media, but everyone from the networks to the supermarket tabloids wants a piece of his story. *Newsweek* has a reporter in town this week. On Monday, Sugar made the network news by putting together a ninety-second report for UBN. There she was on the *Evening News with Ryan Billings*. The network hasn't deemed the story big enough yet to send one of its own reporters. After all, it is only Bakersfield. But it has provided Sugar with her first coast-to-coast exposure on the network. Hunter predicts it won't be her last.

Sam's arrest and all the publicity surrounding it have put him in a fighting mood. Sugar wonders if he is simply playing to the media, but she fears he's become—what did they call that in her psychology class, hypo-manic? She studies the tape. Reverend Sam is clearly agitated; his speech is rapid and his paranoia acute. Yes, she decides, classic symptoms. It's not the Sam she knew before the crisis. And she worries.

As far as the media are concerned, Reverend Sam may not always make sense, but he makes great headlines.

Sugar straightens up, poised to pick up the thread of her story when she hears a whoop just behind the crowd. Kathy is plowing through it like a little train engine with boxcars in tow. She has one hand firmly on the elbow of a small man in glasses. He, in turn, is dragging a taller fellow whose scowl accentuates the single, hairy eyebrow stretching from temple to temple. The caboose of this train is a bulky and bored-looking black man.

Kathy cups her free hand to the side of her mouth. "Lawyers. Lawyers. Lawwww-yers." She mouths the word, silently at first and ending in a whispered singsong. She lines them up next to Sugar and then takes up a position blocking their most convenient escape route. Sugar is thankful for that. Hunter's suggestion that they station

Kathy at City Hall with Sugar tonight, instead of her usual post in the control room at the station, is paying off. He had predicted the crowd and the chaos would be too much for one reporter. Kathy may have been grumpy lately, but she knows her stuff.

The videotape ends. Reverend Sam is gone. Sugar is back on camera. "If the Emerald Arms is forced to close, the Davenport Development Company could tear it down and build on that land. Lawyers for the company have just arrived here at City Hall. These men are from the law firm of Ketcham, Payne and Smith."

Sugar recognizes their faces from the stories other reporters have done. Little Jerry Ketcham is the senior partner. The other men in the legal troika are scowling Sidney Payne and the bored, black lawyer Robert Smith.

Sugar steps closer to Ketcham. "You're the ones who drew up the petition to cut off funding for the Emerald Arms that the council will consider. Is that right?"

He nods in response.

Sugar points to the overflowing council chambers behind them. "This is quite a hornet's nest you've stirred up. Why the petition? Why now?"

He ignores her gesture, choosing instead to stare straight into her eyes. He has flat features, most notably a flat nose, wide at the nostrils as if he pressed it against a window as a young boy and it never recovered. He may be a head shorter than Sugar, but his voice is gruff and his demeanor is perpetually superior and intimidating.

"That housing project and the people who run it have become an embarrassment to our community. And we feel that until the matter is resolved, the city should not waste another nickel on it."

"You're talking about Reverend Sam Cross, here. Isn't it premature to take this action? Sam Cross hasn't had his day in court."

"And he will," the lawyer sniffs. He looks past Sugar as if hoping to find a more worthy adversary in the crowd. "But we are calling for a suspension of funding until the matter is resolved in court. That—and a full audit of the Emerald Arms to account for prior grants and make sure it has been following proper spending procedures."

"And if the seniors who live at the Emerald Arms are turned out into the street in the process?" she asks.

"If you look at the financial problems this organization has faced for the past several months, this should come as no surprise to those residents and their families. In fact, I should say they have received proper and due notice, more than enough to find new homes.

"In addition," he continues, "The investors we represent are willing to help residents. We've already made a very generous offer to relocate the residents, even placing them in a proper institution if necessary."

Institution? Somewhere in her mind Sugar hears a door slamming on the last bit of independence for those folks. "Institution? Do you really believe these people need to be institutionalized? They appear healthy enough to decide that for themselves."

"Certainly. Let them choose. But it is in the interest of the community that we pull the plug on this financially irresponsible, possibly criminal project and move on with our vision of a progressive and equitable city."

Sugar grips the microphone tighter. She'd like to rap the little legalese-speaking twerp on the noggin. "Isn't it a conflict of interest? Your client is bringing this petition to the city council to cut off funding for the Emerald Arms while holding the development rights on that property. Why, that's... that's..."

"Bullshit! It's all bullshit."

The words echo inside Sugar. She quickly raises an embarrassed hand to her lips, afraid once again her thoughts had escaped and been captured on camera. Wait. That voice wasn't hers, but make no mistake, someone just said "bullshit" on the air.

At the edge of the crowd, the light from the KDOA camera bounces off a polished walnut cane as it comes down with a feeble thwack on the elbow of the black lawyer from Ketcham, Payne and Smith. He flinches. They all turn. The buzz of the crowd transforms into a mixture of astonished gasps and delight.

Mr. Marika, the cigar-chomping geriatric pixie from the Emerald Arms, shuffles out of the lawyer's shadow and into the glare of the TV lights. He brandishes his cane in front of him like a swordsman. In his mouth, he swings his stogie from left to right in unison with the wooden weapon in his hand. He whacks the middle lawyer on the knee just hard enough to draw a yelp. They are all too stunned by the little man's actions to stop the blow. Mr. Marika backs away to a safe distance before anyone fully understands the situation.

"C'mon, tough guy," Marika growls. "Show us what you got. How can you go on like that? Shooting crap about what's good for the community, when all you really want is to steal our home so you can put up another God-damned shopping mall!"

The crowd moves closer. The buzz increases, and the only distinguishable reaction is definitely on Marika's side. It's David versus Goliath. And the spectators are rooting for David.

"We don't have to stand here and take this," Ketcham states coolly.

He is trapped in the public spotlight and knows any movement against the feisty, gray-haired gladiator will look like they are bullying a weaker opponent.

Marika reaches out and pokes at Ketcham, who bats the cane away. "You have no right to hit me. I'm warning you right now to stop it," the lawyer says.

"Oh yeah? You ain't got no right to steal my home."

From behind the crowd, Reverend Sam calls out. "Arnold? Is that you? Stop that."

Sugar turns. She can see the reverend's head bouncing up and down behind the mob. He is hopping, trying to snatch a better view of the situation.

The crowd wants more. It is shouting encouragement to Marika, while hurling insults at the lawyers.

Marika shuffles to his right, and then back to the left, as the third lawyer, Smith, reaches out to grab the cane. "You all have been looking to get your greedy mitts on our home for a long time. Tell 'em how you raised the rent. Again and again and again. We're going hungry in order to pay off your money-grubbing landlords."

"Yeah," someone in the crowd yells. "What if that was your mother, huh?"

Ketcham's head snaps in that direction. He snarls, "My mother had the good sense to take care of herself. You old people don't have a right..."

"Your momma's lucky she ain't here to see you now," someone shouts.

Reverend Sam calls out again and tries to muscle through the mass of bodies separating him from the ring where Mr. Marika is staring down the lawyers. It's too late. Mr. Marika raises the cane above his head, wheezing and unsteady as he measures another blow. Smith steps up and catches the cane easily as Marika lashes out. He gives it a tug, and the momentum carries the old man forward, down to the floor.

"Hey! The big guy hit him," someone cries. The throng reacts with a babble of disgust.

"Wait! Everyone just settle down," Sugar shouts. She starts toward Mr. Marika, but she's swept aside by Ketcham. He bends over the old man, whether to apologize or gloat, no one will ever know.

All you see is Ketcham straightening up to swing a harsh elbow at a man who stepped up to defend Marika. Lanny the photographer has moved the camera from its tripod to his shoulder, and he is draping a protective arm over it as he stands against the surf of the crowd.

Sugar is surrounded by several young men who have surged forward. They are the same ones who, at the beginning of the broadcast, had tried to distract her by making faces and lewd noises. Now they take advantage of the chaos, and Sugar has to brush hands away from her hip, her butt and her breasts. First here and then there. So many hands, so many innocent faces each time Sugar turns to catch the culprit.

More bodies are joining the pile in the middle of the vestibule. Kathy has climbed a chair against the wall. Stretching up, she waves to catch Sugar's attention. Sugar has lost track of the camera. She can't hear Kathy above the din. Kathy makes a motion as if lobbing a softball across the room. She follows that with a charade of breaking a rod with her hands.

"Throw," she says with the pitching motion. "To break," she snaps her wrists apart.

Sugar surveys the chaos swirling around her. *Live @ Five* has turned into a barroom brawl scene from an old TV western. It's the pie-throwing melee—minus the custard—that the Three Stooges made famous. It's Saturday afternoon with the World Wrestling Federation. It is moronic yet captivating television.

So it is, in this case, our heroine Sugar Kane, disheveled and disheartened, clears enough space between herself and the TV camera, looks her Bakersfield audience in the eye, and says in a calm, clear and controlled voice, "Bob Moorman will have our weather forecast for you in just a moment. This is Live at Five. We'll be right back."

Slug: Defiant Seniors

Anchor intro:

If you dig deeply enough, you'll find the "big" news story is very rarely a random episode or simple twist of fate. Each has its own history of development predating the moment it grabs the public's attention.

Too often the big story has its roots in something the news media not only covers, but actively cultivates the way a gardener grows a special flower.

The battle over the Emerald Arms is one such story. But it has sprouted into an ugly headline-grabbing weed.

Desperation may have been its seed, but KDOA spread the manure that made it grow.

Roll tape

The fan is on full speed, and today the shit hit just in time for the start of the November ratings period. We've had three days of calm while authorities try to sort out that melee at the city council meeting. Now the newsroom is responding like firefighters to an alarm. Kathy is holding a phone to her ear with one hand while waving the other frantically, as if trying to cool burned fingers. "Someone is shooting up the Emerald Arms."

She slams the phone down. "I can't get any information from the cops downtown," she snaps. "Lanny. Get the live truck rolling," she yells. "Andy. You go with him."

The chaos squawking from the police scanner and Kathy's inflamed state have sucked Hunter away from the phone where he had finally connected with the station owner. Hunter assumes D.O.A. was about to fire him, but couldn't stick around to find out when all hell broke loose. D.O.A.'s anger had been loud and relentless, leaving Hunter's head buzzing like the reverberating effect of a rock concert long after the music has died. "I should fire you right now," D.O.A. had said. "I'll do it tomorrow. I swear..."

Was that a reprieve or a threat? It's still ringing in Hunter's ears as he slides up to Kathy's desk.

Hunter smacks the Local section of the *Bakersfield Californian* against his palm. Most of its front page is covered with the story of last night's raucous city council meeting. A companion column on the page puts most of the blame for the tussle between the lawyers and the senior citizens on Sugar Kane and the specter of live television. That was the focus of D.O.A.'s ranting when Hunter cut him off.

And oh, by the way. City Council voted four-to-three to cut off funding for Reverend Sam and the Emerald Arms, dooming the senior housing program.

"I've got shots fired, and an officer down," Kathy uses the scanner lingo curtly.

Hunter's stomach sinks. "My God. What the hell have we done?"

"They're blocking off the neighborhood from A to D Avenue and down to the railroad tracks," Kathy says. She jabs her finger into a map book on her desk as if it is the source of her vexation. "I don't know how close we'll be able to get."

She looks up and shouts to no one in particular. "Anyone hear from Sugar yet?"

"Where is Sugar?" Hunter asks.

"She's out there at the Emerald Arms."

"Already?"

Now Kathy smiles. It's a thin, guilty smile brought on by the mere thought of breaking news. "Hey it was a hunch, okay? I called a friend at the Sheriff's office this morning and he said they were sending the constables down there to serve an eviction notice on Reverend Sam and the old folks. The developers aren't wasting any time. We got Sugar there before the constables even arrived. And then this shooting went down. We don't know what's up with that yet."

A shooting. At the Emerald Arms? Hunter shakes his head. The story he has carefully guided is now running on its own at a full gallop. No one is supposed to get hurt. Things are out of control. In a quiet, saner moment, he might step back and say "Enough, already." But then the commotion of breaking news tugs at him, drawing him up like a roller coaster heading to its next peak.

Kathy jumps over to the scanner and turns up the volume. "They have an ambulance out there. Nothing about them transporting. No one is going to the hospital yet."

"Do we have anyone to stake out the emergency room with a camera in case they bring someone in?"

"We would have," Kathy says, "if you hadn't fired Valerie."

"Hey, she said she wanted to resign. She said it right here, in front of the whole newsroom."

"You didn't take anyone else's resignation."

"None of them pissed me off," Hunter sniffs. Then he adds, "She won't be out of work long. There are plenty of newsrooms that can handle a reporter with an attitude. Don't fret on her account."

The phone rings. Kathy snatches it, carries on a six-sentence conversation and then slams the receiver back into the cradle. "They've towed the live truck again—Hunter, aren't you ever going to get that transmission fixed? They're about two blocks away from the Emerald Arms. The cops have set up a roadblock. We can't get any closer."

"Damn. We need pictures," Hunter says. "What's out there, homes?"

Kathy shakes her head. "Mostly older places converted to small offices. Lawyers and dentists. I think there's a hair salon directly across the street. According to what I can get from the scanner, the cops have evacuated the whole block."

Hunter picks up the map book from the desk. "All right. Here's what we need right now. Get the art department to draw up a map," he says. "Then we'll..."

Kathy stops him. "No one's in the art department. She's on vacation." Kathy suggests the low-tech graphics generator they use for newscasts. "The Chyron machine can probably crank out something crude for us."

"I can do it much better than that."

Hunter turns. Kathy leans to look over his shoulder. Ray the Web-Guy, the newsroom's producer for KDOA's Internet site, has wandered away from his cyber-cubbyhole near the station's weather computers.

"I heard all this shit going down and came foraging for something to put on our web page," Ray says. He adjusts the hip, black frames of his glasses on his dark brown face.

"You can give us a map of this neighborhood?" Hunter asks. He circles the location with his index finger.

"Just need to access an ISP portal with layout of the city in a size-altering interface dot-com cache download modem Microsoft pollywog carburetor-driven enhancement."

It's all Geek Greek. Hunter doesn't have a clue about what Ray is saying. "Yeah, but can you put it on the air?"

Ray nods. "We've already wired my seven hundred gigabytes and streamlined the peripheral megahertz data digital analog compression cable do-wah through quasar coded ram-a-lam-a ding dong."

What the hell is he saying? Hunter stares blankly at the WebGuy. Ray sighs. "If I can get it on my computer, I can put it on TV."

Whatever. "Just do it."

Hunter turns to Kathy. "How soon before we have a live shot ready?"

"Lanny can have something in a few minutes, but there's nothing to see from his location."

Hunter eyes the clock on the newsroom wall and steals

a glance at the monitors across from it, fearing that, at any moment, Channel 17 or 29 will break in with a special report and scoop them. "Call Lanny, and tell him he has ten minutes. He either finds a better location or just sets up at the roadblock with the cop cars in the background. I want to break into programming with this as soon as possible."

"But…"

The phone rings. The back door slams. Van Thompson comes skidding into the newsroom.

"I was just pulling up in the parking lot, and KLUK Radio is reporting some kind of shooting. Are we on it?"

"Sugar's on the cell phone," Andy Blackman is shouting from his desk. He's holding the telephone high over his head. "Sugar's breaking up. There's so much static on the line, I'm not sure what's going on. But it sounds big."

Hunter claps his hands together. "Golden." He points at Kathy and fires off a list of commands. "Tell Sugar to find Lanny at the truck and get ready for a live report. Call Lanny and tell him he has five minutes. Track down Lee. Get the studio crew up there in the booth and ready in five, too."

"But…" Kathy tries to protest.

Hunter whirls and puts a hand on Thompson's shoulder. "Pull up some video from the archives on Reverend Sam and the Emerald Arms. Plus a minute's worth of copy for background. How it all started."

And the wrestling match at the city council meeting?" Thompson asks. "You know. Defiant seniors. That's good shit."

Hunter taps the newspaper, still in his hand, against his thigh. He looks down. His palms are sweating, creating a moist circle that makes ink on the page bleed. The headline scolds him. *Shame on you.*

"Edit some of last night's video. But hold it until we know for certain we can connect the two. My guess is yes. But it's not really our fault, is it?"

Thompson's reply is a puzzled look.

Hunter sends the folded Local section spinning onto a nearby desk like a dealer delivering the last card in a poker hand. "Let's go," he says, as he heads for the door that leads down the hall to the studio. "I want to cut into programming with a special report in five minutes. Five minutes."

Kathy races to catch him, stumbling when he stops and turns abruptly. She squeezes his elbow. "Hunter. We haven't gotten hold of Kent. We don't have anyone to anchor the report."

Hunter guides her hand from his arm. He places a crooked finger beneath her chin, raising it as he gently tilts her head the way an adult might try to perk up a pouting child.

"We don't have an anchor," Kathy repeats.

Hunter scoffs. "Of course we do."

Slug: Seniors Shoot Back

Anchor intro:

> *Think of the fairy tales we grew up with. Compelling stories with simple yet powerful morals. And think how different those stories would play out on the news if written for this new millennium.*
>
> *Cinderella isn't concerned with a lost glass slipper. She's busy trying to break through the corporate glass ceiling.*
>
> *Jack sells his cow for seeds in an Internet start-up and climbs to riches on beanstalk.com.*
>
> *When the wolf goes to blow down the home of the three little pigs, the pigs are armed and loaded for bear.*
>
> *That really happened in Bakersfield. We saw it Live at Five.*

Roll tape

Look at that sky.

The weather is perfect for a shoot-out with police. The morning fog has lifted and the sun is playing hide-and-seek behind scattered, marshmallow clouds.

Sugar is lying flat on her back, looking up at the sky. It takes her back to the bedroom of her first steady boyfriend. He had tacked a poster of a similar sky above the bed. And Sugar, not nearly as impressed with her boyfriend's sexual prowess as he seemed to be, had spent a few afternoons memorizing the shapes of those clouds.

This afternoon she is pinned beneath the weight of Kern County Constable BillyBobJoeBubba, or some such name that's more suitable to the *Dukes of Hazzard* than even the reddest redneck in California. He had pulled her to safety beneath the nandina bush near the porch when the shot was fired.

"Throw down your weapons and surrender!" The voice is stern and uncompromising. It rains down on them from overhead, confusing Sugar because she knows the officers are here at ground level with her. Sugar squirms away from the constable, trying to raise her head enough to see where the second officer and her photographer landed. Is anyone hurt?

"Stay down." BillyBobJoeBubba fumbles with the radio handset mounted on his shoulder. "Baker One," he says breathlessly. He is hyperventilating from an uppercut of adrenaline. "We need backup at 1938 Nineteenth Street. Shots fired. Officer down."

Sugar takes advantage of the constable's distraction with his radio. She slides back just far enough to see past the small portico above the doorway. Major Tom is leaning out of the second-story window waving a gun. "I repeat," he yells. "Put down your weapons and surrender!" He turns to someone behind him. He calls to someone inside, "Sergeant, we have an enemy breach on the south perimeter."

Major Tom, the retired soldier and self-appointed guardian of
the Emerald Arms, leans out of the window again and waves his
arms to the left. "Collins. Deploy your men along the ridge, but
hold your fire." Then he ducks into the building with a shriek.

"Incoming!"

Sugar whips her head around, startled. She is looking for the
missile that chased Major Tom back inside. There is none. There
is no enemy out on the street to return fire. The threat is all in the
major's head, at least at that moment. Sugar rolls over and drops
back into the soft bed of mulch beneath the nandina and stares
up at the tranquil sky. Poor Major Tom. He's snapped. Just like
Reverend Sam. One more casualty in the long battle to save the
Emerald Arms.

She brushes bits of bark from her hair and strains her neck to
locate her photographer. Raul was at the gate near the street when
Major Tom fired the shot heard 'round Bakersfield. Now he is
shielded behind a low utility box on the corner of the property. His
camera is raised like a submarine's periscope. It rotates to the left
and then to the right. The other county constable is crabbing his
way to the safety of the patrol car. He looks ridiculous but appears
unharmed.

"We have multiple shots fired! And civilians out here," BillyBobJoeBubba repeats. He is shouting into the microphone now.
His gun is drawn, and his knee is bleeding from scraping the edge
of the sidewalk in their dive for cover.

"I think he only shot once," Sugar corrects him. She listens for
more commotion. The breeze rustles the leaves of the bush above

her head. The constable fumbles with the radio strapped to his belt, and it burps static back at him. But by and large, it appears the battle that has them hunkered down behind a flimsy fortress of green is over.

Hear the sirens. Bakersfield P.D. is getting close.

Sugar is angry. The cell phone, her only link to the newsroom, is sitting on the front seat of the Humvee a block away. She struggles to get away, but Constable BillyBob-whatever tugs her back. He growls at her and makes it clear she is not going anywhere anytime soon.

"Wouldn't we be safer out there?" She waves a hand toward the patrol car.

"Not with some nut ready to drill us from the second story if we make a run for it. Not until backup arrives."

Resigned but unable to relax, Sugar strains to see Major Tom, but the window is empty. The front door is shut tight. In the corner of the yard, Raul is still recording the scene with his periscope method of photography. He has everything on videotape; she's certain of that. Sugar checks her watch. They still have a little more than three hours until the newscast. She begins mentally editing the videotape, visualizing the way she hopes it will play on *Live @ Five*.

Start with the shot of Reverend Sam standing in the doorway of the Emerald Arms, guarding the threshold as the constables approach. The door is open only one-quarter of the way. Zoom in on a trio of troubled faces just in the shadows beyond.

There is anger in Reverend Sam's eyes. His voice is crackling like thunder. Sugar knows he would be much more docile without a TV camera in his front yard.

He takes the eviction notice from the constable. "You are doing your job. I understand that," Reverend Sam says. "Honor and duty to country and the uniform you're wearing are all fine and well, but when the power of those you serve has been so badly corrupted…" he pauses for effect and Sugar would swear he was looking for the tally light of Raul's camera to confirm it was recording. Then raises his voice as if preaching to a congregation. It was a congregation of three: two county constables and a TV camera. "We. Must. Make a stand.

"Take this filthy document back to that shameless, spineless bunch of politicians. Politicians who would deprive their constituents of shelter and throw them onto the street just because these folks are poor. They think we won't fight back. Ha!" Reverend Sam is on a roll.

He holds the document at arm's length and reads, "Thirty days." Then he crumples the notice and lets the ball of paper roll from his palm and across his fingertips. In her mind, Sugar can see it in slow motion. It falls like a boulder rolling off a cliff, falling until it bounces on the concrete and the single step of the porch. It stops with a gentle bump at the toe of the constable's black leather boot.

"Go back and tell the city council that *we* took a vote here at the Emerald Arms. We vote to stay put. It will take more than a piece of paper to drag us from our home."

From behind the door, whispers. Then chatter. A then someone claps just before a cheer slices through the narrow opening. It's audible proof that Reverend Sam's proclamation of defiance is as much for the small audience of seniors huddled inside the building as it is for the TV audience Sugar hopes will be there when this videotape airs tonight.

And what of the gunfire? The shot from the second floor which sent them scrambling, did Raul get any of that on videotape? Sugar remembers the startled look on Reverend Sam's face before he slammed the door. He didn't plan on gunfire; Sugar is convinced.

She checks her watch again. Two-thirty. They don't have much time to put together a report.

One. Two. Three. Bakersfield Police cars pull up hard on their brakes in the middle of the street. Sugar makes a run for it. She dodges an officer on the street who tries to corral her. She steers clear of another officer running in the opposite direction. He's wearing a flak jacket and carrying a shotgun. Sugar dives into the Humvee, scoops up the phone and begins frantically punching numbers. She wonders if anyone back in the newsroom has a clue about what's happening. There is too much to do. Too much story to tell. How will she get it all on TV?

Shots fired. Reporter down. Send backup.

Slug: Studio Blues

Anchor intro:

You would be hard-pressed to find any place in America where ego distorts a mirror's reflection more than in a TV studio. No flaw is so big that it can't be covered by makeup, good lighting and a little self-indulgence.

If we are fat, we see the thin person inside. If we are old, we see the youth of our prime. If we are dull, we see the vivacious character we want to be. The mirror may show us one thing, but the reflection in our head is what we want to see.

And then comes reality.

Reality—Visine for the mind's eye.

Roll tape

Hunter dabs highlight under his eyes and inspects his face. Look at the bags. They are heavier than you might expect. They are certainly more than Hunter wants to see.

He is standing in front of a mirror in the corner of the studio. He rummages for something to shrink them in his battered shaving kit and wonders why he doesn't have some Preparation-H. Hunter hasn't used any of his makeup since the night he got off the six o'clock newscast in Des Moines and the boss told him not to come back for the late news. Fired without so much as a chance to say goodbye to the folks at home. Did they notice?

The studio dogs, a crew of two, are hustling, hauling cables and dragging cameras into position. They are energized by the sense of urgency. Hunter stands at the mirror in a corner next to the news set and sponges some Revlon Number Three—Sandy Cream Bronze Toast—onto his nose and cheeks. A darker shade for the hollows of his cheeks, a dusting of powder, and he's ready.

He sighs. He is twenty years and three thousand miles away from the studio in New York where he started. And here he is, putting on his own makeup. His whole career has been ass-backwards, sliding down the ladder of success. If this works, he'll be back in a city where they hire people to prep your face for you. John Tuttle is holding the door for him on that anchor job with the network's twenty-four hour cable division, MS-UBN in Los Angeles. All Hunter has to do is turn on the charm for the next half-hour or so while they feed this live report back to the network. So what if it's cable? It's still the network. The big time. Prime time.

He can see it clearly now. Bakersfield. The senior housing crisis has come at just the right moment. It was meant to be, because timing is everything. This time, he's in the right place at the right time. For once.

"Here you are. I thought we'd lost you."

Hunter doesn't turn. He can see Kathy in the mirror. She's at the studio door over his left shoulder. Her lips, normally soft and full, are pressed thin, and she is rubbing her palms together slowly, as if to grind away the tension. "You want to explain this to me?" she asks.

"I thought you'd be in the control room."

Kathy coolly says, "I told Van to take over."

"No. I want you there," Hunter says. "This is a golden opportunity. I want the A-team."

"Then why not wait another fifteen minutes? Kent is on his way. He can anchor the special report."

"What? And let Channel 29 beat us?" Hunter turns and jumps over a thick cable that is slithering its way across the studio floor. At the other end, a studio crew member is tugging a camera into position in front of the desk. Hunter gives Kathy a disgusted look as he passes. "What's gotten into you? This is happening now. When did you ever sit on a breaking news story? This is what you live for."

Kathy is right behind Hunter as he steps onto the elevated platform at the anchor desk. He has to push her gently aside in order to take his chair. Van Thompson runs in and slaps a handful of script paper on the desk.

"I'll talk to you on the headsets," he yells as he runs out again.

Hunter starts to scribble a note on the top page, then pauses to insert the earphone that is dangling from a clip on the back of his collar.

Kathy snatches the pages of Hunter's script and fans herself. She looks up, whether uncomfortable with the glare of the studio lights or uncomfortable with the situation, Hunter can only guess.

"This isn't at all about the news," Kathy declares. "This is about that anchor job in L.A."

Hunter doesn't answer. He gives her a slender smile of concession, like a player who has been out-maneuvered. He waits for her next move.

"I just got off the phone with a producer from the network. MS-UBN is going to take our report—live," she says. "I didn't know we were feeding them anything… live."

"John Tuttle said they want it right away." It's a half-truth.

Kathy says, "Tuttle. Right. That producer mentioned in passing that Tuttle and his boss will be watching. Very strange."

"Strange that they would be watching?"

"Strange the way she said it. She said they want to see you. You, Hunter. That's how she said it. You're auditioning, aren't you? That's what this is all about."

Hunter shakes his head. "Not entirely. Yes, they're watching. But we also need to get this on the air, and we need to do it now. You want to do it? We have no one else at the moment, and I've done this a million times."

Hunter can see the floor crew—a mousy college intern named Brandi and some fellow whose name he can't recall—exchange troubled glances. "Two minutes," Brandi sings out. "Two minutes to the open." She puts her hands on her hips and stares at Kathy the way she might chastise an insensitive neighbor who showed up on the doorstep at midnight.

Kathy lowers her voice, but the raspy whisper cuts just as sharply. "You arrogant, selfish basta…ah," She can't finish the word. "Don't do this."

Hunter latches on to the scripts in Kathy's hand. He wins a token tug of war and then spreads them out on the desk in front of him. "You'll never understand," Hunter says. He taps his pencil on the desk. "You've never been an anchor. You don't know what it's like. You don't know how seldom we get to hit a fat pitch like this, and I'm going to hit this baby out of the park. It's golden."

He levels her with a steely look. "This is my last shot."

Hunter makes a note to page four of the script. He has to get focused. He is wasting valuable energy arguing with Kathy.

"One minute!" From the shadows behind the camera, Brandi waves at them to clear the set. Kathy ignores her.

"Tell me," Kathy presses. "What is it you're looking for?"

Hunter slams his pencil on the desk. "What the hell do you think?" he asks. "I want success. Just like everyone else. I want to make it in this business."

Hunter raises a finger to the plastic earpiece. He can hear the News-13 theme music.

Brandi is bouncing nervously on the balls of her feet and looking at Hunter for help. "Stand by," she says. She raises one arm and stands next to the studio camera.

Kathy stares at Hunter as if seeing him for the first time. And it's not a pretty sight. "Success isn't who you are. It's what you do."

She flops to the floor at Hunter's feet behind the desk just as Brandi brings her hand down with a chop toward Hunter the way an executioner might wield her ax. A red tally light above Camera-1 blinks on, telling Hunter he's on the air. "Good afternoon.

This is a News-13 special report. I'm Hunter Riley," he begins.

"More than two-dozen senior citizens are defying authorities at the Emerald Arms in north Bakersfield right now. It is a battle for one of the basic necessities of life."

While Hunter continues to talk, Van Thompson whispers instructions to him through the earpiece. Turn to the second studio camera. Hunter swivels in his chair. With his peripheral vision, he can see the studio monitor. He is now sharing the screen with Sugar. She's standing in front of a police car and yellow tape.

Hunter finishes his sentence and says, "News 13's Sugar Kane was on the scene when at least one gunshot sent officers scrambling just over an hour ago. Sugar, what's the latest?"

Pause. Sugar seems surprised to find Hunter—not Kent—at the anchor desk. "Ah… Hunter. Bakersfield police have the building surrounded right now. I was with the county constables as they tried to serve an eviction notice on the thirty-one residents at the Emerald Arms."

The tally light on Hunter's camera flicks off. The monitor is all Sugar now. Everyone in the studio relaxes while Sugar delivers her report from the street near the Emerald Arms.

Hunter looks down at Kathy, sitting cross-legged on the floor beside him. "Come on. Quit acting so naive." He punches the word, his voice rising from the controlled baritone of his on-camera delivery.

"You know what Sugar said the first time I met her?" Hunter asks. "She looked at me and said, 'Didn't you used to be somebody?' *Used* to be. Let's face it. If you're on TV, you are somebody.

If you're not—you're not."

"Bull. Shit! It sounds like you're on a big ego trip, and you've got a suitcase full of attitude."

"If I anchor the news, I can do it my way. My way. If that's ego, it's the kind that says I want to give the folks at home an honest look at the world around them. The world as I see it, as honestly and accurately as I can paint it."

Hunter's chest is tight. Kathy starts to respond, but he hushes her with a hand. He can hear Sugar's voice in his earpiece. The inflection tells him she is wrapping up. Hunter turns to the camera again.

"Stand by," Brandi wails. The words are barely out of her mouth when she swings her arm down again. Again, the tally light blinks on.

Hunter acknowledges Sugar and begins reading the prepared script from the teleprompter. It's the background information that Van Thompson whipped up. Hunter continues to read, adding his own thoughts to the narrative with each paragraph, while video of the Emerald Arms fills the screen.

Tally light off. Without having to worry about being seen by the audience, Hunter tries to nudge Kathy off the news set. She responds by raising her head above the desk and frowning at him.

Hunter puts his left hand on the top of her head to push Kathy out of sight just as the videotape ends. She grabs his wrist and won't let go, leaving Hunter to lean forward. It has the effect of bringing him intimately closer to the audience.

Tally light on. On camera again, Hunter says, "Now let's go

to Andy Blackman, who is with neighbors of the Emerald Arms."

Tally light off. "Let's have this out later, okay? What are you trying to do?" Hunter hisses at Kathy.

"I'm trying to bring you to your senses," she replies.

"Get off the set. Don't make me pull rank on you."

"Go ahead. At least you'll be doing your job instead of someone else's. You're not the news anchor here. You want the news done your way? It isn't going to happen in L.A. You'll just end up reading somebody else's words. Just another talking head."

"Give me a break."

"You know it's true. You know what the trouble with you is, Hunter? You don't know who you are. You've already been there. Haven't you learned anything?"

Hunter looks anxiously at the monitor, then at Brandi near the camera. He can hear Andy still talking over the video. Hunter keeps his eye on the camera and tries to ignore the woman at his knee. Kathy is not going away.

"You're like two different people," she says. "One is this really nice guy, funny and relaxed and likeable. Then you sit out here, all puffed up with ego, and you become Anchorman," she says this with as much deep timbre as she can put in her voice. "We need to put a big 'A' on your chest. Anchorman. Fighting for truth, justice and the American way. Of course, I can think of something else that 'A' can stand for right now."

"Don't be silly," Hunter says.

"You come here and turn everything upside down. You were the one who said the news business is full of phonies and people acting out the news. You told us—no, you taught us—to be different. 'Just be ourselves', you said, and people would listen."

She raises her hands in mock surrender. "I know. I thought it was crazy, but I've been here a long time, and I've never seen this place run so well before.

"Let's face it, the newscast stunk. We didn't want to admit it. We were so bad, and we were so down on ourselves that we'd given up. You made it fun to come to work again. Even with the whole Sugar-is-a-stripper thing, we have some pride now. That's your talent, Hunter. You can lead. You can inspire the dead."

Hunter shakes his head. "Look. All I need is this audition and I'll be back in the game. I'm every bit as good an anchor as Ryan Billings. I'll show them. And then I can shake the pesticide-ridden dust of this hick town off my feet and be somebody again."

Take it back. Take it back. God, how he wants to take it back. Hunter had stopped thinking and the words fell hard.

Kathy climbs to her feet, digging her nails into Hunter's leg a little more deeply than she needs for support. "You sanctimonious, two-faced… market snob!" she spits. "Go ahead. I hope you get the job. It'll serve you right, although I'm beginning to wonder why anyone would want you in the first place. The only reason you came here is because you couldn't do the job in New York, or even Duluth."

"Des Moines."

"Des Moines. Right. Now there's a paradise for news. And if this town is such a loser, what does that make us?" Kathy storms off the set.

Tally light on. It takes Hunter a moment to realize he is on the air. He watches Kathy wrap her arms across her body, head down, just out of the reach of the studio lights. To you, at home, it looks like Hunter is moved by Andy's thought-provoking interview.

He says, "That was Andy Blackman, live at the scene of what has now become a standoff between police and the senior citizens inside the Emerald Arms." Hunter shuffles his pages. "We will pause here for a commercial, a chance to collect our thoughts and the latest information for you. And we'll be back in a moment."

"We're clear," Brandi announces.

Hunter sits in silence while the commercial rolls.

Van Thompson is in Hunter's earpiece. He passes along new information from Sugar. Hunter raises a finger to his ear and nods to acknowledge Thompson's instructions. He needs to wrap this up after the commercial. He tries to make notes for some final thoughts to share with the viewers. Nothing comes to mind.

"One minute. As if anyone cares," Brandi shouts.

Hunter fidgets. "I'm sorry. I didn't mean it to sound like that," he says to Kathy. She's still standing in the shadows near the door. "Maybe I'm not the best anchor in the world. But when people let you into their homes each night like that, it's as if you become one of their best friends. You'll just never understand how good that makes you feel."

Kathy runs her hands across her face and through her hair, pulling thick strands back on each side. "Good God, Hunter. You sound like Sally Field at the Oscars." Kathy lays her hands above her heart and says in a pathetically flustered voice, "You like me. You really like me."

Hunter shakes his head.

Kathy continues, "Isn't it more important to have one real friend? One true friend you can share things with, instead of this silly one-way relationship with a mass of faces you'll never get to know?

"And I'll tell you—as a friend, Hunter. You want success? Then practice what you preach."

Brandi steps forward. She doesn't want to intrude, she says, but just wanted to remind them that the last commercial is running, and we'll be back on television live in a moment. Thank you for listening. Are you listening?

Hunter isn't. "Practice what?" he asks Kathy.

"Just find yourself, and success will find you. Isn't that what you've been telling us since you got here? You're the one who has to find himself. Then maybe you can stop chasing these damned studio lights all over the country."

Kathy spins for the studio door, leaving Hunter less than ten seconds to pick his jaw off the floor.

Tally light on.

Slug: Standoff—Day Three

Anchor intro:

> *The Doldrums.*
>
> *It's not just a state of mind. It's an actual spot on the ocean near the equator where inconsistent and meager winds can leave a sailor drifting aimlessly for days on end.*
>
> *News stories like the crisis at the Emerald Arms have their doldrums if they carry on too long. By the second or third day, inconsistent and meager information can leave a reporter adrift in something of a topical depression...*
>
> *Adrift and praying for a small storm, a medium squall or a hurricane...*

Roll tape

"That really blows!"

Lee Richards scrunches his nose as he pulls the pink umbrella from a frosty glass filled with sunset-colored daiquiri.

"Blows big time," he says. "The cops are being hard-nosed bastards just because they can."

Six heads around the table nod in weary agreement. By now, the argument is as tired as they are. It's Saturday, the third full day of what has become the siege at the Emerald Arms. The cops have the building surrounded. Reverend Sam and his followers are barricaded inside. They're refusing to come out until they get a fair hearing from the city. The cops are refusing to give them any slack, and are offering even less to the news folks who are starved for information back at the roadblock where reporters have camped out with satellite trucks and cameras.

"I can't get any of my sources downtown to talk," Kathy says. "A total news gag." She shakes her head. Bakersfield P.D. won't stage a photo opportunity or even schedule a press briefing to say nothing is new. "And no leaks? Very strange."

"Blame Waco," Hunter says. "Ever since the Feds took it on the chin for that, everyone spends more time watching their backs than dealing with the kooks in front of them."

"Those kooks," Sugar says with a hard look at Hunter, "have enough food for a couple of weeks. And they're going to stay there just as long as Reverend Sam wants. It's all about making some kind of political statement with all this. That's what Reverend Sam is all about."

"Great. Don't they know we ran out of things to talk about yesterday?" Kathy stares down at cold fried rice and scallops that are rapidly turning to rubber in the bottom of a hollowed-out pineapple. It was tasty enough half an hour ago. She can't finish it; fatigue has sapped her appetite. But then, no one comes to this restaurant for the food anyway. It's the large and cheap tropical drinks that draw a crowd to Tai Won Nyong.

Hunter gets up and steps over to the bar. A large television set on the wall facing them is tuned to Channel 17. He takes a remote control from the bartender and returns to their table. Sugar, Kathy and the others on what Hunter has dubbed their "A-shift" should be home resting. Twelve hours on and twelve hours off. Hunter has divided the staff and assigned everyone a task so that each key job is covered around the clock for the duration of the standoff.

Who knows when the FBI or the ATF might move in? Or a renegade pack of girl scouts might pelt the building with Thin Mints and storm the Emerald Arms to end the siege. Maybe Sam will get bored and surrender. Who knows? The cops aren't talking, but Hunter wants to be prepared.

The "Z-shift", as in covering the story A-to-Z, is on duty. Andy Blackman is out at the scene, and Kent is back in the newsroom to give anyone who is watching updates every hour on the hour. So far the script has been simple.

"Nothing new. More at five o'clock."

"Nothing new. More at six o'clock."

"Nothing new..."

It's seven o'clock. They all turn to the TV. Hunter switches to Channel 13.

"From the heart of the Golden Empire. This is a News-13 Special Report." The announcer's voice fades and Kent Abernathy is on the air. His wig is slightly askew and his tie is loose at the collar, but he appears to be holding up well. He tells Bakersfield the standoff continues and police are negotiating with Reverend Sam. More in an hour. Now back to Saturday Night Theater. The movie: "The Alamo" with John Wayne.

It was a last-minute programming coup by someone in the corner office at KDOA to have the Duke under siege in prime time, while the senior citizens are holed up and in the news.

"And details at eleven." Hunter wonders what they could possibly come up with in the next three hours to give the story new legs. He sinks into the booth next to Sugar; exhaustion pushes him deep into what little padding it provides. The adrenaline that permeated the start of the story has run its course. They've spent fourteen hours on the air with the Emerald Arms in two days.

As if that hasn't been enough to wear Hunter down, the war on the second front has added to his fatigue. That battle with the station owner, Andrews, has reached a stalemate not much different than the one they were covering at the Emerald Arms. The station owner keeps putting off a decision to just fire Hunter outright. Or maybe he's doing it out of spite. Andrews' story is that he'd rather not fire Hunter in the middle of the ratings period, no matter how much of a fuckup he is. So he tells Hunter that he'll keep him until the November numbers are back. Unless, of course, he changes his mind in the morning. Each successive morning. So stay tuned.

"We need to generate something new," Hunter says.

"We need to find a way to get this over with," Sugar says.

"Wrap it. Put a bow on it and move on," Kathy agrees.

Ray the WebGuy says something like, "Input data download nary a binary html three-point-oh and multi-task a memory crash on the vinyl server."

Hunter just nods in agreement. Whatever.

A drunk with a beer belly too big for his XXL USC jersey wanders out of the men's room and back to his barstool. "Hey! Who turned off the friggin' game?" He glares at Hunter and the others. By the time he drains the last of his mug and orders another, the bartender has switched channels and replaced John Wayne with the Trojans-Longhorns' shootout from some football field north of the Alamo. The dudes from California are driving on the Texans, looking to score before halftime.

Sugar says, "Maybe we should just let Reverend Sam have his say. We can do that. We can tell the police we'll promise him some air time if he'll give up."

"Been there," Kathy says.

"Done that," Hunter finishes. "Everybody in town has offered to be the exclusive camera for a one-on-one with Sam."

"Yeah, but don't you think he'd pick us first? After all we've done for him," Richards says.

"Either way, the cops won't allow it. It would only encourage other nut cases," Hunter says.

First kooks and now nut cases. Sugar bangs her drink on the table and glares at Hunter. "Don't call them names. That's cruel. We should be trying to help these folks. I thought that's what we were trying to do."

"We were doing a great job. Sam's the one who went postal on us," Hunter replies. It's an anemic attempt to deflect any blame, and at least part of the guilt that has been dogging him. Hunter knows he is the one who provided Reverend Sam with the platform. And he is the one who had encouraged Sam's grandstanding style that has turned the story into a crisis. The table is silent. They also know blaming Sam is only half the answer.

Hunter looks at Kathy—Kathy who wears her heart on her sleeve, and her thoughts on yellow sticky notes pasted where the entire world can read them. Her mouth twitches as she watches him. She must have expected a better answer than that.

Slowly, he eases into a confession of remorse and regret. He shouldn't have jumped on the story as a quick fix for their ratings. Thinking it through now… Maybe the combination of fatigue and strong drink helps grease his squeaky emotional wheel, but Hunter is finding some comfort there. It's a new experience to let his guard down so completely. He drones on and he rambles, and he loses their attention long before his soul is bare enough to be interesting.

"It's a situation that is even more disturbing when you look at it from this angle." The voice floats over Hunter's shoulder. One look at the faces around the table, and he realizes they haven't heard a word he's said. They're riveted to the scene on the bar television.

Halftime at the football game has given the competition a window for its own update on the standoff. Right now, they're showing you an aerial view of the neighborhood.

"They put up a helicopter this afternoon," Kathy moans. "Why can't we have a chopper?"

"D.O.A. nixed it. Too expensive," Hunter says. It was one of the first items Hunter had asked for, but the station owner just laughed and half-jokingly pleaded with Hunter, "Don't make me fire you in the morning."

It has been hard enough for Hunter to get approval for all the overtime. "I guess he figures with all the advertising revenue we've lost since Thursday, he won't spend a dime more than he has to."

As for the rest of the world, it is as if Los Angeles and the networks suddenly woke up to find this big story under a rock. Helicopters, satellite vans and a small army of reporters have invaded Bakersfield, each one trying to outmaneuver the others for a tidbit of fresh information. Hunter can barely compete with the better financed local TV stations, let alone the slick-looking, slick-talking big markets. He is outgunned, and he knows it.

And then, as if to rub salt into his wounds, *she* pops up on TV.

"Hey! It's Valerie."

They all knew Valerie Watson had walked out the door at KDOA and marched directly over to the competition. She has joined the enemy, and now she is in their face with this live report.

Hunter grabs the remote control and turns up the volume.

"...And I have just been told that the FBI has moved in and set up its own command post. Federal agents are taking over as this drama unfolds."

Hunter looks at the others. "Did we have that?" He goes fishing in his pocket for a cell phone. It's not there. "Kathy, do you have the cell phone?"

She shakes her head. "One is back at the station charging the battery, and Andy has the other out at the live truck."

"Son of a ... " Hunter jumps up. "I'll call the newsroom. I hope Van knows about this already."

He looks down the length of the bar for a telephone and barely takes two steps before Valerie's words stop him.

"The bigger story tonight is the true identity of the Senior Bandit. Ever since his arrest, many people have assumed Reverend Sam Cross is guilty of robbing banks to keep the Emerald Arms from going under. If he isn't guilty, why have police responded with such a strong show of force? If Sam Cross isn't guilty, why won't he surrender? It may be mistaken identity. It appears the police have the wrong man. We have exclusive…"

There's that word. Exclusive. It turns Hunter's stomach to hear the competition flaunt it.

"…Exclusive information on that. Hear the *real* bandit's dramatic confession tonight on the news at eleven."

The picture cuts back to the news anchor in the studio. His slow response suggests that even he didn't know Valerie was about to drop that bombshell. He recaps the story and advises viewers to tune in for that exclusive—did we mention it was exclusive—Valerie Watson report tonight at eleven.

Decimated by the news, they sit at the table looking to each other for an explanation that doesn't exist.

Finally Sugar says, "That can't be. I mean, it can. But it can't."

"A confession?"

"If Reverend Sam isn't the bandit, who is?"

Hunter locks his fingers together and cups the top of his head as if trying to keep it from erupting. Spontaneous combustion might be a pleasant alternative to living with the aftermath of Valerie's scoop.

"Who has she been talking to?"

No one has an answer. If Reverend Sam is not the Senior

Bandit, he's the biggest con man Hunter has ever encountered. And Hunter is the victim. All that news coverage KDOA provided in exchange for what? No wonder Sam surrendered so easily. He's not guilty. He knows they can't prove anything.

"But what about the money?" Kathy asks.

"And the security video? Even with that funny wig and hat, it looks like Sam."

"Yeah. And what about the witness who says she thinks Sam's the bandit?"

Too many questions. Still, the only one that matters tonight is what does Valerie know?

Hunter turns to Sugar. "You know Sam best. You said he wasn't guilty before. Do you know something?"

"I… I don't know. Really I don't. We need to talk to Sam."

"We can't, oh bodacious one," Richards says. "The cops have locked up the phone line, and we can't get anywhere near the building. So what's a mother to do?"

Ray the WebGuy has been leaning against the table, twirling Lee Richards' discarded pink umbrella. "Just a thought," he says.

And then he asks a question. It takes a moment to sink in, but it is the only thing Ray has ever said that Hunter doesn't need a Geek-speak translator for. It is simple. It is clear. And if God has a sense of humor at all, it is brilliant.

"Are they on the Internet?"

Slug: Day Three—Reverend Sam

Anchor intro:

> *Since the days of Thomas Paine and Benjamin Franklin, revolutionaries in America have used the press to spread their message. It's a powerful tool when you're locked in a battle over principle.*
>
> *Reverend Sam Cross understands this. He has been holed up inside the Emerald Arms with his senior citizens and his ideals for three days, taking advantage of the standoff and using it as a media event to grab the spotlight for his own attempt at social revolution.*
>
> *Carpe diem. He has not only seized the day, he has seized the night, and the 11 o'clock Report as well.*
>
> *Carpe newsum.*

Roll tape

First you hear the deep sigh and then angry mutters. A human shadow slides across the lobby floor of the Emerald Arms, and if you follow its shape, you'll find the feet attached to Reverend Sam as he paces in front of the open door to his apartment. The lamp beyond that door lays a narrow carpet of light across the dark lobby.

On the opposite side, Sam Junior leans against the wall near his office and worries. "You look exhausted. Aren't you ready to raise the white flag yet?"

"I have asked for a meeting with the Secretary of Housing. They're working on it." Reverend Sam chuckles. "I told them not to call back until he's ready to talk."

Sam Junior shakes his head. "Seriously? Why not ask to see President Clinton while you're at it? The police are not going to set up a meeting with Washington, even if you could get someone out there to agree to it."

"But it makes a great headline."

"Will you stop that?" The uneasiness Junior has been feeling since they locked up the Emerald Arms two days ago is swelling into anger. "I'm tired of headlines and TV interviews. We're all tired of it, and we want our lives back. Nice, quiet lives."

"I don't hear any complaints." Reverend Sam points to the ceiling and makes a little circle in the air. "Ask them. Everyone is behind me on this. It will be over when I say it is over."

"Right. That's why Mrs. Henderson and the Bartons and the others are hiding in their rooms upstairs right now. They don't want any part of this," Junior counters. "Dad, you dragged them into it. They're just too scared to stand up to you. Everyone except Major Tom. But we've got him back on his meds and, anyway, he won't come out of the closet since we took his gun away."

Reverend Sam stands there with his hands on his hips, staring at Junior. They seldom exchange cross words, but every time they do, Junior comes away feeling like a small boy. Even as he approaches fifty years old, taking on his father is not a battle Junior goes into lightly.

Sam Junior looks over his shoulder. Their angry voices have disturbed J.B. Hickok dozing in his usual spot, the easy chair on the far side of the room. The actor shifts and drapes a leg over the armrest, and his head drops heavily to his chest.

"Well," Reverend Sam says. "It's nice to see a little fire in you. Even if it is misdirected."

He folds his arms and resumes his pacing. He moves out of the light and into the middle of the lobby. "This may be our last chance to shake things up. If they don't have the moral backbone at City Hall and in Washington to deal with the aged and the poor and the homeless, then we will have to force their hand."

Junior makes an obvious turn to his left and then to his right, searching for something.

"What is it?" Reverend Sam asks.

"The way you were preaching at me, I was sure someone had turned on a TV camera," Junior says. He lobs this at Reverend Sam with derision, but inside Junior is frightened.

Over the years, Reverend Sam has managed to keep his public and his private personalities separate. Junior could joke about his father keeping a special suit of indignation in a secret closet that he would pull out and wear just for the media. Like Superman's cape.

But as the battle over the Emerald Arms has escalated, Reverend Sam's use of his alter ego has become less calculated. It's as if Media Sam is taking over. Media Sam shows up for breakfast and lectures them over dinner. He is there morning, noon and night.

And you only have to peek through the window at the glare of the spotlights and the police with their guns surrounding the Emerald Arms to see the trouble Media Sam has stirred up. It's no longer a war of words. Those are real guns.

Reverend Sam says, "Don't try to tell me you disagree. This is something that is bigger than us all. And we have a chance to do something about it. We have to look beyond the Emerald Arms."

"And lose it in the process? I don't care about the big picture or marching on Washington or fighting the injustice of it all. I just want our folks to have a roof over their heads and keep them from starving. I haven't the time to worry about the masses," Junior says. "I'm worried about Louisa and Mrs. Henderson and the others. What are *they* going to do if we have to close the Emerald Arms?"

Reverend Sam looks at his son. "That's your soft heart. I've always said you have your mother's compassion; God rest her soul. But haven't I taught you anything? You rely too much on others. Sometimes you just have to take matters into your own hands."

"You have no idea what I've had to do to keep us going. What you've done has alienated a lot of people with the money to help us. These are people we could tap for donations if you weren't constantly criticizing them in public. And now this."

"What?"

"Jumping up and claiming to be the Senior Bandit. That's exactly what I've been talking about. Grabbing all that attention and damn the consequences. On top of it all, it's a lie!"

"Is it?" Reverend Sam asks.

"You know it is." A faint tremble begins making its way through Sam Junior's body. He can feel it rising to the surface. "That's it. I'm going to go out there. It's time to end this thing."

Junior is three steps to the door when Reverend Sam grabs his arm and swings him around. The preacher has considerable strength for someone his age. "What are you going to tell them? You can't stop this alone."

"I don't know. Maybe I'll just tell them that *I'm* the bandit. If it's good enough for you..." Sam Junior wonders. What would he tell the police?

"That's ludicrous; it won't solve anything."

"No? Tell me why not?" Sam Junior raises his voice. The words are rough and scrape his throat as they escape.

"Just shut up!"

Now the anger is hurled from across the room. Both men turn to see Hickok standing now. "Shit or get off the pot! We're trying to sleep over here. Do you mind?" Hickok shakes his head and shuffles toward the kitchen, possibly headed for Mr. Marika's quiet cubbyhole in the basement.

When the actor is out of sight, Reverend Sam lowers his voice and says, "The point is, I know who the bandit is..."

The words stop Sam Junior more than any strong-arm tug on his elbow could have. "Oh yeah? Who?"

Reverend Sam looks past his son and then at each of the walls as if inspecting them for spies. He raises a finger to his lips. "It doesn't matter, Junior. Surely you can see that the real identity of the bandit is immaterial. All that really matters is that we can use this to our advantage."

Advantage? He stares into the eyes of his father. The old man may know the bandit's identity but he truly could not care less. Even if Sam Junior had pulled off the robberies himself, it wouldn't matter. The bandit could be one of the poor residents at the Emerald Arms, or a misguided ex-con—part of that blindly loyal congregation that followed Sam out of prison. The bandit could be the devil or Mother Teresa; it would all be the same to Reverend Sam—just one more puppet, one more opportunity to be controlled by the preacher. The thought is disgusting, and it stings Sam Junior more than he wants to admit.

"You... fool!" Sam Junior doesn't use that word comfortably in the shadow of his father. "You—pretending to be the bandit—got us where we are tonight! If you hadn't done that, we wouldn't have lost the city's money, and we wouldn't have an eviction notice. And we wouldn't have residents hiding upstairs, and we wouldn't have police surrounding the building. This time you have really gone too far!"

"How many times must I say this? Every worthy cause needs a lightning rod. That's how things get done. I am that lightning rod. Do you hear me? I am a lightning rod."

Sam Junior can almost hear the thunder. The words raise hair on the back of his neck. Reverend Sam has fought many battles, but he's never before seemed so dangerous. Now he has drawn a black cloud over everyone at the Emerald Arms. They don't need a lightning rod, not with an army of police outside their front door ready to strike.

But Reverend Sam won't be dissuaded. "As long as they think I'm the bandit, the media, the public and maybe those spineless creatures down at City Hall will pay attention. Without that... they don't care about us. And if they don't care about us, we'll shrivel up and die."

"But you are not the bandit, and they're going to throw you in jail unless you set them straight."

"I've been in jail before, and it doesn't scare me. Besides, they'll never be able to prove it. They can't prove it. That is the beauty of this. It's also something the bandit couldn't anticipate. Since the bandit wore that bit of disguise, what must have been a wig and that silly baseball cap, the witnesses aren't reliable. And he didn't leave any fingerprints behind."

"No, but they have all that money with the serial numbers they've traced back here. And with what you gave away to Mr. Shurman for their refrigerator, and Mrs. Hall's funeral, and those little handouts to the others, that's like putting your fingerprints all over the place."

"Circumstantial. The money was stolen from the bank and deposited in our collection box." Reverend Sam points to the chapel. "And if anyone asks..."

Father and son stare at each other, knowing that long ago they had resolved the answer to that one.

"It's a gift from God," they say in unison.

Junior folds his arms, adopting his father's posture as they stand in the box of light coming from Reverend Sam's apartment. "Too bad the bandit can't help us now. Really, Dad. We can't go on much longer. This has to stop."

Reverend Sam agrees. "But we need to hold out as long as possible, or until we get a fair hearing. Anything less is defeat."

"So a three-day sit-in isn't enough for you to make your point?"

"Tomorrow is Sunday. I'd say three days is enough as long as they give us an opportunity for one last public statement."

"The chances of that are pretty slim." Sam Junior's heart sinks. He looks at his father in the eerie and inconsistent light of the hotel lobby. It has come down to interviews and sound bites. Access to the media has turned the reverend into something larger—and in Junior's mind, uglier than life.

If they had access to the media right now, Reverend Sam could have his say and surrender. But for the first time in the long battle over the Emerald Arms, that vital link to the outside is being denied to them. Authorities control their telephone lines. You can't get a dial tone from the office or any of the apartments upstairs. Months ago, Junior tried to justify spending the money on a cell phone but couldn't find room for it in the budget.

The police have made it clear they won't let reporters anywhere near Reverend Sam and the Emerald Arms. No interview? No surrender. So the standoff continues.

It turns out the solution is at his fingertips. Sam Junior still doesn't realize that as he sits at his computer half an hour later. At least the cops hadn't yet cut off the cable line that feeds his internet connection. He is sending an email to Ginny and Chuck Barton's son in San Jose. Jerry Barton has been following the story up in the Bay Area and—Jerry being Jerry—he wouldn't bother to pick up the phone when he can communicate by computer. Ironically, tonight it's his only option.

As he sits in front of the screen, Sam Junior is grateful Bakersfield P.D. has overlooked this. He hasn't used a conventional telephone line for the Internet since the local cable company began offering the service. It was an easy deal to get. Reverend Sam promised not to raise a ruckus over the cable TV company's abysmal record of meeting community service standards under its contract with the city. In exchange, the Emerald Arms and other vital non-profit groups get free TV and access to the Internet.

Sam Junior rubs his chin. It's hard to ignore some of the benefits of his father's selective use of blackmail for charity. Email is one. And it eases some of Junior's anger at being trapped inside the Emerald Arms.

But his father has changed. He's become more volatile than ever, and he has no right to risk the well being of the residents here. They are frightened. They will run out of food and medicine soon. The stress of living under siege, alone, is enough to cause a heart attack. And the longer this standoff lasts, the greater the risk. They have to end it soon.

After sending his reply to Jerry Barton's message on its way, Sam Junior finds a new one in the electronic mailbox. This email is from Sugar Kane and Channel 13 News.

"Do you...?"

"Can you...?"

"Will you...?"

He reads the question twice and then dives for a box under his desk. He digs until he finds the long-forgotten computer software and equipment he had toyed with the day Sugar Kane made her first visit to the Emerald Arms. He studies the contents of the box for a moment. If he can make this work, they can end the standoff peacefully tonight. All he needs is his father's cooperation. Given the allure of the spotlight and the size of Media Sam's ego lately, that should be the easy part.

Peace tonight. He taps his reply on the keyboard and sends out the message. He'll find a way to make it work.

Channel 13 has a plan.

And Junior has hope.

Slug: Valerie's Scoop

Anchor intro:

> Sometimes you eat the bear, and sometimes the bear eats you. That's life.
>
> Sometimes you scoop the competition, and sometimes it scoops you. That's TV news.
>
> Beating the competition is also the sweetest form of revenge in this business—but not the only one. So it is wise to be careful of whom you scoop, because payback's a bitch.
>
> And sometimes she carries a microphone.

Roll tape

The little mailbox icon sits on the computer screen and mocks you with its silence. It is still empty.

You've got *no* mail.

You've got no hope.

Everything hinges on Reverend Sam responding to Hunter's urgent email. That, and pulling it all together on Sam's end of the line.

The clock is pushing ten. They still haven't hooked up with the preacher. Ray the WebGuy says he's ready. "Phat City," was the term he used. Hunter suspects that's a good thing.

Kathy has assigned Hunter the most critical job: baby-sit the computer to catch Reverend Sam's message the moment he sends it. He waits at his desk.

Two raps on the door. Monsanto Head is leaning into the office. Kent Abernathy's space-age fiber hair appears to be on backwards.

"Kent? Your wwwi...your hair is a bit out of sorts." Hunter swirls his hands around his own head to demonstrate.

Kent puts a hand on the wig, pressing it into his head. "Oh," he says. He stands there for a long time. The silence is getting on Hunter's nerves when Kent says, "I heard Valerie has an exclusive scoop on the Senior Bandit."

Hunter tells him what they had heard at the bar.

With one hand still holding the wig in place, Kent puts the thumbnail of his other hand against his teeth as he smiles. The smile grows. Impish, he looks like a child with a five o'clock shadow.

"What?" Hunter wants to know.

Kent just nods and bounces across the newsroom to where Kathy is busy at her desk. He fails to interrupt her, so he just bounces out of sight.

Hunter is still scratching his own head over Kent's behavior as his eyes rest on the amazing Kathy Wright. Kathy is juggling two phone conversations, a dozen assignments and assorted staff, while walking a tight rope of civility with every source she has around the Bakersfield Police Department. If just one of them has even a hint of what Valerie Watson is up to, Kathy will get it out of them.

Hunter tries to remember what Kathy had said in the studio. He could have her fired for talking to him like that in front of the staff. What did she say about friends? Did she mean as in "Friends"—with a capital "F"? Friends as in potential lovers? He watches her, and the picture in his mind has a soft focus around all the edges. She is gorgeous. If different people shine under different conditions, under the stress of breaking news, Kathy radiates beauty. Or maybe Hunter just sees it that way.

Ring.

Distracted, Hunter snatches the computer mouse.

Click. The mailbox is still empty.

Ring.

No, it's the telephone.

"Yeah?" Hunter grouses.

John Tuttle. Tuttle says he counted on catching Hunter in the office, at his post in the middle of this big story. Tuttle, on the other hand, is in some L.A. bar with a drink in one hand and a cell phone in the other. If he had a third hand, it would be on the waitress.

"Bad timing, John," Hunter says. "We're in the middle of breaking something."

Oh? UBN, like all the other itinerant organizations that moved crews to Bakersfield for only as long as the story is hot, is simply waiting for the standoff to end. To the network, the siege at the Emerald Arms has slipped from lead story to the third segment. What's so new?

With nothing to do but wait on Reverend Sam, Hunter

explains the threat Valerie poses. "She has something on this. We can't figure it out. What's worse, we can't find out," Hunter says.

"But on the other hand…" Hunter explains his plan to put Reverend Sam on the Internet, and from there—on TV, if they can make it work.

In 1996, before Facebook and YouTube and even Google, for God's sake, this is a brilliant idea. Tuttle is genuinely impressed, and first thing Monday morning he will have his own internet staff look into how it can be used for future stories. Which brings us to Monday morning.

"What about it?" Hunter asks. His heartbeat picks up. Tuttle tells him the boss, Walter Redmond, wants to make a decision on the L.A. anchor job for their cable news arm. If Hunter is in town Monday morning, they could seal it with an interview and probably have a contract in hand by happy hour.

"So Redmond liked the live report I did?"

He was adequately impressed.

"Adequately?" Hunter asks, unsatisfied. "What does that mean?"

The answer is somewhere between nominally enthused and knocking his socks off. But Tuttle swears a face-to-face meeting Monday would swing it in Hunter's favor. Definitely. Tuttle will set it up.

"I'm not sure I can make it if this story is still happening," Hunter says. He feels "adequately" interested in the offer right now. "This is a really big story. I can't run off to L.A. right in the middle of it."

Tuttle poses a question. Does Hunter want this one big story or a career? It may come down to that.

Yes folks, it's time for *Let's Make a Deal.* Hunter can trade what he has in the box for whatever is behind door number two. Hmmm. Before he can decide, Hunter's computer pings.

"Gotta run, John. Set up the meeting. I'll see you in L.A."

Hunter's fingers leap from the mouse to the keyboard, where they tap dance across the keys. Reverend Sam got his email.

"Instant chat?" Hunter types.

"Hello." The chat message box pops up on Hunter's screen. Reverend Sam is online right now. This might work.

"We don't have much time," Hunter types. He explains his plan. Is Reverend Sam willing? And do they have the equipment?

"Yes. And yes."

"Yessss!" Hunter bangs a fist on the keyboard and sends a line of dashes across the screen. He types instructions to Reverend Sam and directs him to Ray the WebGuy, who is waiting for him at his own souped-up computer terminal down the hall. Hunter logs off and rushes out to the newsroom.

Kathy is at her desk. Her face is buried in her hands, and she's wearing a rogue yellow sticky note like a tiny hat on top of her head. It says R.I.P.

"We're dead." Kathy doesn't look up.

"Dead?"

"They just ran another promo. Valerie is going to have the Senior Bandit—the *real* Senior Bandit—surrender live on the news at eleven."

"Damn! Okay. Okay." Hunter holds his hands out, palms down and measures the implications. "It's okay." It's not as okay as he'd like.

Kathy responds as if Hunter had said nothing. "I tried everything, and called everyone. I can't get a line on Valerie's guy. All I know is she cut a deal with the guy to surrender. The cops didn't even know about it until the promos started running."

"Let her have the bandit," Hunter says. "The big story is going on at the Emerald Arms. The whole world is watching that. We've got Sam, and he'll give us what we need. Screw Valerie."

"You got him?" Kathy snaps up in her chair. "Is it going to work?"

Hunter nods.

"Hunter, I could kiss you." Her laugh is coy. Her eyes have an unmistakable spark of hope.

Now there's a thought. Hunter places his palms on her desk and leans forward. "Okay," his voice dares her.

Sugar buzzes past them and waves as she heads for the door. She's on her way to the Emerald Arms for a live report at eleven. She bumps a photographer who is headed in the opposite direction. A phone rings. Van Thompson slides up to his desk nearby with a stack of scripts. All the activity is swirling around Hunter and Kathy like the wind around the eye of a storm.

Kathy leans tantalizingly closer. She takes a pencil from the desk and writes a line with a slow, deliberate hand on the tiny yellow note pad there. She peels the top page and slaps it into place just below her neckline. "I'm busy right now. But this will remind me." Then she spins away, picks up the phone and begins barking instructions.

Too much to do. Too little time to prepare. Kathy and Van get to work on last-minute scripts for the eleven o'clock news. Hunter searches out Kent in the studio. The anchor is adjusting his wig and putting another layer of powder on his nose in front of the makeup mirror. Hunter gives him a quick briefing on what to expect.

"What about Valerie?" Kent wants to know.

"It sounds like she's going live with the bandit," Hunter replies. "But screw Valerie."

Kent sticks out his lower lip and puts on a mock frown. "Yeah. Screw Valerie."

Hunter darts off to the control room where the director, Lee, is wearing his crash helmet.

"Fly or die. That's my motto," Lee says.

Ray the WebGuy has the hookups and the downloads. He is as serene as Hunter is roused. What's the worst that could happen?

"The gateway interloper could resist a mega source video stream lock up Cuisinart with photon diddle and may The Force be with you," Ray says.

"We could byte the big one?"

"A veritable cyber face plant!"

It's a scary thought as Hunter returns to his office. He drops in front of the computer and begins composing a series of questions for Reverend Sam. He's racing the clock but he is careful with the wording. No softball interview here. Fine-tuning the question frequently makes the difference between getting a telling answer and a slippery evasion.

Hunter wants Sam to account for his actions and the danger he has thrust on the seniors. It's time for Sam to own up to his role in what has turned out to be nothing more than a grandstanding public relations campaign that has brought them to the brink of disaster.

"For our part, we can share the blame," Hunter types.

More importantly, it's time to let it end. Let Valerie Watson have her bandit. Reverend Sam can surrender to them live on News-13 and end the standoff.

Hunter prints out a copy of the questions and takes the page to Kathy. "Get on the phone to Sugar and pass these along to her."

Eleven o'clock.

Fancy graphics—the familiar peacock and the unblinking CBS eye, the network logos and the local stations' identities all dance across the bank of monitors in Hunter's newsroom like carnival barkers competing for attention. All of the local channels open their newscasts with the latest from the Emerald Arms, except Valerie Watson's station.

No. It begins with its "exclusive, breaking news story. Valerie Watson is live at the Sycamore Hills apartments in east Bakersfield with this shocking report."

Hunter and Kathy stand in the center of the newsroom. It's deserted. They have their own newscast to worry about. Hunter tries to concentrate on the monitor on the far left—KDOA. He agonizes. Torn between duty and the voyeur inside, curiosity gets the best of him. Valerie steals his attention.

"Don't waste my time, Valerie," Hunter mumbles. He turns up the volume on her station. "This had better be worth it."

Valerie strolls confidently into the picture of a large sign in front of the apartment complex. The Sycamore Hills Apartments. There is no mistaking Valerie's location, and she calls attention to that. "The man who has robbed a number of Bakersfield banks lives here, in this non-descript complex on the east side."

Kathy looks at Hunter. "Can you say… 'allegedly'?"

"Vintage Valerie. She'll never be slowed down by anything like that," Hunter replies. It's easy to smile, but the bitterness of being scooped is hard to swallow. His insides are churning.

"Joining me now is Rory Calhoun," Valerie continues. "If his face looks familiar, you've seen it here on Channel 26 and in the newspapers. And in the photos from the security cameras at four different South Valley Bank branches."

A tall, thin man with collar-length gray hair and a baseball cap steps into the glare of the television lights. He's wearing a nylon jogging suit and holding a leather strap. The camera pulls back. It's a dog leash with a black Chihuahua on the other end. The dog appears more nervous than its master. But then, it *is* a Chihuahua. All in all, neither strikes much fear into the heart.

"Is that him?" Kathy asks.

"It kind of looks like him. I think it's him."

Valerie steps closer, like a vulture about to tear bits of flesh from a carcass on highway asphalt. "For months, no one has known the identity of the Senior Bandit," she says. "Why have you come forward tonight?"

Rory Calhoun pauses. "I've been watching you on the news. I like the way you've been reporting it. I wouldn't think of talking to anyone else. You know, you're even better looking in person than you are on TV."

What the hell kind of answer is that?

All business, Valerie replies. "Yes. But why rob banks?"

"Why does someone rob banks? Because that's where the money is." Rory chuckles. It's an old joke. He's not taking the interview nearly as seriously as Valerie Watson. He scratches his head.

Kent Abernathy streaks into the newsroom and skids to a stop at Hunter's elbow. He straightens up and tries to compose himself, though he's clearly out of breath.

"What are you doing down here?" Kathy asks.

"Sugar has the live shot. She's going to talk straight through until we hit the first commercial." Kent thrusts his hands into his pockets. "I just wanted to see how it's going."

He points and directs their attention again to the television where you can now see a close-up of the Senior Bandit. "And I didn't want to miss this. Nice wig."

"If anyone would know about wearing a rug, Monsanto Head would," Kathy mumbles.

Hunter jabs an elbow in her side and shifts his eyes back and forth between the anchor and the TV monitor where Valerie is struggling to get a straight answer from the mysterious bandit. Oh shit! The bandit is a phony.

"I'll bet you know where he got it, too," Hunter says.

Kent Abernathy nods and scratches the corner of his mouth. "My… ah, my barber."

Only Kent could say that with a straight face, Hunter thinks.

"My barber. I bet him he couldn't fool her into an interview. It's going to cost me a hundred dollars."

Hunter's stares at Kent, and his mind flashes back to the first time he saw the Channel 13 anchor. It was that quarrel in the newsroom with Valerie. The shrieking, troublesome Valerie who sends everyone running for cover. Now Hunter gawks at Kent with amazement and no small amount of new admiration. "A hundred dollars? It's worth it at twice the price."

Kent shrugs. "I knew I'd lose. That's Valerie, right? Never checks her facts, but really, I didn't think it would be this easy."

On the television, the fake bandit asks, "Did I mention how much better you look in person than on TV? No wonder you used to dance naked at that nightclub. That's okay. It doesn't bother me."

Valerie had been so intent on bending the bizarre interview to fit her story, it has taken until now to realize she's been snookered. The reality sets in. It's in her face, and it doesn't take much imagination to see her growing devil's horns and snorting flames. "You are thinking of someone else," she says with so much venom even Hunter shudders.

She places a hand firmly on Rory Calhoun's chest and forces him aside as she squares to the camera.

"What? You're not the nice lady from Channel 13? That's the only station…"

The rest is obscured by the sound of wrestling from somewhere off camera and Valerie's attempt to explain away the fiasco.

Hunter's knees go weak. He leans back against the desk. "Holy shit," he says. "Kathy. Hand me one of your little yellow stickies. I want to make a note to find that guy and kiss him."

Someone back at Valerie's station should have had enough heart and good sense to pull the plug on her. But they leave her dangling on the air, attempting to wrap up the story with rambling thoughts on the pitfalls of live television. All the while, Valerie keeps dropping her head and looking at her feet. Her photographer takes that as a cue, and he zooms out to a wider angle just in time to see the little Chihuahua lower his hind leg and pad off into the night.

A voice floats out of the darkness. "Ah, Montezuma. You shouldn't have done that."

In the News-13 newsroom, they are doubled up with laughter. Hunter can barely breathe. Kathy is wiping a tear from her eye when she jumps up.

"Oh my God. Here it is. Sugar's starting the interview with Reverend Sam. Turn it up. Turn it up!"

Hunter kills the volume on the piddled-upon Valerie Watson and turns up Sugar Kane. "Kent," he commands. Hunter makes a feeble attempt to be stern. "Get your ass up on the set where you belong. And I want you in my office when the newscast is over."

"Right." Kent swaggers to the door. Still smiling he asks, "We're going to catch hell for this, aren't we?"

The question doesn't need an answer. Hunter simply points a finger past Kent to shoo him down the hall.

Amused, Kent takes a sliding step that direction. "You know what they say. Payback's a bitch. And so is that dog."

Slug: Day Three—Sam's Interview

Anchor intro:

A news story is like an onion. Peel away one layer, and you find another. And another. Each one gets you closer to its heart.

The last layer in the Senior Bandit's story is ironic. The very act of charity that has helped keep the old folks home open may ultimately bring about its demise.

It is rapidly turning into a story that—like a pungent onion—may bring on tears as you slice it and dice it and serve it as news.

Roll tape

"Microphone check. Testing."

"Let's put another light on this side. Get rid of that shadow."

"Which anchor do I toss back to?"

"Roll the video when I say…"

"Tell them to cut the fucking sports segment down. I need that extra thirty seconds!"

Sugar walks quickly past a line of reporters. Each one is facing lights and cameras, boxed in by the others like racehorses at the starting gate. Each one is relaying or receiving last-minute instructions from the folks back at their TV station or the network.

It's nearly eleven o'clock.

Lanny the photographer is waiting for Sugar at the News 13 camera on the far end. It's a prime location that he staked out early in the standoff. In the daytime, you can just barely see a corner of the Emerald Arms down the block. At night, the camera's glare bounces off a white barricade and provides some backlighting to give the picture more depth. Wary of encroachment by the invading army of news teams, Lanny has defended his territory with the determination of a lion around his lair.

Right now, he is keeping an eye on the competition and munching pizza.

"I see you ordered pizza again," Sugar says.

Lanny shakes his head. "About an hour ago, a couple of Domino's guys show up with stacks and stacks of pizzas. Reverend Sam ordered them. He had them delivered to the cops. I guess he feels sorry for them out here."

"That was nice of him."

"Yeah. Except one of the commanders—you know, that one with the big ears and the flat head—came through and caught a couple of officers eating it. He was really pissed. So they threw the rest away. I intercepted this one before it hit the trash can." He jerks his thumb toward the News-13 van. "There's some left in the truck if you want it. It's vegetarian, but what the hell."

Sugar declines and steps into place between the camera and a Bakersfield P.D. patrol car. She checks her notes and the questions Hunter had typed up. They are questions she'll put to Reverend

Sam if this interview comes off the way Hunter and Ray the Web-Guy think it will.

She looks over her shoulder. She can't see the building, but an eerie glow from the Emerald Arms is one of the few signs of life out there beyond the roadblock. Police have covered every wall and every crevice of the old boarding house with spotlights, while officers continue their watch from the shadows.

This is all so crazy, she thinks. Reverend Sam has gone overboard in his crusade to save the Emerald Arms. The reporters—she looks around sheepishly at the cameras along the street— have gone overboard to cover the crisis. Even the police have responded with such a heavy hand that it's become difficult for Sam to surrender and save face. But no one really seems to be too worried about how this is affecting the poor residents in there. Who is really watching out for them? That's what she wants to ask. She checks her notes one last time.

Lanny waves at her from behind the camera and points to his ear. "Put in your earpiece. Thompson needs to talk to you. They've got the video from inside the building and they're all going ape back in the control room."

Sugar gives him a relieved thumbs up. So far, so good. And she smiles as she thinks about that day she watched Reverend Sam on the phone, berating the son of that couple living there at the Emerald Arms—the one who sent his parents video email equipment. That seems so long ago. Who would have thought?

They had laughed about it afterwards in the newsroom. But then Hunter had seen it as another story, one more piece of the puzzle they put into their ongoing coverage of the Emerald Arms. Old folks who barely have enough money to live on have children who send them expensive high-tech gadgets. Ironic. And sad. Now if only they can make it work tonight.

It's eleven o'clock.

Stand by.

The reporters are lined up in the spotlights along Nineteenth Street. They straighten their shoulders. They run hands through their hair to make sure everything is in place. They rehearse the first lines of their scripts. And then, one by one, they respond to cues and launch into the reports that are beaming back to their individual slice of tonight's viewing audience. Soon they are all talking at once.

In her earpiece, Sugar can hear Kent Abernathy talking to the viewers at home. Then he's talking to her, and she can see herself on the monitor about three steps away. What's the latest?

That's her cue.

"Frankly, Kent, not much has happened since our last report at six o'clock. At least not much out here on the street. The key to all this is what is going on inside the Emerald Arms about two blocks from where I'm standing."

Sugar explains that police have sealed off the area and no one but the FBI negotiators has been able to contact Reverend Sam or anyone else inside to find out what is going on "…until now.

"We are attempting something different tonight to bring you this story. We've established a connection through the internet with the residents of the Emerald Arms."

"The tape is rolling," she hears Thompson say.

On her monitor, Sugar can see what amounts to home video of the residents waving at the camera. The lighting is poor and the picture is slightly out of focus. Sugar can identify the residents by name. She shares that with the viewers.

"This was recorded earlier this evening," Sugar says. Some of the seniors are more animated than others, but none appears distraught or suffering. She narrates slowly, explaining to the viewers that this is her first look inside the Emerald Arms as well.

"We got him. He's up." Thompson's voice in her earpiece is so loud, Sugar flinches.

She can see Reverend Sam sitting at his computer in the office of the Emerald Arms. He is an arm's length away from a television set tuned to KDOA in order to hear Sugar's questions.

"We've used this camera to put Reverend Sam on the Internet, live right now," Sugar says. "How are the residents holding up?"

"Fine, Ms. Kane. We are tired but healthy." The picture jumps and jerks. It is out of sync with the preacher's voice. But it is magical to Sugar.

"The police believe you are holding the residents hostage. Is that true?"

Sam's answer to her question is delayed by technology. It takes time to relay pictures and sound through the Internet to the TV and back. But it adds to the drama.

"Not at all," comes Sam's reply. "Everyone here has chosen to stay and see this through to the end. Any one of them can leave at any time. We have no hostages here."

Sugar places a finger next to her ear. "Reverend. Some suggest that this entire incident could have been, and should have been, avoided. And some blame you for rejecting common sense in order to push a political agenda. Haven't you put that ahead of the welfare of the residents and put them at risk? Hasn't this gone too far and for too long? And what will it take to convince you to surrender?"

"No one is at risk here, as long as authorities keep their word and do not use their weapons to force us out of our home. But then, ask the victims of Ruby Ridge and Waco about how much we can trust the authorities.

"Secondly. We will surrender tomorrow morning."

Just like that, Sugar thinks. Tomorrow. It'll all be over?

Tomorrow morning, Reverend Sam says, if the city agrees to find a suitable replacement for the Emerald Arms. "Ms. Kane, do you realize four million senior citizens die every year in insufferable living conditions." Reverend Sam jumps back on his soapbox. Sugar knows the statistics and the pitiful stories by now. The audience does too; she's convinced.

She cuts in. "You are charged with bank robbery. That's why police have responded like this. You are a suspected criminal. You are accused of instigating this standoff. At the very least, you've alienated City Hall. How can you expect anyone to listen to you?"

"I understand. Yep, I have become something of a distraction. So if the city agrees to establish a program to replace the Emerald Arms, I will step aside. Our residents won't really be free if they step out of here and have nowhere to go. I'll give up tomorrow morning as promised. Just don't penalize them for anything I may have done."

"Sam. Are you the Senior Bandit?"

His pause is long and painful. "I am going to jail for it. Isn't that enough?"

Reverend Sam stands and walks away from his desk. The interview is over.

Sugar stands thoughtfully in the harsh pool of light for the TV camera, and then wonders aloud if city leaders are willing to take Reverend Sam up on his offer. Will they end the standoff? She recaps the story and promises viewers that Kent Abernathy will return. Andy Blackman is at the KDOA newsroom with one councilwoman who is watching this interview and will have her response. "That, and the rest of the day's news in a moment."

They go to the commercial. Van Thompson is in her ear, gushing. "Great job. You're clear. We whupped ass. And by the way, Valerie's interview with the bandit? Totally bogus."

To her right, Sugar can see one of the reporters squatting in front of his own television monitor and pointing her out to a colleague. They had been watching. A network reporter gives her a smile and pumps his fist. Out-maneuvered but not out-classed, he offers congratulations.

One by one, the harsh TV lights click off, and with them the aura of competition. Reporters and photographers mingle. The buzz is strong. Have you heard about the prank someone played on Channel 26? Some reporter got her butt burned live on the air. That Internet interview was something. Why didn't we think of that? Talk and critique. Laughter. Someone suggests a round of drinks at that little dive over on Gunther's Alley.

The photographers and engineers pack up and store the equipment in their trucks, keeping it readily accessible for the next newscast. They draw straws. Who will have to stay out here through the next shift? They call their newsrooms for any last-minute instructions before standing at ease for the night. And they head for the bar.

Sugar lingers. Raul has come to replace Lanny and will stay on the scene through the night. He is picking at the cold pizza.

"Go home and get some sleep," he says. "You need it."

Sugar pulls on a light jacket. She writes her phone number on a page from her notebook and hands it to him. "If anything happens, call me first."

He knows. He nods.

Sugar's car is two blocks away from the News 13 truck. She starts in that direction. Her bones are weary, but her mind isn't ready to rest. Still, it takes a minute for the sound reaching her ear to register in her brain.

Sirens.

Slowly she turns and looks down the street toward the Emerald Arms. Activity has picked up. Figures are scrambling, silhouetted and racing through the light around the old hotel. The white glow from the spotlights has changed to yellow. It flickers with orange. Smoke rises, and the sirens grow louder.

The Emerald Arms is on fire.

Date: November 3, 1996
Slug: Emerald Arms

Fire Transcript from 12:44 am live news cut-in

This is Sugar Kane reporting.

A horrible turn of events in the standoff between Bakersfield Police and senior citizens at the Emerald Arms Hotel. A fire swept through the building about an hour ago. We know many of the residents got out alive, but we haven't been able to find out yet how many.

Take a look at this videotape. You can see the flames, as they lit up the sky over Bakersfield. We were only a block away when the fire started, but as you can see, the fire is shooting out of windows on the second floor when we recorded this.

Firefighters and police officers have been on standby around the Emerald Arms throughout this weekend's standoff. They rushed in to rescue the residents. If they hadn't already been on the scene at that very moment, there is no telling how many people would have died in this fire.

*Streaked with soot and sweat, officers
carried the residents from the building. They
risked their lives to save the senior citizens. It
was heroic.*

And it was awful.

*Mrs. Maxine Henderson was one of those
senior citizens who got out of the burning building alive. This is what she told us just moments
ago:*

"Oh Lord. I was getting ready for bed when someone came
down the hall pounding on all the doors. Then there was smoke
everywhere. And heat. My God, the heat. I couldn't breathe. I
couldn't see anything. But someone took me by the hand and led
me down the stairs. They saved my life. But this… This is terrible.
This is terrible."

*The officers carried residents out here to
the street, not far from where I'm standing.
Dozens of victims sitting or kneeling on the
cold pavement. They wrapped some in blan-
kets. Some needed oxygen and immediate
medical attention. Others needed to be held
and comforted as they cried.*

*We know that at least four of the residents
have been rushed to the hospital.*

*Reverend Sam Cross is the founder and
director of the housing program at the Emerald Arms. You can see him here in this video,
as he rushed around outside the building*

helping the victims.

*Sam Cross, you may remember, is fac-
ing charges—accused of being the city's
Senior Bandit, responsible for several bank
robberies in Bakersfield. Prosecutors tell us
they will file charges against him, for that,
and for his role in the standoff, as well.
Police officers are looking for him right now.
It seems in all the confusion, Reverend Sam
has disappeared.*

*One witness told us she saw him running
back into the building even as firefighters
were carrying more residents to safety:*

"One minute he was over there with Major Tom and some of
the others. Then I seen him running that way. The fire was still
burning! But he was running to the flames like a crazy man."

*It is certain the residents lost everything
in this fire. It is difficult for us to really comprehend the devastation—certainly on this
building—but even more so on the lives of its
residents. Mrs. Henderson said this:*

"We got out alive. Alive, thank God. But now what? My furni-
ture and my clothes. Oh dear! My cat. Where's my cat? My whole
life was in there. What will I do now?"

*There is no word yet on how the fire
started. You can see the fire crews behind me
now, still spraying water to put out the last of*

*the flames. I talked with the commander out
here, and he says...*

Excuse me.

What? Is that confirmed?

No.

No!

*This is horrible. I have just been told that
they have found two bodies in the building.
Officials have confirmed that. And they are all
but certain that one of the victims is Reverend
Sam Cross.*

Reverend Sam Cross is dead.

We will...

What can we do?

I... I must apologize for the tears.

*We will... we will take a commercial
break while we try to get more information for
you. This is Sugar Kane reporting.*

Are we clear?

Sam's dead. Oh my God!

Date: December 20, 1996
Slug: Bandit Returns

Anchor intro:

With all due respect, a martyr is seldom the best role model, no matter how noble the cause may be, because you cannot win the battle by giving up your life; you must force the opposition to change his. That is the point.

So Bakersfield Police are searching once again for the so-called Senior Bandit. They had all but closed the books on the case after their prime suspect, Reverend Sam Cross, died in the Emerald Arms fire last month.

But it seems a martyr's work is never done.

Roll tape:

You can see him best on the wide-angle picture of the bank security video. He's the tall one limping through the front doors with the help of a cane. A digital read-out of the time on the security video says it's 1:53 pm.

Only three tellers are working the long marble counter at the bank. The lunch crowd is gone, and the tellers are chatting with each other.

The Senior Bandit hobbles forward. He's glad to finally have the cast off his leg. He should never have tried to slide down that ladder on his own after helping Louisa Witherspoon out the second-story window and into the arms of the firefighter. Then that incompetent witch doctor at the community clinic made matters worse, badly setting the broken bone in his leg.

Even more painful these past weeks has been watching the press vilify Reverend Sam as a crazed robber and malcontent who was bent on destroying himself and the Emerald Arms in the process. Most of the press simply convicted Reverend Sam in absentia. Dead men don't sue.

The bandit brushes the ends of the gray wig away from his long neck and over the collar of his jogging suit. He adjusts the Brooklyn Dodger's cap that holds the hairpiece in place and raises his tinted glasses high on his nose.

For six weeks he has lived with dread, afraid that Reverend Sam will forever be linked to the crime of bank robbery the way rumors have linked actor Richard Gere and gerbils. Who knows if they're true, but you can't think of one without the other. And everyone snickers. It's time to set the record straight.

The three tellers have stopped chatting. Surely, they must recognize him. They exchange worried glances. Sam Junior doesn't pause.

He nods to one of the tellers and moves stiffly to her window. Melissa is working the far end of the counter. Just like last time.

"Melissa," he says in that voice that is raspy and firm, but not much stronger than a whisper. "I remember you. Do you remember me?"

She responds with a nervous smile. "Who could forget you?"

Sam Junior says, "We don't have much time. I'm sure your friends over there have already alerted security. But since you and I have shared the intimacy of a bank robbery before, this should be child's play."

Melissa opens her cash drawer, as he lays his battered and smoke-stained briefcase on the counter. "Do you want it all?" she asks.

The question makes him laugh. If she only knew about the book and movie deals, the offers that have been pouring in from Hollywood and New York. Everyone wants to get rich from Reverend Sam and the Emerald Arms story. NBC was first on the scene and is shooting a made-for-TV movie that should be ready just in time for Christmas: *Bakersfield Burnout—The Reverend Sam Cross Story*. Maybe Richard Gere could play Reverend Sam?

Sam Junior had an agonizing emotional battle over selling the story at all. But the money will not only build a new housing facility for the Emerald Arms residents, it will provide a healthy start for a permanent endowment to keep the new facility going. Once that was abundantly clear, his decision was easy. Father would have wanted it that way. The plans for a new home are already being drawn.

Of course, Mr. Marika won't be there to see it. He will be forever known as "the other victim in the Emerald Arms fire." Poor Mr. Marika. It was his cigar and all those *Playboy* magazines he hid in the basement that started the inferno in the first place. At least that's the official cause of the fire. Sam Junior believes it.

But as long as the FBI and Bakersfield Police deny that officers used any tear gas or other devices that night, conspiracy theorists will hound them with charges of a cover-up. It will keep them on the defensive for months and keep the story alive.

The fake hair makes the back of Sam Junior's neck itch. He brushes it away and thinks that this time he won't return it. Taking the wig from J.B.'s collection of costumes the actor kept in his mother's room at the Emerald Arms, and targeting South Valley Bank—the source of Hickok's financial stress—was poetic justice.

He looks at Melissa, standing with her cash drawer open, waiting.

"I suppose to make this official, I should take something," he says. "One dollar will do it."

"One dollar?"

He nods and takes a newspaper from his briefcase. He slides it across the counter to her as she hands him the dollar. The paper is folded so that the headline faces her.

"Senior Bandit Dies in Fire," it screams.

The bandit snaps his briefcase shut and takes Melissa's dollar. He studies the bill for a moment. Maybe he should have it framed. It is loot from the Senior Bandit's last holdup. Thank God, it's the last holdup.

"If anyone asks, tell them they got the story wrong. I'm alive and well. And if I may say so, Melissa, of all the robberies, you are my favorite teller. Keep up the good work."

With that, Sam Cross Junior moves as swiftly as possible across the lobby and out the door.

The clock on the security video reads 2:01.

Slug: Finally Tonight

Anchor intro:

> Finally tonight...
>
> The universe of TV news is no different than life. They are both made up of rising stars and falling stars, while most just hang above you and twinkle with their own faint glow. That is not to suggest any one of them is less important than the rest. Even the most unassuming stars have their purpose.
>
> Sailors navigate by them.
>
> Astrologers predict the future by them.
>
> Dreamers wish upon them.
>
> And isn't there a little Jiminy Cricket in each of us?

Roll tape

Three sharp raps and a loud "God dammit!"

Hunter drops the hammer and jams a wounded thumb between his teeth. It's been three days, and the station's maintenance man still hasn't shown up to hang the plaque on Hunter's office wall. Now, Hunter thinks it wasn't so wise to take matters into his own hands.

When the pain subsides, he lifts the award and places it carefully on the nail. Associated Press. First Place for News Excellence in November. He looks around the office, assessing each wall, each open space that might be perfect for a golden Emmy statue. The buzz around the industry is getting louder. KDOA is the favorite to take home that award for their region. How about a national one? Could happen.

From the start of the Emerald Arms siege, through the fire and the investigation that followed, no one could touch their coverage. True, they had a head start. All that coverage they gave Reverend Sam before the City Council vote and the siege provided Hunter's team with everything at their fingertips to own the story. His reporters had used it all wisely and out-hustled the competition the rest of the way. No flash, just good solid journalism this time around. And people were watching. He felt it in the checkout line at the grocery store, and in the chatter at the barber shop.

Hunter peers through the vertical blinds separating his office from the newsroom. That's where the Emmy belongs, he decides. If he can only lure the maintenance man out of whatever cave he lives in long enough to build them a shelf. A shrine, maybe, right above the assignment desk, he thinks. St. Emmy. May she bless us with journalistic integrity, forgive us our inaccuracies, and protect us from poor ratings.

It wouldn't look out of place, either. Kathy has Christmas lights over and around the white board on the wall she uses to keep track of her reporters and photographers. She swears they will stay there until after the results of the Emmy ballots are counted. Hunter turns to the window facing the back parking lot and Highway 99. This isn't Christmas weather. Seventy-five degrees and sunny.

He smiles. It sure beats the hell out of shoveling snow in Des Moines.

He picks up another picture frame to hang, bites his bruised thumbnail again, and thinks better of it. He places a hand on the photograph in the frame. It's a picture from the Local section of the *Bakersfield Californian* after the seniors rioted at City Hall. Reverend Sam and Sugar stand out amid the flailing bodies. Now his heart aches, too.

"You miss them, don't you?" Kathy asks.

Hunter turns. She's standing not more than a foot away, sneaking a peek at the picture in his hand. Why didn't he hear her sneak in like that? Or notice her perfume? He's been very good at that lately. Whenever Kathy isn't in his face, she's on his mind. Neither is objectionable. Damn her.

"Yeah. I miss them both," Hunter says. "Sugar called today. She wanted some advice again. She doesn't like the snow in Denver, but it's going to be okay. They're going to start her on the air in the dead week between Christmas and New Year."

Kathy says, "She sounds homesick. Did they really make her change her name to Sally?"

"Or Sarah, Suzanne or something like that."

"Boring."

"Yeah," Hunter agrees. "And you know that mole? The little beauty mark right there above the corner of her mouth?" Hunter gently touches that spot on Kathy's face. She is warm to his touch.

"Her new boss scheduled surgery to have it removed without even asking her. Sugar says she draws the line at messing with her face. Big fight. She won. She's keeping it."

Kathy takes the picture from Hunter's hands. "Smart move. So when you get around to finding her replacement, no more strippers. Okay?"

Hunter snorts. "Of course not. You can't catch lightning in a bottle twice." He moves to the chair behind his desk and plops down, and then he locks his hands behind his head.

Kathy sets the picture down on the desk. "What about Sam?"

"I told you, I don't want to talk about that."

"You didn't even go to his funeral."

"I watched it on the news."

"You should have been there, Hunter."

"I didn't want to be part of the spectacle."

"What's that supposed to mean?"

Hunter leans forward on the desk. Kathy's looking at him with those eyes, ever inviting, pulling him to open up. "I've said it before. Enough already. Sam would probably be alive today if I hadn't pushed him and taken advantage of this whole mess in the name of news. It just seems that a made-for-TV funeral is a bad time to say you're sorry."

"Hunter," she says gently. "You are such an idiot sometimes. Reverend Sam wanted it this way. That's why he ran back into the building."

Hunter shakes his head and holds up a finger, but Kathy doesn't give him a chance to reply.

"And don't try to tell me how guilty you feel. You can't take responsibility for the standoff. Reverend Sam did that. It was a train wreck waiting to happen. He was the engineer. Not you."

"Yeah, but I feel like the guy who pulled the switch and put him on that track."

Kathy stands there, quiet and measuring the man behind the desk with her eyes.

Hunter shakes his head. "Funny thing, this business. We do the reporting, and we anchor the news and, if we're successful, we make the viewers feel that they are really affected by what we tell them. And we convince them that we're affected, too. Then after we shut down the studio lights, we go out for a beer. We go home. We sleep easily. The next day, we get up and start our pseudo-empathetic lives all over again. But this one… this story got to me."

Now it's Kathy's turn. She moves behind the desk next to him and leans forward, supporting herself with her elbows so that they are both looking across the office towards the newsroom. "You know what I think? I think this got you because, for the first time, you didn't anchor the story. You didn't even report it. For the first time, you didn't have put up that wall between you and your feelings about it."

"Thank you Doctor Laura. Or Doctor Kathy, I guess. TV psychologist. I feel better already." He's tempted to take her hand, but knows he'll have to wait until they walk out the door tonight. They are trying to keep it professional, at least between the morning assignment meeting and the credits at the end of the day's news. Some days that works better than others.

Hunter says, "Hmm. You know, I've been thinking about New Mexico lately. Have you ever been to New Mexico?"

"Nooo."

"Just outside of Taos, there is a pueblo where the Indians live. It's a closed society, but on certain days they let you take a tour for four bucks. For an extra ten dollars, you can bring a camera. But you're not allowed to take pictures of any of the natives."

"Why not?"

"The Indians believe that in order to capture their image on film, the camera steals their soul."

"Really."

Hunter nods. "I'm beginning to believe them. Maybe the TV camera steals just a little of us, bit by bit. Day in and day out, it steals the part of our souls that helps us be compassion- ate. I mean really compassionate. So the more time we spend in front of the camera, the less we have to fight off all the bad news every day that makes us such wonderful cynics. Pretty soon we can't feel anymore. Anyway, that's what I've been thinking about lately."

Kathy shrugs. "I guess some people have a deeper reservoir of compassion than others."

"And others are drained overnight." Hunter runs his thumb across the fingers of one hand, counting the years. "I've spent a long time in front of the camera. So that means I'm…"

"Running on fumes," Kathy answers. "Maybe that's why it feels so strange to be touched by Reverend Sam and his story. Your gas tank is empty."

Hunter wonders aloud, if that's true, is this something you can fill up again? Can you get it back?

"I don't see why not," Kathy says. With a steady diet of granola, a few intense sessions with a psychotherapist, pyramid crystals around your neck, and magnets in your shoes, we could restore your aura in no time."

Hunter tells her it sounds much too involved.

Kathy takes his hand. "We could do it on our own, I suppose. But that would take a lot longer."

"How long?"

"If you have to ask, you're not making much progress."

"Okay," Screw the rules. He stands up, reaches for Kathy and tries to slip an arm around her waist. "Let's start now."

She backs away.

"What's wrong?" he asks.

"I'm trying not to listen to the scanner."

"What? I don't hear anything."

Kathy rolls her eyes toward the ceiling. "Bank robbery."

"Ignore it," he says.

She moves closer and puts a tentative hand against his chest. "Okay. Can we start after I take care of this teeny little robbery?"

Before Hunter can answer, she spins toward the door and sweeps into the newsroom. "Did anyone get the address on that?" she calls out. "Andy! Get on your horse. It sounds like the Ming Avenue branch. Wait! Wasn't that one of the banks Reverend Sam stuck up once? I'll start making calls."

Hunter bobs his head back and forth, trying to follow her

movements through those blasted vertical blinds. Finally he sweeps them to one side with a satisfying sense of liberation. He watches Kathy dispatch her troops and begin working the phones. It's under control. He looks at his watch. It's just after two o'clock—plenty of time to get it covered for the evening news.

Hunter moves to the corner window. Out across the highway, the *Live @ Five* news team smiles down at him from a billboard. Kent and Sugar. Weatherman Bob and Boog Powell, sports.

Sugar has been gone two weeks. The billboards should have come down already. He studies their faces. Something is missing in the Sugar who stares down at him from the sign. It's something the photographer didn't quite catch in her eyes. The picture is a good likeness, but lacks the energy, the magical spark they call "it" that makes her such a compelling television news reporter.

He sighs. You can't capture "it" on film. Maybe a master artist could do "it" justice. DaVinci did. He understood "it". Mona Lisa had "it". Or maybe DaVinci just painted "it".

Hunter mulls this over as he crosses to a tall stack of videotapes on the floor against the opposite wall. Audition tapes from anchor wanna-bes. He checks their labels and picks a few promising suspects with nice-sounding names. There's a knock on his door as he feeds the first tape into his videotape player.

"Mr. Riley?"

Hunter swivels his head for a cock-eyed look at a young man in the doorway. Baggy clothes with an open collar and a tie that doesn't even reach his navel, the boy's attire screams college intern.

"Mr. Riley. Miss Drake, I'm from the promotions department,

Miss Drake asked me to bring these to you. They're the November ratings."

Hunter growls, "Are they good?"

"She, ah, well, she seemed happy," College Boy says, as he places a large flat white envelope carefully on Hunter's desk and backs out.

Hunter straightens slowly as the videotape begins to roll. The face of a perky blond pops up on his TV screen. Hunter ignores her and takes the envelope. The numbers are in. They have been his Holy Grail since he sweated out his first day in Bakersfield nine months ago. The chase derailed him. Kept him from finding another job. Kept him in Bakersfield.

The ratings are his reward—or his punishment—for manipulating Sugar and Sam and the seniors. He bounces the package on his fingertips and on his palms, as if weight alone could tell Hunter the results. And then he lets the envelope slide from his hands into the wastebasket at his feet.

He uses the remote control to increase the volume on his TV monitor and watches the first audition tape as he sinks back into the chair behind the desk. Thirty seconds. He pulls the blond from the videotape machine. That wasn't "it". Hunter places another tape in the machine and leans back. Replacing Sugar won't be easy.

Hunter is on his fifth audition tape when he shifts his attention to a different television screen. There is a face speaking to him from one of the small set on the far end of his desk that he keeps tuned KDOA unless he needs to monitor one of the other stations. He studies it for only a moment, but that's all he needs.

He scoops up the phone and begins punching the numbers that scroll constantly across the bottom of the screen. He wrestles with the phone as he digs the envelope with November's ratings from the trashcan. He places it gingerly on the desktop and drums the envelope with his fingers.

"Hello. Psychic Buddies Hotline? I'd like to speak to Madam Laura. No. It has to be Madam Laura. I just saw her on TV."

It takes a considerable amount of haggling and insistence on Hunter's part, but he finally connects with Madam Laura herself. He knows her voice immediately. It's a sultry voice that could make your bed vibrate, and it is perfect for the dark hair and mysterious eyes that had stolen Hunter away from the audition tapes.

"Madam Laura? This is Hunter Riley. KDOA-TV in Bakersfield," he begins.

"What? You knew I would call?" Of course she would say that.

"Listen, Laura. I was sitting here watching one of your spots for the Psychic Buddies Hotline.

"Have you ever considered a career in TV news?

"No? Well, we need to talk."

Hunter props his chin on his fists while he makes his pitch. His mind dances on the stage the possibilities.

A psychic anchor. She delivers the news before it happens.

It would be crazy.

It could be golden.

Roll credits

An excerpt from

THE PATTERER

By Larry Brill

Available from Black Tie Books Fall 2013

In *The Patterer*, Larry Brill takes a step back.
Back in time, that is. Imagine the zany chaos that
would ensue if Hunter Riley could have invented
the modern-day newscast 250 years ago. Fortunately for us, Leeds Merriweather, an eighteenth
century patterer, beat him to it. Yes, *Live@Five*
meets Jane Austen with hilarious results. **Turn the
page to read an excerpt.**

Chapter 1

London-1765.

Blood and lust make the world go 'round I say. You may argue that it is money—the pound or the pence, the farthing, the bob, the crown, gold or silver—that makes it spin. God knows money is good. I will tell you straight away, I have personally found it quite handy when bartering for a wench or wine in those rare exquisite moments of self-indulgence. But if you believe that, you'd be as wrong as tits on a bull.

Ladies, forgive me. A crude turn of phrase, that. Men, you expect it. But I will, for the ladies sake, attempt to rein in the crude-osity of my tale. It won't be easy what with britches dropping nearly as often as your jaw. What I offer is a tawdry tale of bullets flying and death-defying antics, but also a tale of love. Man on woman. Man on man. Camel on...well, let's have none of that here, shall we?

Mostly, this is a story about oral stimulation.

Wait! Don't run. No need to even blush. It's not at all what you imagine. Although your imagination did just have a go with you, now didn't it? Cheeky devils. Yes, you are my kind of crowd, and you have proven my point. Blood and lust make the world go 'round. Repeat it with me. That, in fact, is my world. And I offer it for sale to you. Got two pence and a halfpenny? Then step up even closer, and let's have at it. You see I am a patterer. At your service.

That is my exceptional skill. It is also my curse, as you will surely see.

Now the first rule of a good patterer is to begin with the most titillating, scandalous or horrific story you can find. Flesh it out whenever possible with references to bodily fluids, and never, *never* let facts get in the way.

Actually, I have a saying, which I made up, entirely original, though you may steal it if you wish: "If it bleeds, it..."

"Leeds!"

That's me. Leeds Merriweather. The roar of my name as it rolled like thunder through the printer's shoppe yanked me rudely from a deep and dreamless sleep. It was so loud, it would have awakened Shakespeare himself. And this just in: Shakespeare is still dead.

"Leeds Merriweather, you lazy son of a twat! The ink's dry an'a day's a-wasting."

Charles McNabb owned the dusty print shoppe where this story begins. He added an exclamation point to his roar with a kick to my ribs. I squinted up at him from the corner of the pressroom where I had curled up for the night with a soft pillow and a hard floor. It seemed as if I had only just closed my eyes before being subjected to the indignity of McNabb's boot. I know for a fact that it was nearly dawn when, like a weary tomcat, I padded in and settled down with a snout full of gin and a head full of stories I had collected from a long night patronizing the public houses along Fleet Street.

"If'n you're not going to sell for me today, it'd be certain I have plenty like you who will," McNabb said. He carried a bundle of the day's edition of his broadsheet, the *London Tattler-Tribune*.

"Aw. Go easy if you please, sir," I said. My ribs where McNabb's boot struck ached, but, oh, how my head throbbed even more. February had just given way to March, and the light from the window danced with particles of dust creating a veil of sorts before my eyes. I sniffed. Oil and ink, parchment and stain. The aroma of the printing press, of literature freshly baked. And turpentine. I love the smell of turpentine in the morning.

McNabb slapped the back of his hand on the broadsheets. "Cannibalism," he cried. "Adultery and ravishing of maidens."

I love the ravishing of maidens. It sells newspapers.

The publisher was a short Scot with a gunpowder temperament, and that morning something put a spark to his britches. "'Tis death on the high seas. By God, I am good."

I asked, "Good for what?"

He aimed his next kick at my privates; I raised a knee just in time. "Don't you be insolent, y'ragged lump of gutter waste. If this story d'nnot draw a decent income today then we have no business doing business in this business."

I used the brick wall behind me as a brace for my back as I inched up—slowly, very, *very* slowly—to a standing position. War drums were beating in my noggin, and the battle for a clear head was most definitely in doubt. Too much gin last night, for certain.

I took the broadsheet McNabb forced upon me and glanced over the all-important lead story beneath the *Tattler-Tribune* banner.

Spank me senseless! "Lord Howell's shipwreck? What the bloody hell is this?" I demanded.

"A fine bit of writing, if I say so myself."

"A fine bit thievery, I say." That weasel McNabb had attached his name to the story—*my story!* I was the one who mined the details of the shipwreck over a bottle of rum from a Portuguese captain whose ship happened upon an uncharted island. The crew was taking on fresh water when they discovered what was left of a tourist yacht in the lagoon and the remains of the rich nobleman, his wife, and the others who perished with him.

"What is this dung you've printed here? What happened to what I wrote?" I wanted to rip that newspaper and wave the tatters in McNabb's ferret face. I had only turned the details over to McNabb on the promise that I could print and sell the story under my name. All I had to do was raise a couple of quid to cover the cost of printing. All the right elements of a great story were there, not the least of which was potential for profit. McNabb understood that. He held out his palm, and the way he rubbed two fingers against this thumb said it all: Show me the money.

I shook my head. "Soon."

"And what of yesterday's sales? D'ya drink it all away as usual last night?"

"'Course not," I lied. Yes, I was penniless again. Even McNabb could read that much in my bloodshot eyes.

"It's a fine story, lad, and I couldn't let it waste away a-waiting for you." That bugger, McNabb, knew a golden story when he saw one.

All they found were the bones of the good Lord Thurston and those six who were shipwrecked with him. The evidence of the extreme hedonistic life they lived and left behind created a tale so repulsive and so enchanting in one, that it was sure to shock and awe and produce profits. More important, this was a story to be told and re-told and remembered for generations. And it was mine to tell first.

"Lad, 'tis a sin to give stock to such profound pride. Be prudent," McNabb said. "You're a better man for surrendering it to me, and the story is better for it; that is my duty as editor. Now run. Run and patter. Patter and run, whichever it is that you do." He waved me off, dismissing me as one might shoo a cat from the supper table.

"Leave the wordsmithing to McNabb," he said. "You have every chance to patter your version on the street. You have a handsome face, a strong voice and straight teeth. You were made to patter, not to publish. That is your proper lot in life. Accept it."

I looked down at McNabb. He was barely as tall as my shoulder. My left hand clenched, balling up a corner of the Tattler-Tribune I held. I snapped at him. "This was mine. You said it was a story beneath you."

"She rose to the occasion," he said with a smirk. McNabb handed the broadsheets to me. "Do you want them or shall I find another patterer today?"

I moved to the window and bent at the waist enough to peek at the sky above the roofs of Fleet Street. The clouds were grey but not dismal. More distressing was the odor of the fish market carried on the wind. Whitefish today, and not a fresh catch apparently. Strong enough to blow down from Billingsgate, the wind would invariably carry my voice away from the crowds I hoped to capture. Bloody hell it was, this would be a difficult day.

I turned to face McNabb, took one of the broadsheets from the bundle and waved the front page at him, not ready to back down from this duel. "You agreed I could rent your press to print my own."

He laughed, "What? You have no money and c'nnot afford it, you foul-breath alley dog. Be intelligent for once. Why should I allow you to compete with me? 'Twould be like lettin' you shag me wife and offer you my own bed for the purpose. I may be a Scot, but I'm not insane, man."

I took a step toward him, and then sharply veered right to the large typesetting table in the pressroom. To my left, near the front door, a wall of books, pamphlets and assorted printed pages for sale stood behind the counter where McNabb serviced his customers. Everything for the literate gentleman, from pens and ink to writing paper and wax seals, sat on display across the counter itself. At the back of the pressroom, McNabb's assistants, Simon and Garfield, were preparing the printing press for another go and pretending to ignore the battle of wills and ink-stained egos.

Pacing back to McNabb, I considered my limited options. No respect, I say. Some day, I knew, I would have my own press and see my words, my ideas in print instead of being cast on the wind as they were now. Even on a calm day words disappeared within the moment at each street corner where I stopped. No one respects the patterer, but put your story in print? That, my friends, is a whole 'nother kettle of carp.

Change would come, of that I was certain. But until then there were meals to be purchased and rent money to be paid. Both, sadly, had been hard to acquire of late, and dodging my landlord who selfishly insisted on being paid for overdue rent had become a daily game.

"How is your head this morning?" McNabb asked, as if the matter was settled and forgotten. "And your rhyme? How will you pitch this?"

"My head? As right as ever. My rhyme? Far too splendid for the drivel you have written here," I said.

"Leeds, 'tis that attitude that makes you so difficult. If I want a bit of criticism I have only to spend more time with my wife. Show some conviction, man. And be positive in your expression. Be cheerful, even. For no one wants to buy death from a grump."

He was right, of course. In pattering, proper disposition is nearly as important as a winning smile and the tale's details. I admitted to McNabb as much, and it placated him. So, I handed him the one copy I had waved in his face a moment earlier and stepped next to the window. I counted only those papers in my hand. "Three and twenty papers," I said. "That is two pence, halfpenny short of three shillings in total."

He shook his head. "No, lad, the count is twenty-four."

"But Mr. McNabb, see for yourself."

I handed him the bundle of papers in my hand and, in return, took the single broadsheet he was holding. I rolled it cylindrical and tapped it like a baton on the palm of my left hand while McNabb counted the papers.

"I am sure I printed out exactly four over twenty," he said. He looked at the table in the center of the room. He looked to his left and to his right, clearly confused. He counted again as if he could perform the Lord's own fish-and-loaves miracle to increase it by at least one, but the stack in his hand had not changed.

Then I pointed my rolled newspaper to the printing press. McNabb's eyes followed the sweeping motion of my paper pointer. "Is it possible you left the final print on the press?" I asked. I took the bundle of broadsheets from him, and while he stumped to the press in the back of his shoppe I unfurled and added the sheet in my hand to the others.

"No, it is not here."

With a shrug I placed the newspapers in my satchel where I still had six as-yet unsold copies of *The London Gentleman's Magazine* and three books I had purchased at discount from Mr. Hawke, the bookseller six doors down. I slung the satchel's long leather strap over my head, collected my hat and turned for the door. "Well," I said, "If by chance the missing copy appears, do send it my way. I should have made three; maybe four stops by then, and will most certainly reach the West End within three hours. I'm certain that with a story so compelling and cleverly written as this, I should be sold out in no time at all."

Mr. McNabb accepted that as certain fact and grinned. "Do your job, and my words will do theirs." Then he demanded payment for the twenty-three *Tattler-Tribunes* he could account for. I sheepishly shook my head.

"I c'nnot go on giving you papers on credit, lad. Why can't you pay like the other patterers? 'Tis no way to run a business."

"You tell me; you're the Scot. And don't I always make good? I am the best patterer you've had, Mr. McNabb. No one sells your trash like me."

"I'm not so very certain of that, me boy. On the soul of my sainted muther I say n'more credit. This is the last time."

"That is precisely what you said last time." I smiled. I was starting out my day with a one-paper profit. And with the extra two pence I could afford a full meal that evening. It would be my first of the week.

With a gulp of the thick London air and a sip of thin potato gin from the flask in my pocket to steady myself, I began my march across uneven cobblestones toward my first stop, a busy corner at Cheapside.

"Hummm." I drew out the sound like a monk's chant to test my vocals. I would need them proper today. The tone sounded strong enough; it carried a depth, timbre, and a bear-like resonance that comes only after a fair night of drinking. Some say London gin will put hair on your chest. I say it'll put baritone balls in your voice. At least for me, more than three nips and I sound like God on high, Himself. With what I could remember of the previous evening's rounds, I was bound to be thrice as strong that day.

I will tell you, I do not fancy the overuse of rhyme in pattering as so many of my compatriots do these days. But this was a story so full of twists, and characters uncommon in London that it demanded just such the fine, Merriweather touch. A wretchedly wealthy, shipwrecked aristocrat, his wife and his five fellow castaways, ("fellows" being a relative description; two were lusty females, harlots, I was happy to note), left to fend for themselves on an island.

I began shouting more than twenty paces before reaching the corner. Drama on the high seas! Cannibalism! Lust on the high seas! Lusty cannibalism! Come hear me out, I have details!

A crowd formed around me like the first innocent swell of high tide when I stopped across from Cheapside Market. I stepped on a small platform I built there and paused. I looked over the faces before me and let tension and their expectations of entertainment build. I held up a copy of the *Tattler-Tribune* and directed their attention to first the masthead, and then the story of Lord Thurston.

"Step right up, and come hear a tale.

"A tale of a fateful trip." My voice was strong. More passers-by paused to listen.

"It started in a distant port—aboard a tiny ship."

I told them of the first mate and the captain who was brave. "And sure, they set sail that day for what was to be a three-hour tour."

"A three-hour tour?" a woman asked, wide-eyed.

Indeed. "A three-hour tour."

www.ingramcontent.com/pod-product-compliance
Lightning Source LLC
Chambersburg PA
CBHW020228180626
46810CB00006B/2085